Outstanding Praise for Previous Novels

Praise for *Hayley Aldridge Is Still Here*

"Calling all smart readers and gossip lovers alike: this novel is an unputdownable ride, fiction inspired by the narratives of stars like Jennette McCurdy (*I'm Glad My Mom Died*) and Britney Spears. Sloan's examination of money, fame, and control is brilliant, necessary . . . and fun as hell."

—Amanda Eyre Ward,
New York Times bestselling author

"Heart-wrenching and riveting, *Hayley Aldridge Is Still Here* is both a sensitive portrait of a young woman trying to take back control of her own life and an acute skewering of a toxic culture that still very much exists. . . . I found it near impossible to look away."

—Ella Berman,
author of *The Comeback*

"Sharp and sparkling, Elissa R. Sloan's tale of a famous wild child turned commodity is filled with high stakes, shocking twists, and pitch-perfect explorations of celebrity and exploitation. If you've ever wondered the truth behind tabloid headlines, you need to read this irresistible and empowering story of a woman reclaiming her own life."

—Sarah Priscus,
uthor of *Groupies*

T0182235

Praise for *The Unraveling of Cassidy Holmes*

"*The Unraveling of Cassidy Holmes* is a page-turning peek inside the glamour and brutality of life as a pop star. Sloan takes us on a wild ride through the world of music video shoots, expensive hotels, and arena tours—showing us the darkness that threatens just below the surface."

—Taylor Jenkins Reid,
New York Times bestselling author of *Daisy Jones & The Six*

"I didn't know I was waiting for a smart, literary writer to craft a novel about the rise and fall of a teen star akin to Britney Spears until I discovered *The Unraveling of Cassidy Holmes*. A witty, bright, hilarious—and at times devastating—read. I loved it."

—Amanda Eyre Ward,
New York Times bestselling author

"A witty, devastating, and ultimately beautiful peek behind the illusion of fame. With a perfect combination of music, drama, and depth, *The Unraveling of Cassidy Holmes* takes us on a journey I won't soon forget. From the opening line to the stunning close, this is a mesmerizing, thrilling, and must-read debut."

—Patti Callahan Henry,
New York Times bestselling author

Double Exposure

Also by Elissa R. Sloan

Hayley Aldridge Is Still Here
The Unraveling of Cassidy Holmes

Double Exposure

A Novel

Elissa R. Sloan

wm

WILLIAM MORROW

An Imprint of HarperCollins*Publishers*

DOUBLE EXPOSURE. Copyright © 2024 by Elissa R. Sloan. All rights reserved. Printed in the United States of America. No part of this book may be used or reproduced in any manner whatsoever without written permission except in the case of brief quotations embodied in critical articles and reviews. For information, address HarperCollins Publishers, 195 Broadway, New York, NY 10007.

HarperCollins books may be purchased for educational, business, or sales promotional use. For information, please email the Special Markets Department at SPsales@harpercollins.com.

FIRST EDITION

Designed by Diahann Sturge-Campbell

Library of Congress Cataloging-in-Publication Data has been applied for.

ISBN 978-0-06-331519-8

24 25 26 27 28 LBC 5 4 3 2 1

To my family,
especially Mom and Dad

Author's Note

This story has contents that may be upsetting. Some of the topics touched upon are medically induced abortion, miscarriage, infertility, and other healthcare issues, as well as gaslighting, drug abuse, parent death, and body dysmorphia. Please read with care.

Part 1

"Madrian"
(2000–2006)

1

2000

Maiko had her first abortion when she was eighteen. After the procedure, when she was dressed and dismissed, she leaned her head against the steering wheel of her car and caught her breath. She wiped streaks of tears away with the back of her hand and wondered why she was emotional. She didn't *want* a baby, especially not now, when she'd just landed a contract with a notoriously difficult-to-get agency and nailed an audition for a brief role on the TV show *Evergreen*.

But Charlie's absence made her wonder if she'd done the right thing, not telling him. Charlie wasn't the type of guy who would go with her to the appointment. She had sat in the waiting room, head down, her long blue-black hair hiding her face, as she assessed the others in the room. There were a few women, but only one with a companion, which struck her as interesting. A white guy had been holding the hand of a woman about the same age as Maiko—maybe a year or two older. He had the chiseled jaw of a man in his early twenties, no baby fat left, and an Adam's apple that bobbed up and down as he swallowed repeatedly, nervously. Their eyes met for a moment and Maiko dropped her gaze to her lap. He looked kind.

Maiko broke up with Charlie that same day.

"But what did I *do*?" he pressed. They were in her apartment, which she shared with Helen, who was somewhere in the depths of her own bedroom. Maiko felt bolstered by the thought that Helen was there; if Charlie tried something, she'd have support. She was in sweatpants with baggy elastic, not wanting to put any pressure on her abdomen after her procedure. She looked and felt like hell and didn't want to draw this out any longer than she had to.

"Nothing; it's me," she said. She couldn't tell him that she wanted him to be someone he was not: a person she barely knew, a kind person who would go to the clinic with her. She was always choosing guys who needed to be fixed. It had finally dawned on her that Charlie was not the type of guy she could ask to go to the clinic with her, and that unkindness, coupled with her current misery, influenced her decision.

"This is bullshit, Mai!" he shouted.

After he had left, slamming the door behind him, Maiko folded in on herself and made a cup of hot tea, even though it was sweltering in her little apartment. It wasn't in the nice part of Hollywood, but the seedy area where broken glass littered the sidewalks and crumpled plastic bags from the Blockbuster Video fluttered along the ground. Helen, who was also a model, sauntered out of her room and lit a cigarette, despite Maiko's repeated declarations that she hated the smell. Tonight, after

Maiko made a face, Helen opened a window and tapped her ash outside, letting it drift down from the second story.

"So, what'd he do?" Helen asked, taking a deep drag.

Maiko plucked at the leg of her sweatpants, wearing them despite the heat and the tepid AC that was now being leaked out the open window. "It's hard to explain," she muttered. Maiko and Helen were not very close; Helen was standoffish and gruff, but somehow they were copacetic in their habitation together. The roommates didn't bond over anything except their grocery list, which they regulated down to the raisin, and they labeled their food obsessively.

Helen raised an eyebrow but said nothing in response. Then: "You look like shit," she offered, and slipped on her clogs to go clomping downstairs to the convenience store for more cigarettes. When she returned, Maiko was still sitting with her legs curled up under her on the dingy sofa, and Helen slipped her a Snickers.

It was the kindest thing Helen had ever done. Never mind that Maiko could barely eat the candy bar. She nibbled on one edge and then put it in the freezer.

Maiko was back at work two days later. The art directors were staring intently at her clavicles trying to decide which pendant would look better on her neck, when Maiko looked up and saw the male model she would be partnered with. The jawline was familiar. Her eyes trailed down his sinewy forearms and she recognized his hands. It was the guy from the clinic.

If he recognized her, he didn't show it. He gave her a small, impersonal smile and she nodded back.

"Adrian," someone called, and the guy turned. He was impeccably clean-shaven, with a perfect line buzzed at the nape of his neck. His hair was brown, but Maiko imagined it would be a hazy red in the sun.

A diamond pendant was chosen for Maiko, clasped around her neck, and she draped her hair over her back. Her agency advertised her with her long, dark hair and cattish shaped eyes. She was tall too: tall for an Asian girl, though it was probably due to her being half-white and her father standing at six-five.

The photographer gave the instructions: "Okay, you two are going to embrace each other. He worships the ground you walk on. Remember to sell the diamond."

Maiko nodded and Adrian joined her on the set. He had been stripped of his shirt and oiled down so his skin was glistening. Maiko could see where the photographers had placed the lights and instinctively knew how to position her face and chest so that the pendant gleamed. She could imagine what the photo would look like, black and white with her skin aglow and her small hands delicately clasping Adrian's face.

His face was so close to hers; his breath was minty. When they were finished with the shoot, he drew away from her with his eyes guarded, and asked, "Are you . . . you know, are you okay?"

And that was how Maiko knew: he remembered her from the clinic too.

She chewed the inside of her lip, wondering how to answer.

"It's just—my girlfriend. She's not . . ." He trailed off. Maiko understood. His girlfriend wasn't up and working yet. But here was Maiko, buffed and polished and looking serene, and she resented her life for more than a split second.

"I have bills to pay," she said simply, and Adrian nodded.

"Take care," he said.

And Maiko was sure she'd never see him again.

THE *EVERGREEN* SET Maiko found herself on several weeks later was outdoors and humid. Lighting riggers placed a giant diffuser in the air to try to soften the light falling on the actors; to Maiko, it looked like a great white parade balloon held down by dozens of strings. She was hovering by craft services, playing with the label on a water bottle, when Adrian ambled up to her and said hello.

"What were the chances of seeing you here?" he asked. "In a city this size?"

Maiko nodded, not answering. The PA who had set her there had asked her to stay quiet, and she didn't want to risk his ire.

"So you play a model in this scene?" he continued. "Must not be a stretch of the imagination for you."

Maiko continued to be silent. It seemed to drive Adrian to want to babble, because he said, "Did you see our billboard on Riverside? We look great together."

Maiko let out a small huff of breath. "Why are you even talking to me?" she asked.

"What?"

Maiko didn't like this cocky version of the kind man she had seen at the clinic. "How's your girlfriend?" she asked, without preamble.

"Oh. Um. She's fine."

She nodded, as if what he'd said confirmed something she'd suspected. "Does she know that you come up to random women during your job and pester them?"

"You're not *random*. We've worked together before."

"I'm not random, hmm? So what's my name?"

Adrian stood very still, thrown for a loop. The photographer had never said her name during the shoot, preferring instead to shout enthused *Yes*es or *A little more!* And the assistant director on this TV show had seen her and acknowledged her but hadn't addressed her. The truth was, Adrian did not know her name.

Maiko left the mangled bottle on the craft services table, walking away from Adrian. She didn't go far, because the PA would need to find her, but she didn't want to be bothered.

Which is why it was *highly* inconvenient when the AD strode toward her and said, "Maiko. There you are. You're playing a b-ball player's model wife. Here." And gestured her to Adrian. "Just hang off of him like he's the planet around which you revolve."

Maiko placed her elbow on his shoulder, leaning against him, hoping that her deodorant had broken down and he would get a good whiff of her armpit.

"Maiko," Adrian said. "What is that? Korean?"

"Japanese," she said between gritted teeth.

"And you're with NRG Models."

"That's right."

"They're tough." When she didn't say anything, he continued. "Ophelia—my girlfriend—tried to get with them. She wasn't tall enough. How tall are you?"

"Five-ten."

"I'm six-one. I was wondering. You're in heels and you're about eye level with me." He regarded her lightly. His eyes were dark brown and Maiko realized she had been right about his hair—it burned red in the sun. She felt a slight turn in her stomach, an attraction for which she'd always been a little weak.

In fact, there was something going on with Adrian at the moment that made her sway slightly under his influence. He was sweating in his jersey, and there must have been pheromones coming off him, because she hadn't felt so woozy in his presence during the jewelry shoot. Then again, she hazarded, maybe it had been because she'd still been recovering from her procedure and dumping Charlie.

"Quiet on the set, please!" came a call, and Maiko leaned heavily against Adrian, opposite hand on her hip, feeling like a groupie.

The scene was shot, wrapped, dismissed. On to the next. Maiko's job here was done.

Before she left the lot, Adrian caught up with her and pressed a scrap of paper into her hand. "If you ever want to get coffee," he said, and gave a smirking smile.

Maiko looked down at her palm and saw *Adrian Hightower 213* . . . She balled up the paper while he watched. "What, so you get your girlfriend pregnant, support her abortion—which is great of you, not going to take that away from you—but then you hit on *me* while you're still with her? What kind of *garbage* are you?"

He looked properly chastised and his ears burned pink. "I meant it as a professional courtesy," he said, and Maiko couldn't tell if he was lying or not. "I figure, we're in the same industry, we're both trying to make it, it'd be nice to have more friends."

"Likely story," Maiko snarled, and she turned on her heel and stalked away. She loved her long legs at that moment, carrying her far, far away from Adrian Hightower.

2

2001

Adrian gazed at the paycheck with hot eyes. He'd never seen so much money made out to him before. There, forty-five hundred dollars and zero cents, to Adrian Hightower, for his work on *Punch Drunk*. It was enough to pay his rent thrice over for his shithole apartment in Pasadena and keep him in gas to commute to auditions for the next couple of months. It had saved his hide.

No matter that the *Punch Drunk* role was a small, bit part on a WB drama. It was *work*. It was good, honest work—the kind of work that his father, Jerome, liked to espouse was the only kind of work there was dignity in doing. So what if he was acting, and pretending to be someone he was not, instead of selling cars off a dealership lot?

Adrian loved the chase of it, the thrill of booking something, *anything*. He wasn't choosy right now because he was still getting his feet wet. The beginning of life in Hollywood was rough. With barely any safety net, Adrian was working his ass off trying to make a name for himself, one small part at a time.

He had recently broken up with his longtime girlfriend, Ophelia, who had not seen eye-to-eye with him about his career trajectory. She was floundering in her modeling career and wanted to take him down with her. Nope, not happening. He was going to make it. *It* being an ever-distant mark. *It* used to be getting a recurring role on a sitcom, but after *Punch Drunk* the idea of *it* became a main character role in a project. Film, TV, whatever. He would make it happen.

It had been a year since he'd been on the set of *Evergreen* and he wondered what had happened to that young model, what was her name? The pretty one, Asian with long hair and cattish shaped eyes. She haunted him sometimes when he was alone, his mind's eye tracing the contour of her pretty upper lip.

"What's that?" his housemate, Tim, said. Tim was a light rigger and was doing well for himself, having a consistent job on an NBC show. He was a brown-eyed blond with a beer gut and one of the nicest guys Adrian had ever known, sometimes floating Adrian his portion of the rent money. But that didn't mean he had health insurance, a fact that he bemoaned every time he got paid.

"My check for *Punch Drunk*," Adrian said excitedly, and held it out to Tim to see. "Look at it!"

Tim whistled through his teeth. "We should celebrate. Get some barbecue out in K-town or something."

"Are you kidding? I'm socking this away. I need it for rent

and gas." Then, feeling bad, he added, "Though I can treat you to a beer if you want."

"Sold! Anyway, aren't you auditioning for *Atomic Crusader* soon?" Tim gave a small guffaw.

Atomic Crusader was a movie that had everyone in Hollywood— and London—gunning for the title role. The chance that Adrian would get it was minuscule. Smaller than small. Insignificant. But Adrian's agent, Jason, wanted him to try for it anyway. He was the right build for it, had the right timbre of voice. An unknown without a pedigree, something that appealed to the casting crew, because the Atomic Crusader was a self-made superhero, not a product of nepotism. Jason had gotten Adrian the audition and told him not to fuck it up. Adrian wasn't convinced he'd get it, but he wasn't about to look a gift horse in the mouth.

"Yeah," Adrian said, feeling slightly deflated.

"If you get it, we're definitely getting steak."

"Yeah," Adrian said again, slightly more enthused this time.

He went to deposit the check, taking his dilapidated old Camry through the bank drive-through and watching the ATM eat the important piece of paper. Then he drove himself to a liquor store, where he bought a six-pack of light beer to celebrate with Tim.

What was the point of living in Hollywood and doing these jobs if he couldn't enjoy his wins?

ADRIAN WAS PAINFULLY shy in his youth. He was good at calculating math, so much so that he was a member of his middle school's Number Sense club. He learned how to do FOIL calculations when he was ten and even won eleventh place in the regional competition. But when he graduated to high school, he had trouble with theoretical math. All of that *imagining,* and not the way he expected it to be.

Jerome, his father, wouldn't help him with homework because he was always at work. Adrian dropped calculus to take a study hall and physics to become a student aide. He was assigned to the drama department. What he learned there would change his life.

Adrian was too timid to audition for anything the first semester of his time in the drama club, but he watched and absorbed. He loved how his peers would disappear into a role. He liked the makeup creating elderly faces on the skin of his youthful friends, the bright lights. He enjoyed the costumes and the *bustle* behind the curtain and the stage manager whispering into their mic headset. And so, when he was a senior, he auditioned for Bottom in *A Midsummer Night's Dream,* not realizing that that character had the most lines out of anyone in the play.

But he learned all of his monologue and delivered it with ease during rehearsals. On the night of the first performance, instead of finding himself jittery with nerves, he was calm and ready. Adrian felt like he was someone else entirely; he'd removed his skin and placed Bottom's on top of his skeleton, and his brain was occupied by Bottom, and he was determined.

His father and mother, Betty, were in the front row on opening night; when the curtain dropped at the end of the performance, he let Bottom out of his lungs and returned to being just Adrian Hightower. Suddenly, it wasn't awful to be himself. He'd found a power within that made him more comfortable in his skin.

"Honey!" his mother said, carrying a bouquet of daisies and carnations in crinkly paper. "We're so proud of you."

Jerome had actually attended the play, eschewing his normal seven o'clock practice of taking a walk around all the cars in his dealership to make sure nothing was dented or scratched or had been the target of a bird. He gruffly cuffed his son on the shoulder and said, "I didn't understand half of what you said, but you did good."

"Marvelous!" Betty said, handing Adrian the flowers.

He held them at his chest and looked down at them. They weren't the expensive kinds of buds that other kids were getting—roses and the like—but he appreciated them because he knew his parents cared.

When Adrian applied to colleges, he chose schools with drama programs. But something about further schooling made him itch. He wanted to do things *now*, while he was still *hungry*. He didn't want to go to classes and get the spontaneity beaten out of him by someone who wanted to relive their glory days of being on Broadway.

And so. Adrian told his parents he was going to graduate high school and go off to Los Angeles to try to become an actor.

Betty was concerned. "What's your backup plan?"

"This is it," Adrian answered. "This is the plan."

Jerome was nonplussed. "Saves us money on schooling, that's for sure," he said. "We can use your college fund to pay off our mortgage."

Betty, still hesitant, asked, "But what if . . . well, what if it doesn't go right?"

"I'll come back and work at the dealership," Adrian promised. "But I think I'm going to make it okay."

"You're a focused young man," Betty said, "so I hope you'll do fine. But, Adrian? If you get hungry, let us know. We'll send you Western Union for rent or groceries."

Adrian left for Los Angeles the week after high school graduation. He wasted no time in securing a shitty shared apartment with someone else who had a job in the industry and threw himself into auditioning. He wasn't going to go groveling back to his parents. He never wanted to work in the car dealership—no offense to his father. He was young, lean, and hungry.

3

Maiko stood on her mark.

"Whenever you're ready," the designer said.

Maiko took a deep breath and strutted down an imaginary runway. She imbued pep into every step, grinning with her entire face, her heels coming down sure and square. She gave a little hip check at the end of the runway—which was really the carpeted floor of a designer's shop—paused, then walked back the way she'd come. When she was done, she turned with her hand still on her hip, as if to say, *What did you think?*

"Thank you, but we won't be using you for this show," said the designer.

Maiko tried to school her facial expression into one of gratefulness instead of sorrow. "Thank you," she said, taking her portfolio of images back from the assistant and walking out of the door with her head held high.

Modeling was excruciating. Long hours, little pay, and tons of rejection. She felt like crying. She wouldn't be able to afford her part of the rent this month. She'd have to rely on her parents again, and she loathed asking them for money. They didn't think modeling was a viable career, and here she was, proving them right.

Just one more booking, she told herself, teeth clenched. All she needed was one more booking. Then she could buy groceries and pay her half of the rent. She'd have to be careful, but she could do it.

She walked along the boulevard until she reached the next designer, Madeleine Alexandra. As she walked in the side door, she wondered if she should be casting her net a little wider. Something more commercial, not as high-end. Maybe she had a Clean & Clear sort of look. Maybe she should be hawking CoverGirl products instead of trying to sell Miu Miu.

If I don't get this one, she thought to herself, *I'll try for a makeup brand*. And in the meantime, she'd still apply to be an extra in some TV shows and movies. They were a dime a dozen here and the pay, paltry as it was, was better than nothing. She'd rather get paid seventy-five dollars for ten hours of her time than sit at home doing nothing but despairing that her dream wouldn't come true.

There were other eager models waiting for their chance at the go-see, so Maiko had to wait her turn. When it was her chance to shine, she did her signature strut, a placid smile on her face this time, a perfunctory pause at the end of the imagined runway, and back. Her mind was zen as she walked. She tried to keep her thoughts clear, as if the audience could mind-read, and concentrated instead on stepping with surety and grace.

"Your look is perfect," said Madeleine. "Are you free on the twenty-fourth to walk my show?"

"Yes!" Maiko said, her enthusiasm apparent. She cleared her throat. "Yes, I'm available."

"Great. We'll follow up with your agency. NRG Models, right?" Both Madeleine and her assistant were leafing through her portfolio. There was an image from the Kriegler's shoot that Maiko could see upside-down, and she thought of that model she had been paired with. Adrian Hightower. He'd tried to give her his number. She should've accepted. She hated that it had been years since that shoot and he was still on her mind. But why?

She stepped out onto the sidewalk with her portfolio in hand and gave a little scream. She was making it! And then she thought: *I can do anything. I should try to model for something big. Like Valentina Posh, the lingerie company. Or* Seventeen *magazine.*

THE COLD BIT through Maiko's thin shirt and she repressed a shiver. The set was outdoors, a made-up town with a fake square. She stood in rickety stilettos, wondering if she had time to pull them off and slip them back on before the director started rolling film. They were the type of heel that had a thousand clasps ribboning up the leg so she didn't think it would be possible, but she could still dream.

Maiko was playing yet another model—this time in a movie, *Summer Haze.* Because modeling also played with the seasons—photographing bikinis in the height of winter, and winter coats photographed during the summer—it barely bothered Maiko that this summery scene was being filmed in February. She had learned to compartmentalize her body's discomfort on shoots, but these shoes were testing her strength. She shifted from one foot to the other.

"Cold?" came a voice, and there he was again, two years after she'd last set eyes on him. Adrian Hightower. She had tried to forget him, but he'd lingered in her memory. She'd seen him on a TV show where he'd had a bit part, and she secretly harbored a crush.

Adrian was a good-looking guy, for sure. He had a great smile, with beautifully shaped teeth and one crooked lateral incisor that made his perfect smile not-so-perfect after all. His dark brown eyes had a lovely depth to them, and he had a cute nose that wasn't too pointy or too buttony. Just an all-around good face. Maiko assumed it had to be the face, because she barely knew Adrian, except that he was the type of guy who would take his girlfriend to the abortion clinic but would also try to scam on other women.

But maybe Adrian had been truthful when he'd said that he'd wanted to grab coffee as a professional courtesy . . .

Maiko shrugged, and the sequined silver shirt she was wearing rippled. It was as large as a handkerchief and had strings for a back. Adrian was already pulling off his windbreaker and settling it on her shoulders, but Maiko shook it off. "I don't need this. It's my feet that are killing me, not the weather."

"I could carry you," Adrian joked, and Maiko flicked a glance at him, as if to say *Don't be so unprofessional.*

"I'll live, thanks."

"Playing another model? What a stretch of the imagination." He said it wryly, without judgment.

"I'm good at it."

"I can see." And he actually gave her a long, roving glance, from her blue-black hair to her tall, gangly frame to her over-size feet stuffed into too-small stilettos. "No complaints."

Maiko pressed her lips together. "How's your girlfriend?" she asked.

"Oh. She's . . . well, we're no longer together."

A sliver of hope opened up in her chest and she said with surprise, "Yeah?"

Adrian's eyes were very warm as he nodded. "Yeah."

There was a zip of energy between the two, from sternum to sternum, as they assessed each other with direct eye contact. "No . . . new girlfriend?" Maiko asked hopefully.

"Nope."

Maiko wanted to ask him if he would still like that coffee and was gathering up her courage when the director came up to them. "Adrian, you're needed for the next shot."

She watched him walk to his mark, and she realized that he was an actual star of *Summer Haze* and that all the other models-turned-extras were chittering excitedly because he'd deigned to talk to one of them. Maiko had not kept tabs on Adrian's career, only lazily checking his IMDb page once in a blue moon, but it seemed like he was doing well for himself.

"You know Adrian?" one of the other extras said to Maiko.

"Um, yeah, we worked together on a TV show a long time ago."

"Ugh, he's so hot."

Maiko watched the director walk a few paces with Adrian, describing the scene that was about to be shot, and she nodded. "Yeah," she agreed.

"You do this a lot?" asked the same extra.

"Yeah, but I'm thinking of stopping. I'm walking Fashion Week."

"Oh, wow!"

"I feel like I should devote my time to my modeling, you know?"

Maiko didn't know this woman but felt comfortable speaking aloud what she'd been thinking. Surely, once she'd walked Fashion Week, the opportunities for her modeling would rise? She hadn't had much luck for the past two years, toiling instead in the same grind.

"Quiet on the set! *Rolling!*" came a shout, and the two women stopped talking to watch Adrian. He walked and delivered his lines with ease. Maiko had been on enough sets to know that it was hard to walk and talk at the same time; even seasoned veterans overthought it and their legs would look unnatural. Adrian had star power.

When "*Cut!*" had been shouted after the scene, the extra said to Maiko, "I wonder how much longer we'll be here."

Maiko shrugged. She'd stay here all day if it meant watching Adrian.

The models were dismissed sometime around eight, but Maiko stuck around in her street clothes for a while, and sure enough, Adrian came sauntering out of one of the trailers parked nearby. Maiko suddenly felt very shy. She had been practicing what she wanted to say, but now that it came time to say it, she wasn't sure how. "Um, Adrian," she said, her throat gone dry.

"Yeah?"

"I was wondering . . . if you ever wanted to grab . . . that coffee . . ." Every word was excruciating to get out, made worse by the fact that the guy didn't give any encouragement whatsoever. Maiko felt her face burning. Then Adrian's face split into a grin. He held out a Post-it. *Adrian Hightower 213 . . .*

"You're not going to throw it away this time?" Adrian laughed.

Maiko took the paper happily.

"I'll call you," she promised.

"I HAVEN'T SEEN you this giddy since . . . well, since I've known you," Christine said to Maiko, the night of her first date with Adrian. Christine was Maiko's oldest friend, having known her since they were both in first grade. She was a short Black woman with dark brown eyes that glimmered when she was excited. They were bright now with anticipation as her friend got ready. The three of them were in Helen's room while Maiko tried on some of Helen's more daring clothes, stuff she'd found at estate sales and thrift stores, some of them name brand.

Maiko was shimmying into a low-waisted miniskirt with a crop top, but decided she didn't want to show so much skin. She threw the skirt onto Helen's twin-size bed and bent over to pull on a pair of ultra-low-rise jeans instead. They buttoned right at her pubic bone.

"Have you ever met someone and just known . . ." Maiko started to say, but then she stopped herself, not wanting to jinx it.

Helen took a drag of her cigarette and breathed out heavily through her nostrils. "Can't say that I have," she said shortly. "All the women I date have been touched in the head." She tapped her forehead with the hand holding her cigarette butt, indicating *crazy*.

"I have," Christine said dreamily.

"We know, we know. You're violently in love. Christine, do you *have* to move to Roanoke to be with Derek?" Maiko tossed the crop top off and tried on a tiny sweater. "I just . . . think he's special, that's all." She whirled around, looking at her exposed back in the mirror, and added a studded belt to her ensemble. "Do I look too . . . Avril?"

"For that, you'd have to wear a tie," Christine said. "You look great. Do you know where you're going?"

"No, it's a surprise." Maiko couldn't contain her excitement. "Maybe I should wear a dress."

When Adrian knocked on the door and led her down to his haphazardly parked jalopy, Maiko was in a ribbed sweater-dress and a pair of her most comfortable heels. She ducked into the car, an early-nineties Toyota sedan, and ignored the fabric peeling off the edges of the ceiling.

"I just got paid for *Summer Haze* and I haven't had a chance to upgrade yet," Adrian said, a little embarrassed. "But I know you're not into me because of my car, so."

Maiko laughed. "I'd be the worst gold-digger ever if I was

into you for your car," she agreed. "I don't care about your ride. I'm just excited to go out with you."

The two looked at each other across the gearshift and Maiko was shy again. What should they talk about? There was an awkward silence that she hastened to fill. She watched him check his side mirror before signaling to pull out from the parking spot.

"We had to get up hideously early for that Kriegler's shoot, didn't we?" she said, wondering what to discuss.

"They went out of business, you know," he replied, easing the car up to speed. "Barely had that billboard up for a week. But I went to go see it. Just because, you know." And he quirked his mouth in a smile as he glanced over at her.

"No, I don't know; tell me," Maiko teased, and he grinned all the way as he navigated down the road.

"We looked good together," he said, shrugging.

"Omigod, you totally had a crush on me," she said.

"Did not."

"Did too!" She gave him a playful shove on his shoulder and he made an exaggerated gasp.

"I'm driving here!"

"It's okay," she said, settling back into her dilapidated seat. She wouldn't admit to him that she'd had a crush on him for two years. It was a little embarrassing. She didn't know anything about him, except that he had gone with his then-girlfriend to the health clinic and that he had a nice smile. She wondered if maybe he was a jerk and she had been letting his good face trick her into this date. She resolved to find out more about him as soon as possible.

"So." She watched him drive. He was a good driver, something that she appreciated. He stopped at all stop signs and looked both ways. That was unusual in a Los Angeles driver. He had his hands on ten and two on the wheel, and she liked that he wasn't trying to feel up her leg—even though she kind of wanted him to.

"So." He gave her a dimpled half grin.

"Can I change the station?" The radio had been warbling some R&B and it was not Maiko's style. "Do you actually listen to this?"

Adrian laughed. "I just clicked it on the most popular tunes. There are CDs in the glove compartment if you want to change it."

She popped the compartment and slid the CDs out of the zippered case. Radiohead, Coldplay, Godspeed You! Black Emperor, and Yo La Tengo were among the groups. *Kid A* would be too melancholy and intense for a first date, she decided, and put in *Parachutes*.

"I didn't take you for a Coldplay fan," he said.

"*Everyone* is a fan of Coldplay. They just don't know it."

"I'll have to tell my housemate that. He hates Chris Martin."

"What's to hate? He has a great voice and he sings about the color yellow. Although yellow is usually the worst flavor of candy. Like a lemon Skittle. What's your favorite Skittles flavor?"

"Lime. But yellow *is* the worst," he added.

"Mine's purple."

Maiko looked at Adrian across the gearshift. The street light was painting his face in red, and she liked tracing the strong outline of his jaw with her eyes.

"You say 'purple' like it's a flavor." He joked. "Isn't it grape or something?"

"It's purple. It's sugar. It tastes like sugar." She was quiet for a moment. "Not that I eat many Skittles in the first place."

"Special occasions only," he said, with a knowing nod. "That's why I don't touch the yellow ones. I throw them out. I'm not wasting calories on an inferior flavor."

"Me too!" Maiko was happy learning this about her date. She felt a kinship. It was so silly, bonding over candy, but candy, to her, was a big deal. She didn't get to eat it all that often.

"How old are you?" he asked.

"Twenty," she said.

"Where are you from?"

She rolled her eyes. "I'm from LA. But if you're asking where I'm *from*, my mom is Japanese and my dad is white."

"I wasn't asking that. I was wondering where you grew up."

"You know Mark Fox?"

Adrian shifted in his seat. "Should I . . . ?"

"Well, he's a world-famous architect. He's my dad."

"That's awesome," Adrian said, feelingly. "My dad is a car dealer in Florida. Mostly new cars—but yeah. I've had this old Toyota since I got my license. It's been with me since high school and it came looking the way it does because I paid for it myself."

"I was wondering!" Maiko said, a hint of teasing in her

voice. "You drive so carefully, like you're afraid to scratch the paint."

"I know it's stupid to baby a car this ugly," Adrian said, "but I can't mishandle a car. Even if it's hideous." He took her hand. To Maiko, it felt as natural as breathing air. She marveled at how their palms fit together. "I'm actually working on a script. I want to make a movie one day."

"That's really amazing," she said, impressed. "What do your folks think of it?"

"My mom is supportive, but my dad . . . well, he doesn't get it. But I just had a callback for a big movie that I'm hoping to land."

"Ooh, which one? Or will you jinx it if you tell me?"

"*Atomic Crusader*," he said, a little shyly.

"Oh wow! Good luck. You have the right build for it."

"You were checking me out?" he asked, voice teasing.

Maiko's cheeks burned. She coughed and changed the subject. "My parents wanted me to go to college to become a lawyer. When I took up modeling, they were like, *Okay, but you're on your own*. My mom sends me some money every now and then for gas and groceries, but for the most part, I'm doing this myself." She plucked at her dress with her free hand.

"And how's it going?" he asked, eyes back on the road.

"I'm going to walk Fashion Week in Milan!"

"Wow, that's a big deal, right?" he asked. "That's really awesome."

"And I got a contract for Valentina Posh," she said proudly. "I'm going to be a Vixen."

"Look at you," he said in awe.

She giggled and ran a hand down her thigh. "Yup, Vixen material, right here. It took two years of auditions but it's finally happening." She grew quiet. "I hope I'm not just a 'diversity hire.'"

"Why would you be?" he asked, sounding indignant.

"I've been told that I was hired not because I was a good model, but because I filled a quota. It wouldn't be the first time."

"I find that very hard to believe," he said. "Not that it's happened to you before, but that you're not a good model. When I saw you on that *Summer Haze* shoot, you took my breath away."

"That's sweet of you. Thanks." She felt a heat in her chest, and deflected the flattery.

"It's not just a line," he said, and his fingers curled around hers. He was still looking at the road, but he squeezed her palm.

"How did you feel when you got the first check for *Summer Haze*?" she asked. "I want to know what to anticipate, for when I get paid for VP."

"I couldn't believe it. All those zeroes, just for me? It made no sense." He smiled ruefully. "But then I had to give a portion to my agent, and my manager, and save some for taxes, and the pie got sliced up. Still, that first glimpse of the check was *otherworldly*."

"I can't wait," she said, sighing happily and leaning back in the seat. She played with her fingers, tapping the side of his hand, as if she were nervous. He glanced down in between them at their hands on the gearshift, but he didn't say anything. "I want a new car. I've been driving a Mitsubishi Eclipse my parents bought me for my sixteenth birthday. It's *sort* of reliable, but starting to have some problems. But I'm so intimidated by car dealers and all their little scare tactics. No offense to your dad."

"I can teach you how to buy a car!" he said excitedly. "I have tons of experience, working at my family's dealership."

"I might take you up on that." She smiled.

"Anyway, we're here." He turned into a driveway, and Maiko crowed with delight.

"Dumplings!"

4

They got dumplings in Chinatown—even though it was out of their way, Adrian said that they "had to" because they were "the best"—and then went dancing at Dublin's. Tipsy off two whiskey sodas, Maiko let her limbs loosen on the dance floor as the percussion reverberated through her spine. Adrian was right next to her, his hairline beaded in sweat.

Giggling, she led Adrian up to her second-story apartment and turned the key in the lock. "I have a roommate, just so you know, so we have to be quiet," Maiko said, and turned the doorknob under the heel of her hand. The door swung open and they stumbled in, not quite drunk on alcohol but definitely inebriated with something else.

Adrian said, "Is something on fire?"

"No, it's just Helen. She smokes."

"I wondered. But you, you smell like . . . lavender." He gave a theatrical sniff of her neck and she giggled.

"Want something to drink? I think we have Grey Goose in the freezer?"

"Nah, I'm good."

Maiko flopped down on the tweedy couch and wrapped her arms around a throw pillow. Adrian settled down next to her, but he didn't attempt to make any romantic moves. They were suddenly shy toward each other, trying to tamp down their animalistic feelings and to know *each other* as people. They peered down at the space between them, the pillow barrier that Maiko was holding, and smiled secret smiles to themselves.

Maiko already knew a bit about Adrian that was available online: he was twenty-two, he was from Tallahassee, he moved out to LA when he was eighteen to try to make it in Hollywood. He had played little bit parts every now and then, like the boyfriend of a side character with one line in a WB show, but *Summer Haze* was his first starring role, and he had auditioned for the *Atomic Crusader* superhero movie. His trajectory was going up.

Maiko studied Adrian as he cast a look around the apartment, which was quite homey despite the models obviously being on a budget. There was a small lamp emitting an orange glow next to the tweedy couch. The walls were covered in thin cloth blankets with designs all over them, like tapestries. A beaded curtain made up of plastic butterflies separated the living room from a minuscule kitchen, the light in it still on and the refrigerator humming loudly.

Maiko was buzzing. She hadn't kissed him in the car, wanting to prolong this moment of knowing Adrian before *knowing* him. She smiled at him and waited for him to make a move.

"Maiko," Adrian said.

"Yes, Adrian?" Her heart thumped wildly.

"Do you want that car dealership lesson now?"

Maiko laughed. She had been expecting something else, but she nodded. "Go for it." She shifted so that she was facing him on the couch, one leg pulled up slightly on the seat cushion. He looked at her bare knee for a moment before composing himself.

"The first rule is, try to buy in cash. And the second rule is, never let them know you want to buy in cash."

"That doesn't make any sense. Isn't cash king? Wouldn't they want to know in advance that I'm going to make their job super easy?"

"Dealerships make their money off financing," he explained. "So it's in their advantage for you to have monthly payments with interest. What you do is, you go in, you look at the cars, you choose one that you like, you sit down, and you say, *I want the out-the-door price.*"

"Out the door," she repeated.

"They'll needle you with questions about how much you want to pay per month, but you just say, *I want the out-the-door price.* And don't sign or initial anything that they put down in front of you."

"Out the door, don't sign or initial," she said, like a mantra.

"Want to try it?" he asked.

"What, like role-play?" She looked at him from under her dark lashes, and he turned pink.

"Just try it." He cleared his throat. "Hi there, miss. I see you've test-driven the Honda Accord."

"I can't afford an Accord," she interrupted.

"Yes, you can. You're a top model in this scenario."

"If I were a top model, I'd buy a Lexus."

"*Mai.*" He said her nickname so easily, it was as if he'd known her for years. She beamed in pleasure. She liked the way her name sounded in his mouth.

"Okay, okay."

"So, the Honda Accord. What do you think?"

"It's a nice car. I want to buy it."

"No, you don't ever say you want to buy it."

"Isn't that the whole point?"

"You tell them that it's a good fit for you and if the price is right, *then* you'll buy."

"This is too complicated."

"They make it complicated for a reason. Okay. Would you like to talk financing?"

"I want the out-the-door price," she parroted.

"If I could just find out what you'd like your monthly payments to be, I can get a good deal for you."

"I want the out-the-door price," she said again, laughing, batting him with a throw pillow.

"Good! That's good practice." Adrian smiled at her. "Mai?"

"Yes, Adrian?"

"I'd really like to kiss you."

"Okay," she said, coy.

An electric jolt passed through them once more as they closed the gap between their faces. Adrian placed a hand on Maiko's cheek and brushed some of her long hair away with a thumb. Maiko closed her eyes. Their lips met, tentatively at first, a quiet exploration of mouth on mouth. But then they grew equally hungry. Maiko had the sense that she wanted to *eat* Adrian; she wanted to consume him with everything she had. The way he responded in kind let her know that he was interested in devouring her as well.

Maiko didn't know how long they sat on the couch, twining closer and closer, but after a while, Adrian pulled back. "I have an early-morning meeting with my agent that I can't miss. If we get started here, I feel like I'll never leave. I don't want to say *I'll call you* because that sounds like I won't. So let's make a plan to see each other on Friday."

"Okay." Maiko smoothed her dress down over her knees. She felt flushed and tired in all the right ways. She sat up on the couch as Adrian stood, and she could see the outline of his erection through his pants. She wanted to press her face into his groin and hear him moan, but she refrained. "I'll walk you out, then."

He kissed her again at the door and gave her a sweet smile. "See you Friday." Then he was gone.

JASON WAS GRINNING widely at Adrian over the tablecloth. He'd ordered mimosas in champagne glasses for their early, in-person meeting. "What's the occasion?" Adrian had asked, because he was expecting coffee at that hour in the morning.

"My man," Jason said. "You got it."

"What do you mean, *I got it*?"

"Your life is about to change, Adrian. You're going to be Atomic Crusader."

Adrian had had a good feeling after his third callback for the movie, but he hadn't expected this news. He'd often felt that he'd nailed auditions and then found out later that he was not chosen for the part.

He breathed, "This is huge."

"It's a huge deal, yes. The best part isn't just the paycheck, which will be substantial. But the merchandising! Atomic Crusader is everywhere kids are. So there will be lunchboxes and posters and Halloween costumes with your picture on the label."

"Wow," Adrian said. His head was swimming. He didn't know what to say.

"We can go over the offer right now, or you can bask in this for a while before we get down to the nitty-gritty," Jason said. "I'm going to try to negotiate a higher salary for you and a portion of residuals."

"Are you sure that won't . . . make them not want to hire me?" Adrian was suddenly afraid of the offer dissipating like smoke.

"Trust me." Jason took a swig of his mimosa and then speared a piece of asparagus covered in hollandaise. Then he pointed his fork at Adrian's midsection. "No beer. Not even light beer. I shouldn't even be giving you champagne right now. Alcohol goes straight to the gut. You're going to need to lose ten pounds of fat to fit into the costume."

Adrian straightened up, sucking in his belly. He pushed away the toast from his poached eggs and said, "No problem."

"You'll be able to hire a dietician to put together a nutrition plan for you."

"Okay."

"And you'll need to work out more. Lose the fat, gain ten pounds of muscle instead. Your thighs need to be tree trunks."

"On it."

Jason grinned again. "I knew you could do it, buddy. You're going to be the goose that laid the golden egg for me. I'm glad I stuck it out with you."

It was true; it had been four grueling years for Adrian. But now it was going to be worth it. *Atomic Crusader.* He was going to be known for decades to come as the vigilante superhero. He'd be able to buy—not just rent—a new place, move out on his own. Maybe someplace flashy. *Not* Pasadena.

He leaned forward. "Tell me all about the deal."

WHEN ADRIAN WAS done with the meeting, all he wanted to do was tell Maiko about his good news. Instead of waiting for Friday, he drove to her apartment that same morning and ran up the stairs to the second story, and only when he reached her door did he wonder if he was being too eager. He knocked tentatively, and Helen opened the door.

"Yes?" she said curtly, cigarette dangling from her mouth.

"Is Maiko in?" he asked hopefully.

"Mai!" she hollered, and the ash floated down. Helen was a dishwater blonde who'd bleached her hair platinum and had a Michelle Pfeiffer look to her. Big lips—perfect for a lipstick campaign—kissed the tip of the cigarette. She smoked like a 1940s glamour girl, her long fingers delicately plucking at the filter. "Who are you?" she asked.

"I'm . . . I'm Adrian," he said, trying not to feel awkward.

He placed his hands in his back pockets and pushed his shoulders back.

"Okay, Adrian," Helen purred.

"Back off, Helen," Maiko said, appearing from behind her in a pair of cutoff shorts and a fluorescent pink tank top. Her face was lit with wonder and excitement at seeing Adrian again so soon. "It's *you!*"

Adrian stepped around Helen and grasped Maiko's hands with his. "I got it," he said in a low voice.

The grin that Maiko gave him confirmed to Adrian what he'd already known: that he wanted to share this good news with Maiko before anyone else. Before his roommate—before his parents, even. "Yeah?" she breathed.

"Yeah," he said, nodding.

She gave a squeal and hugged him around the neck. "That's amazing! Congratulations!" She pulled back and looked at him fully in the eyes. He was about to kiss her when Helen said, "Got *what?*" and Adrian remembered she was still there. He whirled around to face Helen.

"I'll tell you when the ink dries," he said. "Mai, want to go out and celebrate?"

"Let me get my shoes!" Maiko said, and she ran back into her room.

"You're the one she went out with last night?" Helen asked, and Adrian nodded. He felt like he should invite Maiko's roommate, for some reason. To share the wealth, share the good news. Helen sized him up while finishing her cigarette and blowing out a long hiss of smoke. She dumped the butt in a nearby Diet

Coke can and gave him a wry smile. "Treat my girl right," she said. A hint of warning was in her voice.

"Yeah. I will."

Maiko dashed back in a pair of clogs that had a two-inch thick sole. She held a small baguette purse in one hand and her flip phone in the other. "Let's go!"

"Do you want to join us?" Adrian asked Helen, and she wrinkled her nose.

"Nah." She turned away. "Threesomes are not my thing."

Giggling, Maiko pulled on Adrian's hand and led him out of the apartment. And this—this was the memory that Adrian held on to for the next night, and the next, and the next. Hell, maybe it was the memory he replayed in his mind when he felt lonely in various days of his life. Maiko, her long hair swirling around her neck like squid ink, looking over her shoulder at him as she tugged on his hand. The sun winked behind her, casting her face in a soft shadow, but her entire face was aglow.

Adrian knew he was a goner in that moment.

5

Maiko and Adrian had kissed on dates (so many movie tickets were used as an excuse to make out in a darkened theater without their roommates looming over them); they had made out in Adrian's car (the gearshift stabbing Adrian in the thigh as he leaned to get closer, closer); Maiko had even encouraged him to feel her up in a dressing room stall at a Pacific Sunwear, until the nosy teen who was in charge of the keys had knocked and said, "Hey, only one person is allowed in there." Adrian had left the cubicle reluctantly, clearing his throat and adjusting the front of his pants while Maiko laughed in the stall. (She did not buy the maxi dress she had been trying on.)

It was November, and the Valentina Posh Fashion Show was imminent. Maiko, a new Vixen, was going to wear three outfits. Maiko had recently been photographed for the catalog, and a huge black-and-white photo of her in a black lace demi bra and matching panties was blown up and hung in every Valentina Posh in the nation. Adrian had a poster framed for Maiko as a gift, though she didn't know where to hang it, so she left it propped up against the accordion doors of her closet.

Every time she looked at it, she marveled at the turn her life had made: She was doing it! She was living her dream!

Maiko was allowed one guest at the show, and she gave her ticket to Adrian. He had to fund his own plane ticket to New York City, and she was technically supposed to room with another model at the hotel, but she knew she could sneak into Adrian's room if he was in the same building.

She was excited. Runway walks were often similar from brand to brand, but the *attitude* was different depending on the designer. Valentina Posh loved playful, approachable models with cheekbones that could cut glass. The Vixens had unattainable beauty, but the average viewer could imagine being *with* them. Some of the other haute couture brands Maiko had walked for would hate what Maiko was rehearsing to do for VP: winking, grinning, *preening* with her rhinestone-studded bra and white panties with stiletto heels.

Adrian had gotten his contract for *Atomic Crusader* and the news had spread like wildfire: this unknown, who had last been in a small spring release called *Summer Haze*, was going to be the new John Jackson. The internet, still in its early days of online forums and bulletin boards, raised the question: Could Adrian Hightower do a creditable job as the 1950s superhero? The masses seemed evenly split between a hearty assent and a negative outlook, and Adrian had been a mess of nerves. Maiko hoped that the fashion show, which would be recorded a month before filming began on *Atomic Crusader*, would help Adrian forget some of his worries.

———

THEY TOOK SEPARATE flights to New York City, as the Vixens were flown on the company's dime, so Maiko didn't see Adrian before the show. Everyone was rushing backstage; there was makeup to be applied *everywhere*, highlighter to be applied to cheeks—face and ass alike—so many tubes of mascara to lose, so many shoes to stumble over, so many tiny garments on hangers with name tags attached. Maiko was hustled into her first outfit and then ducked behind a video camera that was recording the already dressed models backstage for the TV broadcast.

When the show began, Maiko felt a humming in her chest. She was thrumming with energy, eager to get out onto the runway and *strut*. When her turn came, she thrust her chest forward and shifted her hips back, holding on to her thong strings with her pinkies, and *walked*. She couldn't see Adrian, but she sensed him in the audience, and she stopped at the end of the runway and posed, winking. Then she slid back into a strut, one foot slightly crossing in front of the other, until she was backstage again. The exhilaration! The heart-pounding of it all!

Before she knew it, she had walked her three outfits and the audience stood, clapping, as the models showed off the lingerie for the last time. Valentina herself walked out at the end to applause and wished everyone a good night, and the stage went dark.

The Vixens all chattered excitedly among one another after the show, changing into warm clothes to battle the November chill outside. Maiko pulled on a soft sweatshirt she'd borrowed from Adrian and tucked her hands into the long sleeves. The models were bussed to their hotel, and Maiko slipped out of her room while still in her tennis shoes to find Adrian.

They'd planned to meet at the hotel bar for a nightcap. Maiko relaxed as well as she could on a stool and realized that this might be the last time she would be able to sit, unbothered, in public. The show would air the next week and her anonymity would be toast. She sipped a vodka soda leisurely as she waited for Adrian.

Within minutes, he slipped into the seat next to hers. "Fancy meeting you here."

She raised an eyebrow and sipped her drink. "Smooth."

"I try." He gestured to her half-filled glass. "Want another?"

"I'm good," she said. "Are you getting anything?"

He signaled to the bartender, who approached. "Old-fashioned," Adrian said. When he got his drink, he clinked glasses with Mai. "To you."

"To Valentina," she said grandly, and tipped the rest of her drink down her throat. She hadn't eaten much that day—too nervous—and was slightly fuzzy-headed from the alcohol. Adrian, as if sensing this, asked, "Wanna eat something?"

She looked at him from under her lashes. "You."

He cleared his throat, flustered. "Want to get out of here?"

Maiko wanted to, badly. A whole hotel room to themselves—no roommates, no gearshift, no mall employees to interrupt them.

She jumped him as soon as they got into the room. With her legs wrapped around his waist, arms clasped about his neck, she devoured his lips as he carried her to the bed. "Mai, Mai, slow down," he said, when his mouth was free. She was now tugging on the back of his shirt, and he let her pull it over his head.

She stared, enraptured, at his body. He had always been in good shape, but the *Atomic Crusader* workouts took him to the next level. He *looked* like a superhero.

"Wow." She touched the planes of muscles on his shoulders and back.

"You're drunk," he said.

"Tipsy," she corrected.

"Is this my sweatshirt?" he asked, noticing the oversize garment.

"I'll give it back," she said, giggling, and pulled it off. She was wearing a black lace bra, no doubt from her employer. Adrian's hands slid down her ribs to her hips.

They kissed some more, and Maiko lost the bra, and her socks and jeans.

She felt him under his pants and tried to take his slacks off.

"You must be exhausted," he said, kissing her leisurely. "You're rushing just so you can go to sleep, aren't you? Mai, don't worry, I fully intend on fucking you. Tomorrow."

She laughed.

In the end, they made out until they were half-asleep. Adrian tucked Maiko under the sheets and spooned her until six in the morning, when they both woke up, Maiko no longer fuzzy-headed, Adrian with a raging hard-on, and they made love for the first time. Maiko felt that she could definitely love this person, but she didn't say it out loud. She'd been burned before. She held the secret deep in her belly as she came.

New Couple Alert!

Valentina Posh model Maiko Fox and Adrian Hightower, recently tapped to feature in the *Atomic Crusader* movie, were seen canoodling at a restaurant in Malibu. Onlookers say they were hot and heavy in between their appetizers and entrees. Pictures below.

Maiko Fox: The Next Gisele Bündchen?!

Move over, Gisele and Adriana, there's a new Vixen in town! Los Angeles–born Maiko Fox strutted her stuff on the runway during the 2002 Valentina Posh Fashion Show. While she wasn't chosen to wear the coveted Gem-Encrusted Fox Ears—that honor went to Mariacarla Boscono—Maiko's initial runway show proved to be a hit with audiences. Online forums lit up with conversations about the Japanese-American stunner, all chattering excitedly about her beautiful form and perfect strut.

Jiji201 (8:36 P.M.): I see it. She has the looks, the confidence, the walk. I remember seeing her walk for Karen Kane last season and I thought she would blow up. I think VP will be great for her.

G0bsmacked (8:42 P.M.): maiko fox is so beautiful, she's got that all-american diverse look that is so hot right now, like her face is so exotic but not alien-looking like a lot of high fashion models, i think she will dominate the industry.

Luster8pearl (8:45 P.M.): I think she's going to be the new face of L'Oréal too. Homegirl is going places. She'll be in every drugstore in America and Europe too.

Exclusive Clip: An Interview with the Actor Playing Atomic Crusader, on *Entertainment Tonight*!

We're excited to bring you the hottest new actor in America, Adrian Hightower. He'll be pulling on the famous gold cape to play Atomic Crusader in the upcoming adaptation.

Maria Menounos: Adrian, tell us how you're feeling. You're about to start filming, right?

Adrian Hightower: In a couple of weeks! Wow. Just wow.

MM: How is it "wow"?

AH: I've never been so thankful to land a role in my life. *(laughs)*

MM: Have you told your parents?

AH: Yes. My mom is over the moon excited for me. She and my sister, Leslie, are talking about going to see it on opening day. I want to tell them—you're my dates to the premiere!

MM: Wouldn't you want to take Maiko?

AH: Oh, of course. How many dates am I allowed to bring?

6

O n the first day of filming, Adrian walked nervously onto the set and tried to look like he belonged. He'd been introduced at Comic-Con to a rousing ovation back in August 2002, but it had been half a year since then, and he felt like he shouldn't even *be* in this space.

"Adrian," said a voice, and he turned to see the director coming toward him, arms outstretched. Martin McGarry had worked on smaller films before this—like some indie movies that had gained cult status and a graphic novel adaptation that had put him in the good graces of the folks running Comic-Con. This was his first big break and he seemed nervous, too, which set Adrian off even more.

"It's going to be great," Martin said, grasping both of Adrian's shoulders.

A PA took Adrian in for hair and makeup, and he put on his wardrobe, shots were set up, and Adrian believed he was John Jackson, Atomic Crusader—and the hours melted away, just like that. When the day's work had wrapped and Adrian had gone home, he had the bone-deep weariness of having done something hard, but something *worthwhile*. He felt like the planets were aligning correctly, that the world was tilted the right way.

By the end of the first week, Adrian was exhausted in the best way possible—wrung out like a damp washcloth. He'd been challenged every minute of his time on set, his workouts had been punishing, the early wakeup calls had grown more excruciating every day that passed. Production ran for six days that first week, with one day off, and Adrian asked Maiko to spend the night on his one "weekend" day.

He was drifting back to sleep that Monday morning when he heard an incessant honking outside of his condo. It jolted him awake, and he wiped a hand down his face as he heard the staccato blasts continuing from the street.

"What the hell?" he muttered, as he pulled open his blinds and peered out into the hazy sunshine. He was irritated; he was tired, and he missed his girlfriend with an ache that felt like cracked ribs.

But down below, parallel parked neatly in front of his condominium, was a silver Audi TT. Maiko was standing outside the driver's side door, pressing her hand against the horn.

Adrian ran downstairs and scooped Maiko into a hug. "Did you pay cash?" he asked.

"I got a great deal on the out-the-door price," she responded, and he kissed her.

"Fuck, I love you."

He hadn't meant to say it, but he realized in that moment that—he did. He loved her. He had missed her through the grueling first week at his job. And he realized that he loved her not because he needed her, but because he really enjoyed his time with her.

She looked at him with those dark eyes, and he could sense that she was thinking of how to respond. "It's okay if you don't say it back," he assured her quickly. "I just . . . wanted to tell you."

And then she smiled. Adrian's heart was alight. "I love you too," she whispered. He wrapped his arms around her again and picked her up, spinning her around in a circle.

"Come upstairs," he said, and Maiko took his hand and followed him to the second story. Adrian didn't know whether he wanted to devour her or just snuggle her as he slept. In the end, he did a little of both; the couple kissed passionately on the bed, peeling off layers of clothes, slowing down as they snuggled closer and closer together. Adrian held Maiko at her waist and kissed her forehead, apologized for being so tired, and napped for four hours.

He woke up groggily, and the first thing he saw was Maiko, topless and in a bikini-cut pair of panties, lounging on his white sheets. "Good morning," she said softly, and he enveloped her in a warm hug, pulling her close, nosing her skin down from her cheek to her neck. They made love languidly, the kind of long, marathoning sex that couples in their twenties with nothing in the fridge but eggs and baking soda would experience. When they finally stopped for the day, it was late; the slanting sunlight slipped through the windows and lit Maiko's face in a hazy glow. "I made you coffee." She laughed, and Adrian saw the mug on the nightstand, the contents no doubt cold.

They got Thai delivery and ate their curry and noodles on the coffee table that was askew in the living room. Adrian groaned softly when he remembered that he was back on the schedule the next day.

But when he received his first paycheck, Adrian's eyes watered at the number of zeroes. Because he was a newcomer, Adrian wasn't paid, say, George Clooney levels of money for playing Atomic Crusader, but it was still more money than he'd ever seen in his entire life. He wrote his mother—"Made it, Ma"—with his first week's wages enclosed.

THE SUPERHERO FLICK was one of a two-picture contract with McKnight Pictures, and Adrian hoped that the first did well enough that he'd be able to reprise his role in a sequel.

John Jackson had been working as a new NSA agent in post–World War II America. He came across a broken spaceship when on a mission and, to his surprise, found that the alien inside the ship looked just like him. After a brief confrontation, where Jackson didn't hurt the extraterrestrial but did demand his face back, the shapeshifting alien resumed its regular appearance and gifted Jackson the ability to scramble molecular structures—namely, himself. When Jackson returned to Washington, D.C., he was able to change his appearance and body like the alien had. At first, he was wary of his new powers, but when he realized that his gift came with super-strength and the ability to fly, Jackson embarked on a superhero's life. When he shapeshifts, his cape wraps around his body then unfurls to reveal his new face and physique.

The fact that Adrian was going to be the default face of John Jackson and Atomic Crusader made him chuckle. He knew that Halloween would be full of kids wearing the iconic red super-suit and gold cape, but he was happy that John Jackson could also be a woman.

Because this film was his origin story, John Jackson, as himself, would be prominently placed. There was a cameo from the original Atomic Crusader, Eugene Waters, who had played him in a 1969 adaptation, but for the most part, John Jackson was Atomic Crusader for the majority of the movie. Adrian was on the cast sheet practically every day of filming.

Production was tough, but Adrian stuck it through. And as the filming progressed, he grew more confident in his portrayal of John Jackson. He believed he could *be* Atomic Crusader. Even on his days off, he parted his hair like John Jackson, he spoke slowly and eloquently like John Jackson, and he ate the diet of John Jackson (high protein, moderate carbs, no added sugar, glass of milk with every meal).

And as his coffers filled up with every paycheck, Adrian began to wonder what to spend the money on.

WHEN *ATOMIC CRUSADER* wrapped and the money was banked, Adrian suggested to Maiko that they take a nice vacation. "Charter a yacht, see the world." She had excitedly flung her arms around him, squealing with surprise.

There they were, floating on one hundred feet of luxury yacht, sunning themselves in prime hours, when the barracuda of paparazzi seized upon them and shot a barrage of photos. What ended up in *In Touch Weekly* and *TMZ* were photos of Adrian and Maiko, or *Madrian*, as they were now called, caressing each other in the Bahamas.

Helicopters overhead didn't deter him from running his hands up and down the curves of her hips, playing with the strings on her bikini bottom, as they kissed. He playfully tugged on one string and she gave a little yelp, jumping up and retying the side of her bathing suit.

They laughed and laughed in the bright sun.

"You know what we should do after this?" Adrian asked.

"What?" Maiko implored, eyes sparkling.

"Get tattoos."

She laughed, but did not say no; when they found landfall, they wandered all around their part of the island until they found a tattoo parlor. On his inner forearm, where Maiko had lit her eyes on him in the clinic, Adrian got an infinity symbol. On her hip, right where the flesh dipped under the bone, Maiko got a matching tattoo.

Madrian's Matching Tats!

Model Maiko Fox and actor Adrian Hightower got matching tattoos while vacationing in the Bahamas. (For pictures of them on a luxury yacht in tiny swimwear, click here.) The lovebirds were photographed in Island Ink getting tatted. We can't wait to see what they got!

ScoutSays900 (9:12 P.M.): This couple. I am obsessed.

Helios34 (9:14 P.M.): can u imagine if they got each others NAMES tattooed and then they broke up? they have only been together for like what 6 months or smth? way 2 soon to get inked imo.

Laprimadonna (9:15 P.M.): these two sure know how to keep themselves in the tabloids, that's for sure. I didn't even know who Adrian Hightower was until a couple of weeks ago and now he's everywhere. Atomic Crusader wrapped, luxury vacation secured, beautiful woman on his arm. Living the life.

7

Maiko was on fire. It felt like every week she was booking new campaigns, returning for old brands, walking in a show, being photographed for an ad. She was everywhere; on billboards off Rodeo Drive, smiling with sparkling gems dripping from her earlobes in a boutique shop, scowling on a runway with her head held high and a self-made wind blowing through her hair as she stomped. Her locks were still long, her cattish eyes still sharp, her body all beautiful planes and angles.

And then.

Maiko skipped a period.

She wasn't worried about it; she had an inconsistent cycle and she was under a lot of stress—not sleeping enough, probably not eating enough, and fighting a cold while still working. She and Adrian had been using condoms, but apparently they were not effective enough. She took a test when she was a couple of weeks late, and there it was: another pink line where it shouldn't be.

Maiko was quietly devastated. She called Christine, who

had recently moved to Roanoke with her boyfriend, Derek, and they discussed her predicament.

"I can't have this baby," she breathed. "I'm booked with jobs until next summer. I have commitments. I'm in my prime. I haven't even peaked. It would ruin everything."

Christine, who had been listening silently, said, "Can't you— you know—give it up for adoption?"

"Christine." Maiko's voice was steelier now.

"I know." The argument was clear. Maiko made her money off her body. What happened if her body was not what the designers and stylists had signed her for?

"Have you told Adrian?"

"No, but I will."

Maiko knew she could. She'd seen him for the first time in a health clinic, after all.

When she told him, he absorbed the shock as best he could. "What do you want to do?" he asked, clasping his fingers together. "I'll be here no matter what you choose."

"I don't know," she hedged. "A baby is a lot of work."

"Right."

"A lifelong commitment."

"Yes," he said.

She was silent. She knew what she had to say.

"I can't keep it, Adrian."

His relief was noticeable. "Okay. Are you sure?"

She nodded. "Will you go to the clinic with me?"

"Of course."

Because she was well-known now, she couldn't go back to

the place she'd seen Adrian for the first time, when she was eighteen. Maiko made an appointment with a reputable doctor and Adrian held her hand through the entire procedure.

She was crying when they left the doctor's office. "I feel so bad," she said softly. "We were so careful, and this happened anyway."

"Listen to me." He stopped her in the parking garage and held her close. He spoke into her hair. "You did the right thing. We aren't ready to be parents. And it's not the right time. But maybe one day . . ."

She nodded into his shoulder. "Yeah," she said tearily. "Someday."

Maiko had a runway show three days later, for Osprey Gold swimwear. She felt awful. She felt like she was coming down with a low-grade fever, and she was still spotting. But models don't get sick days; she tucked a tampon in, popped some Advil, and went in for her hair and makeup.

Maiko walked the show, but declined to return to Osprey Gold for any subsequent campaigns. She couldn't shake the association between her second abortion and the swimwear label, and when she thought of wearing those tiny bikini bottoms again while worrying about spotting, she felt sick.

She spent the days after the show alternating between crying and calling Christine for support. She felt the need to purge herself of all bad feelings and heaved a few times over the toilet, but nothing came out. Maiko was tired.

MAIKO AND CHRISTINE were inseparable that first year together at school. They'd been seated next to each other in their homeroom and played together every recess too. Tanya, Christine's mother, got a job at Cedars-Sinai hospital and worked the night shift, so she was somewhat available in the afternoons when Michiyo, Maiko's mother, was at her pediatric practice, and when Tanya went to work, Michiyo took over and let the girls have slumber parties, even on school nights. Christine's father had divorced Tanya when Christine was a baby, so it was just the two of them in their house, and Tanya appreciated knowing where Christine was in the evenings.

One day, during the winter holidays, Christine asked Maiko if she wanted to go to her church with her for Christmas. Maiko raised a brow. "Church?" she said, as if the word was unfamiliar on her tongue.

"It's kind of fun on Christmas," Christine said. "There's cookies and cider and everyone is friendly and happy because it's the holidays."

"I'll have to ask my mom," Maiko said.

But when she brought it up to her parents, Michiyo was reserved. "Church, Maiko-chan?" she said, her nose wrinkling.

"Christine said there are cookies."

"But what do they want from you, for those cookies?" Michiyo answered. Still, she gave her permission, and Maiko put on an emerald green velvet dress and scratchy white tights with patent leather shoes, and went with Christine to church that Christmas Eve.

The sermon didn't make any sense to Maiko—too many characters to keep track of—but afterward there were indeed cider and cookies, the stained-glass windows were beautiful, and Christine proudly showed off her friend to all of the congregation. And everyone was friendly to Maiko. It seemed like a nice place. But she didn't see the point in going back. If Christmas was the best time to go, she reasoned, she'd already seen its peak.

Still, as the years passed, Christine told Maiko a little bit more about her faith, things she learned, lessons she was challenged with, without pushing Maiko to join the congregation itself. As the girls reached high school, Christine passed along the information about teenage pregnancy: that it was to be avoided, and the only way to avoid it was to abstain from sex.

Maiko, at fourteen, was not that interested in sex, but she took Christine's advice to heart as they started ninth grade. Now, at age twenty-two, Maiko's internalized conversations with Christine about unwanted pregnancies seemed to smack her right in the face.

She couldn't tell her colleagues, the other models, about it—they all complained about various ailments, working while injured, working while on their periods, but they never broached a serious subject with one another. A rumor about a pregnancy would become vicious in a second; they would turn on one another like hungry wolves.

So Maiko lived with her shame and pretended nothing was amiss when backstage at a photo shoot or fashion show, and she tried to get back to her life as normal. Until she saw Helen at a Balenciaga sunglasses shoot.

The two women had not seen each other in almost a year. Maiko had moved out of the shared Hollywood Boulevard apartment when her star began to rise and had gotten her own place, an apartment with a walk-in closet where she could have a wall of shoes, if she so wished. Helen had been like a genial older sister; she was a few years older than Maiko, had been in the industry longer, and was moderately successful, but not at Maiko's level now. *Helen* had never been asked to model for Valentina Posh. Her once-blond hair was now dyed red, and when she saw Maiko, her blue eyes lit up.

"Hey, girl!" she said from her makeup chair.

"Helen!" Maiko was surprised to find herself thrilled to see her old roommate. "We need to catch up!"

Maiko sat down and had her hair plaited for the shoot. The stylist touched Maiko on the neck and said, "Have you ever considered chopping your hair up to here?"

"No," Maiko said.

"It would look really good on you." He continued to braid.

Maiko wondered what it would be like to have short hair. She hadn't had her hair cut into a bob since she was in high school.

The two women were released from their chairs after hair and makeup and were sent to wardrobe, where their outfits would be rounded-collar T-shirts with blazers. They waited their turn for the photographer while other models were decked out in eyewear and lipstick. Helen turned to Maiko. "How have you been?"

Maiko felt herself crumbling. She had never cried in front of Helen when they lived together—they were both too stoic for that—but she was vulnerable, and Helen was the closest friend she had besides Adrian, and she felt that she couldn't talk to Christine about it anymore—not after she'd spent the last few weeks calling her best friend and crying. She swallowed the lump in her throat and said, "Good."

Helen glanced at her. "Uh-huh," she said disbelievingly.

"Work has been great," Maiko said. "I'm booked up until next year, at the very least, and the offers keep on coming."

"I heard you turned down Osprey Gold's magazine campaign. What's the deal? Did they treat you badly? Because if they come calling to me, I want to know if I should tell them no."

"No, nothing like that!" Maiko panicked for a moment, thinking that the news of her turning down the swim brand would reverberate across the modeling world and be taken the wrong way. "They were great. It was just . . . personal."

Helen sucked on her teeth, no doubt wanting to smoke a cigarette. "Personal, like . . . the way you broke up with your last boyfriend, personal?"

Maiko knew then that Helen had known what she'd gone through back in 2000.

"I saw the test in the bathroom trash, Mai," Helen said softly. "You could've talked to me then, you know. Like you can talk to me now."

Maiko felt her eyes prick with tears. "I can't discuss it here," she said. "Can we grab coffee sometime this week?"

"Sure," Helen said kindly, and Maiko felt that she was getting a friend back.

———

AFTER SOME TIME, Maiko felt herself return to normal. She went back to kickboxing and cardio; she stopped second-guessing her decision and made her peace with it. Adrian had been right: they had not been ready to be parents. She'd known that. She'd told Christine that. But she hadn't accepted it until after the due date had passed and she realized, with a start, that she was busier than ever before. Her star just kept rising. And she was *happy*.

She and Helen had gone out for that coffee, stopping at a Starbucks and getting papped holding iced Americanos with two Sweet'N Lows. Then they went to Helen's new pad, which was in La Brea. "What an upgrade," gasped Maiko, as she took in a chandelier that was as big as her old closet in their Hollywood apartment.

"I'm doing well," Helen said.

The two women settled on the couch and Helen tapped out a cigarette. They talked about the weather, modeling gossip, which designers assigned shoes that were the wrong sizes for the models' feet, everything under the sun, except the topic that Helen was curious about. Finally, she said, "So tell me."

Maiko took a deep breath and explained about the unplanned pregnancy. How she had gotten an abortion that time in 2000 and then met Adrian at the Kriegler's photo shoot two days later. How she knew he would be the type of guy who would go with her to the clinic. How he'd held her hand during their abortion. How lucky she felt, and yet how guilty she felt as well.

"Fuck that," Helen said, breathing out two smoke trails from her nostrils and taking a long drink of her coffee through the iconic green straw. "Don't feel bad about that. Abortion is healthcare."

"I know. It's just that—Christine—she thinks—"

"Fuck what Christine thinks," Helen interrupted. "I know dozens of girls like Christine, who grew up with the best intentions, but their faith has misled them. Don't let her make you feel bad about what is necessary." She paused. "Though, don't tell her I said that."

Maiko was silent for a moment. She swirled her coffee with the straw.

"I know you love your friend," Helen said, gentler this time. "But she's not you. And you're not her. And it's *your* body. Don't forget that."

Helen paused, then probed lightly. "Do you still hear from Christine?"

"We talk every week, though it all depends on our schedules. Why?"

"Is she still with that guy?"

"Derek? Yeah."

Helen hummed in response.

"I know your type, Helen. Christine isn't one of them." Maiko knew that Helen liked other models, leggy blondes being her specialty. If they weren't Amazon women, six feet or above, she didn't care for them. Christine was short, barely at Helen's chin.

"How do *you* know?" Helen stretched her tight calves. "I'm tired of other models. They're so bitchy."

"Well, she doesn't swing that way. I know that for a fact."

Helen shrugged. "People get curious. I can be very enticing. But I'll drop it."

The conversation the two women had had about Maiko's body lived in her mind for weeks after the women had hugged and parted ways. Maiko had driven home in her Audi ruminating on it. She'd always been the type of girl who heeded the rules of everyone else. She had disappointed her parents by not going to college, and by pursuing modeling she had lost their monetary support. So she'd put her dependence on Christine. Maybe Christine shouldn't have had to deal with Maiko's big life problems.

She unlocked her apartment and found her phone. She flipped it open and dialed. "Hello? Maiko-chan?" Michiyo's voice.

"Mom?"

8

Adrian knew that Maiko had barely talked to her parents in the last four years, ever since they cut her off after she told them she was pursuing modeling instead of going to college. He was surprised when she rolled over in his bed and said, out of the blue, "Want to go to Calabasas?"

He knew what was in Calabasas. Maiko had told him about growing up there, going to private schools, living it up with Christine. She had told him animatedly about how she and Christine went to their junior prom with two guys, but Christine's date ghosted her as soon as he stepped into the dance. Maiko and Christine danced together, ignoring Maiko's date, the senior who had invited her. When it was time to go, Maiko insisted that her date take Christine home, too, and the guy did as he was told, grumbling all the while. Maiko was so grateful that she slept with him. It was her first time.

"In a car?" Adrian had asked.

"It was a Cadillac. Those things are boats. There was enough room, I guess." But Maiko had sounded a little sad, as if she had been cheated out of a perfect first time, so Adrian gave her a hug.

Now Adrian asked, "What's in Calabasas?"

"I thought you might like to meet my parents," she said vaguely, and Adrian knew that whatever was happening, it was not about him—it was something *she* wanted to do, and that she wanted his support.

He said yes.

When Maiko and Adrian pulled into the expansive driveway, Michiyo met their car outside, excitedly opening the passenger door to see her daughter. Mark Fox stood framed in the front door with his arms crossed. He looked sanguine, though, and he hugged Maiko as she stepped into the doorway.

"Nice to meet you, sir," Adrian said, holding out a hand to shake, and Mark grasped it firmly. Adrian sensed the distinct feeling of being sized up.

The house was very angular, made of textured concrete. The inside was sterile as well, stark with very little to show in terms of personality. Adrian wondered how Maiko had grown up in such an austere house.

But the inside smelled delicious, like ham and yams and casseroles, and Adrian smiled benignly as he was led to the living room, which was decorated with pearl-white couches that looked like they were made of blocks.

Michiyo said, "Adrian, can I offer you a beverage?"

"That's so kind of you. Anything is fine."

She swept a ruby-colored drink into his hand momentarily, before popping back into the kitchen, and he sipped at it. Apple-cranberry juice, no vodka. Were Maiko's parents teetotalers?

"So, Adrian," Mark Fox said, "I understand you've been seeing my daughter."

"Yes, sir," Adrian said, and touched Maiko's hand. He didn't want to wrap his arms around her waist in front of her parents. He didn't know how strict they were about touching.

"How long now?" Mark asked.

"About a year and a half."

"A year and a half," Mark mused.

Michiyo popped out of the dining room. "Everything is ready. Let's eat."

They filed into the dining room and took turns filling their plates at the buffet. Then they sat down and Adrian waited for some sort of prayer. But the Nakamoto-Foxes started biting into their sweet potatoes as soon as they had touched their cutlery. "We don't stand on ceremony here," Mark said, as he looked at Adrian's hesitant face. "We give thanks every day, so we eat when the food is hot."

Adrian spread a napkin on his lap and reached for a fork. "This looks amazing," he offered, as he speared a green bean. "It must have taken forever to cook all this."

Michiyo laughed, raising a hand to cover her mouth. "I requested that our cook, Gloria, make all of this for Maiko before she left on vacation. It's Maiko-chan's favorite. I just had to pop it all in the oven and make the rolls fresh from the tube. But I do appreciate that you think I did it."

Adrian felt his ears warm. He hadn't realized that Maiko had grown up this rich, to have an everyday cook. He thought of his mother, Betty, who had slaved over every holiday meal and the other three hundred sixty-three days' worth of food. How McDonald's was a treat, that he now knew was because Betty was too tired to give a damn in the kitchen that day.

"So." Mark buttered a roll. "Tell us how the career is going, Mai."

"It's going great," she said carefully, as if walking around a landmine. "I'm booked up until next year."

"And Adrian? You're going to be a household name, I hear." Mark took a bite of the roll.

"*Atomic Crusader* is in postproduction now. It'll come out this summer." He watched Maiko, making sure he didn't say too much.

"That's exciting," Michiyo said.

"Yes, I'm very lucky."

"It sounds like it," Mark said. "From what we hear, it's difficult to eke out a living in this business. Hollywood is so fickle. I work with everyone there, you know. I build their opera houses, and the stuff those people say! It's terrifying that my daughter is rubbing elbows with those types all the time."

"*Dad*," Maiko said, but without bite.

"They'd sell you to the highest bidder without caring about you at all. You're a beautiful woman, Maiko, and you were a beautiful child too. There's a reason we didn't put you in acting classes or submit you to be a Gerber baby."

"I *like* modeling," Maiko said, an edge in her voice now.

"But do they treat you well?"

"Sure."

"You don't get health insurance, you don't get sick days, you're barely eating your ham—are you sure you're doing all right?" Mark's voice held a touch of concern.

"I'm fine," Maiko said. But she put her fork down and sipped her glass of Perrier. Adrian's throat ached as he watched her drink. He was thirsty for some alcohol. He didn't like the way Maiko's dad was grilling her; Adrian understood now why they had been estranged.

Michiyo, as if feeling the tension at the table, said, "Adrian, what's next for you?"

Adrian gave her a wan smile. "I hope a sequel. *Atomic Crusader* is a summer blockbuster, so the studio is hoping it will be a big movie. And if it does well enough at the box office, they'll probably greenlight a second."

"Here's hoping, then," Michiyo said, and Adrian knew that she was trying to bridge the divide between her daughter and herself.

"Excuse me," Maiko said, and pushed out of her chair. She headed in the direction of a well-lit hallway, and Adrian heard a door close. He chewed slowly on a piece of ham, wondering if he should go see if she needed anything. But he stayed in his seat, feeling awkward as the silence extended longer and longer.

"This is a beautiful home," he said finally.

"Thank you." Mark put down his fork and looked at Adrian. "I'm going to be frank with you. I don't like Hollywood people. I take their money and design their buildings, but I don't make friends with them. I am not interested in being friends with you, Adrian. But if my daughter wants to be with you, and she is in the business as well, I hope to hell that you treat her well and watch her back. I don't want my little girl getting hurt."

Adrian nodded, swallowing. "I'll do my best, sir." He hated how thin his voice sounded.

Maiko reappeared from the depths of the house but didn't sit down again. "Adrian, are you ready to go?" she asked.

He stood, and his hosts stood as well. Mark said, "Is it necessary to leave *now*? You haven't had any dessert."

"I can't have dessert. I can't show up bloated to my fitting tomorrow."

The parents followed the couple to the front door and Michiyo said, "It was good to see you again, Maiko-chan." She hugged her daughter tentatively. "Call me whenever you want. I'll always pick up."

When they started driving away, Adrian glanced over at Maiko in the passenger seat. "Are you okay?" he asked.

"Yeah. Fine," she said distantly. She turned a little in the seat, her knees toward the gearshift. "Did my dad say anything to you while I was in the bathroom?"

"Um . . ."

"I hope he wasn't inappropriate."

"No, he was fine. Just . . . not that friendly, I guess."

"Not surprising. But my mom . . . she was trying, right?"

"Yeah, seemed like it." Adrian concentrated on the twisty roads leading out of the mountain.

Maiko sat back against the seat and hummed in thought. "She always sent me money when I was starting out. She never wanted to lose me. I think she wants to be close again."

"Could be." Adrian was noncommittal, not wanting to influence whatever thoughts Maiko was having. If she and her folks could reconcile, maybe she'd be happier. He hadn't been ignorant of the fact that she cried more often than before and leaned on Christine harder than she used to. He ached with wanting to protect her, and guilt gnawed at him too: it was *his* fault she'd gotten pregnant.

After all, it takes two to tango.

"How about a trip?" he suggested.

"Where?"

"Florida."

Maiko smiled at him, her first smile that night. "You want me to meet your parents?"

"It's only fair," he said.

She looked out the window and laid her head on her fist. "It sounds like a great idea. When can we go?"

"THIS IS ADRIAN when he was ten. He sang the national anthem at a baseball game." Adrian's father, Jerome, lovingly turned the page in the album. "And here he is with Leslie. She did everything he did in those days. He joined soccer so she had to buy cleats too. When he was in the school play, she had to audition for the chorus."

"I sang better than he did, but I never got to sing at a baseball game," Leslie said with a mock pout.

"Pop, please," Adrian said in a begging tone, but his smile was wide and Maiko knew that he was enjoying Jerome's bragging. Maiko and Adrian had flown to Tallahassee for Christmas and

despite the tepid weather and the abundance of palm trees—
the Hightowers had decorated one in their yard as a joke for the
holidays—Maiko had felt at home as soon as she stepped in the
door. Betty, Adrian's mother, had embraced her with fervor and
Jerome stood with his arms outstretched right behind her. Leslie,
Adrian's sister, offered Maiko wine immediately, which she accepted.

Betty had excused herself to go finish the cooking, and instead of standing awkwardly in the foyer like she expected,
Maiko was led to the couch, where Jerome offered her fresh
nuts and a nutcracker and a photo album with plasticky pages.

"Do you have any siblings?" Jerome asked interestedly, and
Maiko had to admit that, no, she was an only child.

"Lucky," Leslie said jokingly.

"Hey, if there was only one child in this house, it would be
me," Adrian retorted. "I came first. You'd be just an idea."

Leslie mock pouted again, then took another tiny sip of her
wine. It was dark red and matched her nail polish. She and
Adrian looked alike: heart-shaped faces with reddish-brown
hair and dark eyes.

"How many years difference is there between you two?"
Maiko wanted to know.

"He's four years older," Leslie said. "So he thinks he knows
everything."

"Correction: I *do* know everything."

"You little shit." Leslie winked.

"I always wanted a sister," Maiko said wistfully.

"Well, maybe you'll get one!" Leslie wrapped her arm around Maiko's shoulder. "Adrian, propose already!"

Maiko laughed a genuine chuckle, and Jerome looked on with a pleased expression on his face. From the kitchen Maiko could hear Betty clanging around. She stood up and set her wineglass down. "Can I help you, Betty?" Maiko asked, raising her voice and poking her head into the warm kitchen. It was bathed in yellow artificial light so everything seemed butter-tinted. The windows were small and set in shadow, which would have annoyed Mark Fox but the Hightowers ignored it.

"Oh, no, dear," Betty said, pulling a casserole from the oven. "Everything is pretty much finished. Just going to let this cool for a second before we dive in. But if you could get everyone settled at the table . . ."

Maiko returned to the dining room to find everyone had moved off the couch and were getting the table ready. Like a well-orchestrated ballet, Adrian and Leslie set plates and glasses at their places while Jerome whisked into the kitchen to grab the turkey.

Maiko sat down when everyone else did, watching them all carefully lest she accidentally commit a faux pas. The group did not hold hands, but they bowed their heads and Jerome said a prayer. Then everyone murmured "amen" and they began passing plates of stuffing and casserole and honey-baked turkey around.

"So, your next project," Betty said, as she scooped salad onto a plate.

"I auditioned for something called *Alphabet Alibi*," Adrian offered. "I don't know if I got it yet, though. There might be an *Atomic Crusader 2*."

"And what would the sequel be about if they make it?" Leslie asked.

"Probably like the 1972 *Atomic Crusader: The Reckoning*," Adrian said.

"Soon all the movies will be reboots," Leslie said jokingly.

"I hope not." Maiko nibbled on some casserole.

"There's still *some* originality left in Hollywood," Adrian said, laughing. "I think."

"I'll be honest with you, son," Jerome said. "I didn't think you would do well in this profession. But you've proven me wrong." He lifted his glass. "To Maiko."

Maiko felt herself blush. Why her? But the rest of the table lifted their glasses, and each murmured, "To Maiko." Maiko twisted the napkin in her lap but felt a red-hot coal glowing in her chest.

That night, at the hotel, as she and Adrian were getting ready for bed, she said, "Why did your dad toast to me?"

"I didn't really have my head screwed on straight before you. I think they want to credit my good fortune to you."

"That's silly," Maiko protested. "You got *Summer Haze* on your own."

"Right, but I don't think my trajectory would've gone as high without you." He grinned and held her against him. "Thank you, Mai."

Atomic Crusader Reviews Come Rolling In, and They're Great!

McKnight Pictures has something to grin about: their newest adaptation of the Atomic Crusader superhero has garnered rave reviews from early viewers. The flick is touting a 97% Fresh rating on Rotten Tomatoes with notable praise for newcomer Adrian Hightower, who plays the golden-caped champion-slash-NSA operative John Jackson.

"With a fresh new face and charming smile, Hightower can disarm those of us in the audience as well as his foes," writes one reviewer for the *Washington Post*.

The Telegraph states, "Hightower is a revelation. Superhero movies shouldn't be this fun, but *Atomic Crusader* is nonstop rollicking action, and *smart* too!"

The film is expected to bring in big bucks on Memorial Day weekend, when it opens.

9

Of all the things that Maiko loved about modeling—the attention from photographers, being primped with hair and makeup, the feel of luxurious fabric, which she once could not afford, against her skin—the high she got from a good walk down the runway was the most addictive. She lived for the moments when her heels would clack on the floor, her hips would slip from side to side, and her stride would lengthen into one of a model walk. Before she knew it, the pose at the end of the runway and the strut back would be over, and she'd remember how to breathe. The cheers, the claps, the spots of light dancing in front of her vision from the camera flashes, all melted away. She felt the best when she was done with a good show and dipped her body into a bathtub filled with hot water. She would let herself dissolve with the bath salts, until her fingertips and toes were prunes and her hair was waterlogged, get out, and splay herself across the bed.

She *thought* that a good model walk was the best high there was. That is, until she found herself in front of a crowd of people at Grauman's Chinese Theatre, holding on to the arm of Adrian Hightower. The *screams*, the energy! It was like a fashion show but with the sound and intensity turned up. Maiko looked at the wall of *Atomic Crusader* fans and was surprised to hear a few of them shouting *her* name as well.

"This is amazing," she said, the well inside of her heart filling up with the admiration from the fans. She clutched Adrian's arm harder as he used his free hand to wave to the crowd.

"I'm overwhelmed," he admitted to her, still smiling for the press.

"They're here for *you*, Adrian." She couldn't leave the sense of wonder out of her voice. "Look at how excited they are for you."

Maiko had been in a few movies before, as an extra, which meant she wasn't invited to the premieres. She watched the movies at home, rented from the Blockbuster down the street, pausing the DVD when she saw an elbow that looked like hers or a shoe she had worn from Wardrobe. The days she saw her face, even in profile, were exciting. But nothing compared to the acknowledgment from the crowd that she and Adrian were a hot commodity. It made her wonder if there was more to life than just modeling. If, in fact, she should pursue acting as well . . .

Adrian stopped in front of the crowd and started signing autographs, and Maiko stood slightly behind him, unsure of what to do. But the maelstrom shifted closer, and people chanted,

"Maiko! Over here! Maiko!" She joined Adrian at the barricades and borrowed Sharpies and signed whatever was handed to her—magazines with her picture in them, whether it was *In Touch Weekly* showing her and Adrian on a paparazzi-attended date or a Prada advertisement in *Harper's Bazaar*; torsos, hands, T-shirts—realizing that they had come to the premiere with the intention of seeing her too. The feeling surprised and pleased her, and she grinned wider and wider as the items kept coming and her hand became tired.

After they had been through the photo grind and Adrian had done a few red-carpet interviews, they made their way into the theater and found their seats. As the lights dimmed, Maiko leaned over and whispered to Adrian, "Do you think I could do this too?"

"'This?'"

"Being in a movie. But, like, as a star."

"Of course, you can." He beamed at her.

"It wouldn't, like, be stepping on your toes?" she asked.

"Why would it?" And he wrapped his arm around her shoulder, settled in, and they enjoyed the movie.

Atomic Crusader was two hours and fourteen minutes of good fun. Maiko marveled at how good Adrian was; the camera loved his face, and every shot of him was lit beautifully, even when he was the dour, taciturn John Jackson. Jason, Adrian's agent, was sitting to the right of the couple and he kept elbowing Adrian in the shoulder and saying, "You did it, buddy! Look at that money shot!" Maiko knew that there would be new fans of Adrian Hightower as soon as this movie went mainstream—people who aspired to be *with* him, and people who aspired to *be* him.

Mine, she thought, as she leaned into his broad, muscled shoulder under the silkiness of his suit.

When they got to Adrian's condo that night, Maiko ravaged him. As they lay on the covers afterward, tired and spent, she knew she was in so deep, she would marry him the next day if he asked.

A COUPLE OF weeks later, Adrian came to Maiko's door and asked her, humbly, if she was interested in some fine dining, no euphemism. "Pack a bag and include a nice dress," he said, and she fumbled excitedly through her closet, pulling out a Gucci sheath still in its dry-cleaning bag and selecting a pair of Manolos from her wall of shoes.

A hired car sped them out toward the airport, and she gasped when they drove right out onto the tarmac to a smallish plane. "Are we *going* somewhere?" she asked.

"Isn't it obvious? I'm taking you to New York."

She laughed. "Sure."

But she climbed into the little airplane anyway and sat down in a buttery leather seat. "This must've cost you a fortune." Marveling, she turned and looked at the armrest with all of its little controls.

"Nah" is all he said in response, and they were off, into the air, flying high. Maiko fell asleep with her shoes kicked off at one point and woke up with a soft Hermès blanket covering her from sternum to shin.

They stopped in New York, but Adrian wouldn't let her deplane; they refueled and started back up again, this time to destination unknown.

It was a long trip, and Maiko ate what was offered to her by the flight attendant, though Adrian said with a smile not to get too full, because he was going to take her to *the best* restaurant when they landed. He advised her to change into her dress so they could go from airport to restaurant without any hesitation. Another car met their plane on the tarmac, and Maiko listened to the chatter of the baggage handlers before realizing that they were speaking Italian.

Excitement growing in her belly (or maybe it was hunger), Maiko watched Florence go by as their car drove them deeper and deeper into the city center. She wondered if Adrian had planned this grand gesture to propose, and tried to talk herself out of it. They didn't even live together yet. But maybe he was a traditionalist and wanted to be engaged before they shared a living space. It was all too much.

When the car deposited them at a restaurant, she was so dizzy with emotion and excitement that she didn't even notice what it was called or the people waiting outside. She ducked into the dining room, which was completely empty except for a waiter in a holding pattern by the only table with a lit candle on it. Adrian pushed in her chair as she marveled at the room: framed portraits hung on the walls and globular light pendants dripped from the ceiling.

The waiter poured Adrian a small amount of wine and let him examine the label. He sipped appreciatively and nodded, and the wine was let loose into their glasses. Maiko plucked at the stem of hers and Adrian smiled his crooked smile and said, "To us."

"Cheers," she said, and took a swallow. It was a revelation.

Adrian set his glass down and said, "*Atomic Crusader* is doing really well. They're talking about greenlighting a sequel."

"That's great, Adrian!" Maiko was happy for him. She leaned across the small table and gave him a kiss.

The first course came out, and Maiko tamped down her impulse to eat it all, because she knew there would be more courses to come.

"They want *you* to be in it too."

Maiko stopped her fork halfway to her mouth. "*Seriously?*"

"Their words were, and I quote, 'Madrian will make this an even bigger blockbuster.' They love our *chemistry*, Mai. They asked me to ask you to come in for an audition."

She was so excited, she forgot all about the food. "For *what?*"

"The role of Lindsey." Lindsey Wilton, alias Ms. Hemlock, was John Jackson's love interest and Atomic Crusader's nemesis. It would be a meaty role.

"I'd look so good in green! When is this happening?"

He laughed. "I knew you'd love that, Mai. When we get back."

"Let's go, then," she said, pretending to grab at her purse.

"Not *immediately* when we get back. Give it a few days. Let them set it up."

She relaxed into her seat and handled her fork again. She was glad; the pasta was divine. "You're cheating on your diet," she said, mock-teasing.

"With the best pasta in the world," he said, the skin around his eyes crinkling. "With the best woman in the world, the most beautiful model in the world—"

Maiko had the sense that it would happen *soon*.

But when the dessert came and there was no ring in the tiramisu, she wondered how she'd gotten it so wrong. She felt her face crumple a little, and Adrian asked, "Are you all right? Too much food?"

"No, I'm fine. I'm just . . . overwhelmed." She forced a smile and tried to remember that her boyfriend had taken her to Italy just for a celebratory meal. It was ostentatious and flirtatious but nothing more than that.

"Too much wine," he said sagely, nodding. "I know you're a bit of a lightweight."

They drove back to the airplane, which was waiting for them, and Maiko looked out the window as Italy disappeared beneath them. The paparazzi had been out in full force and they'd gotten their photo taken, as usual, both on arrival at the restaurant and departure from the airport, and she knew that the gossip rags would talk about this whirlwind date in a way that would keep her and Adrian in the cycle for more than just a few days.

"Hey." Adrian's hand was on hers. "I feel like I did something wrong."

"No, it's just . . ." Her eyes filled with tears as she realized her mistake. "PMS," she said.

"Oh. *Oh*. Okay."

"But thank you. This was wonderful. And I'm glad you got your pasta."

He stretched out with his legs extended in front of him, and he said contentedly, "Right?"

Then he leaned forward. "Mai."

"Yes?" She held her breath.

"Do you want to move in with me?"

She wasn't expecting that question, but she felt herself growing excited. "Are you sure? You'll see me at work, you'll see me at home . . . You might get tired of me."

"How could I get tired of you?"

Maiko felt a sparkling in her chest. She was happy again. "Yes, of course I'll move in with you!"

He unclasped her seatbelt and pulled her onto his lap. She shucked her heels, nuzzled her face into his neck, and tucked her feet into the space between his thighs and the seat. The flight attendant surreptitiously made herself disappear, and Maiko felt Adrian's hardness beneath her.

"I love you," he murmured into her ear.

"I love you too."

They made love, high above the Atlantic. Maiko sorted her feelings afterward. She was going to audition for *Atomic Crusader 2*. She was going to move in with Adrian. She was fine. She was happy.

October 16, 2004
Madrian's 36-Hour Date!

The two lovebirds, Maiko Fox and Adrian Hightower, left the country for just one day. Nay, for just one MEAL. They were photographed landing in Florence, Italy, and going to Trattoria Antico Fattore for dinner. The restaurant was cleared out for the couple, who dined for two and a half hours and were seen exiting around 9:00 P.M. local time. They returned to Los Angeles sixteen hours later. Must be nice to be Madrian!

Good4U622 (8:09 P.M.): How wasteful.

TooBB (8:12 P.M.): I think it's dreamy af. He's sweeping her off her feet! Going to Italy just for a meal . . . So romantic

Galaba3 (8:14 P.M.): Adrian is such a dreamy guy. M is so lucky.

TooBB (8:15 P.M.): You just KNOW that he fucks good

Good4U622 (8:17 P.M.): Jesus take the wheel

Atomic Crusader 2 Begins Filming

Adrian Hightower puts on the golden cape again, for the next installment of *Atomic Crusader*. The second movie in the duology is expected to have more action, more excitement, and more hype than the first. Plus, an added bonus—Adrian's real-life counterpart, Maiko Fox, will be taking up the green suit as Lindsey Wilton, aka Ms. Hemlock.

Martin McGarry, who was at the director's helm in the first movie, returns as well. "Obviously, we are excited about making a second *Atomic Crusader*. The first was a summer blockbuster turned huge hit—who knew that people would be into a 1950s comic book character in the year 2004? But the outpouring of support from fans, young and old, has been amazing."

We asked Hightower how he feels about the second movie being greenlit. He told us, "I'm excited to bring justice to the character again! I hope the fans have a great time!"

Atomic Crusader 2: Rise of Hemlock will arrive in theaters around the winter holidays, 2006.

10

Adrian wanted to wipe his bleary eyes with his fingers, but stopped himself. He and Maiko were in the makeup trailer together and getting foundation blended meant he couldn't touch his face.

The days on set were long and hard. They were up at three or four in the morning to exercise, have a balanced breakfast, go in for hair and makeup, and then finally start filming *Atomic Crusader 2*. There were many breaks throughout the day, but none enough for them to get a restful amount of sleep. Sometimes, they would finish a scene, wrap for the night, and then get up again in six hours to start filming once more.

"Gosh, I feel so haggard," Maiko said. The makeup crew dabbed concealer on her under-eye circles and she added, with feeling, "Thank you."

Maiko had accepted the role of Ms. Hemlock to further her career—to brighten her already bright star. She was being paid a paltry sum to get her foot in the door, but the couple agreed it was for the best. The next film she'd be in, she reasoned to Adrian, she would get a more respectable wage. After all, she was just a model moonlighting as an actress, without any theatrical training.

"You look beautiful, babe," Adrian assured her, but he was half asleep. He let his eyes flutter closed as he attempted to take a nap after his punishing workout that morning. His makeup artist spritzed him with setting spray and said, "You're done, Adrian." Giving a muffled groan, he stretched and got out of the seat.

"I'll see you out there," he told his girlfriend and stepped out of the trailer.

"Hey, Adrian, my man." Dave, his costar, caught up to him. "I've noticed you've been kind of dragging lately. Here's an espresso."

Adrian accepted the paper cup and downed the espresso. "I think I need something stronger than coffee," he said, grimacing.

"If you're serious . . . " Dave said.

Adrian looked at him closely. "Whatcha got?"

Dave fished into his pocket and pulled out a loose pill. "This'll wake you up," he promised.

"What is it?" Adrian said, scrutinizing the tablet, which was somewhat familiar to him.

"Adderall. My manager gives them to me."

Adrian was no stranger to Adderall. He had been a student once, after all, and the attention-focusing drug had been all over his school before test days and research paper deadlines.

He'd gotten the pills from his best friend's sister, who'd had a mild case of ADHD. What Adrian's parents didn't know wouldn't hurt them. He had purchased the tablets from Emilie and used them when the need was dire—he was a soccer and volleyball jock whose time was dominated by practices, so when big homework projects were due, he'd taken half a pill at a time to ration them out.

Adrian proffered his hand and Dave dropped the pill into it. He slipped it into his mouth and swallowed it dry.

"Adrian! Martin is looking for you." A PA had come jogging up. Adrian whirled around guiltily and then remembered that he was the star. He didn't have to feel guilty for doing what he had to do to keep the production running smoothly.

Nodding at Dave, he followed the PA to the set.

Adrian started taking Adderall twice a day; he asked his agent to procure it for him, and Jason was happy to oblige. He was careful about his usage, trying to take them only at the same times, like a habit: once before his workout, once after lunch. He had some Klonopin to help him sleep, and he took that before bed, the pill case hidden in his pocket so as not to raise suspicion with Mai.

It wasn't that he was feeling *in the wrong*, per se, but something about taking the pills made him think that Maiko wouldn't approve.

He bulldozed through *Atomic Crusader 2* workouts and shoots using his new crutch, and things seemed fine. When the couple had a lull in filming, Adrian thought it was time for another grand gesture.

"Pack a bag, and bring a dress," Adrian said to his girlfriend. "I'm taking you out on an adventure."

Again, there was a private plane, and again, they flew off across the Atlantic with Maiko not knowing the destination. When they touched down, in France this time, Maiko was dressed in head-to-toe Givenchy—a red above-the-knee dress with a sheer red top and red heels—and Adrian was in a navy suit and tie. They took the stairs down to the tarmac and were whisked away by car to whatever restaurant Adrian had chosen.

Adrian held the small of her back as they entered the restaurant, this time with other patrons, though they were shuffled to a table in a private room. Adrian swept two glass flutes off the table and held them both as their waiter filled them with champagne. Adrian placed a flute in front of her on the table.

There was a ring at the bottom of the glass.

Not just any ring. A beautiful, gleaming, albeit bubbly, diamond ring.

She raised her eyes and saw Adrian's grinning face. "I wanted to wait until the dinner was over, but I can't," he said, rising from his seat and then kneeling down. "Maiko Fox, you're the most brilliant woman I've ever met. You're my soul mate, the person who truly understands me. I love you so much. Will you marry me?"

Maiko didn't seem to know how to get the ring out of the flute without getting her fingers full of champagne. Laughing, she drank the entire glass and let the ring fall into her mouth, then spit it out onto her hand. The diamond was cut into an oval and surrounded by more gems on a rose gold band.

Adrian felt like he was going to burst, waiting for her answer.

"Of course, I'll marry you," she burbled, and he placed the ring on her finger.

THE TWO RETURNED to the States in a highly publicized flight home. There went Madrian, enraptured with each other, Adrian's arm around Maiko's waist as they walked off the tarmac into a firestorm of photographers.

"Maiko! Show us the ring!" the paparazzi shouted. She flashed them a grin and a glimpse of the diamond.

Adrian went out with Dave and Adrian's old roommate, Tim, and a few other buddies the next night to celebrate. At the Viper Room, their corner table filled with cheers as shot glasses were raised to toast Adrian and his ability to not only bed, but wed, one of the hottest supermodels of their era.

"To Adrian! You lucky son of a bitch," Tim yelled, and the table threw back their shots of Jäger.

Dave nudged Adrian under the table and murmured, "Want some?"

He was offering a baggie of something, and Adrian wanted to say yes to everything—yes to life, and to his engagement, and to whatever Dave was giving him. So they cut a few lines in the shadow of the table and snorted the cocaine and all was good. It was Adrian's first time using coke and he marveled at what he'd been missing all his life. It was like a firecracker bursting behind his eyes, and his heart sped up so it felt like it was beating double-time. He could feel his body constrict, coiled like a cobra's, and he laughed: maybe he should take some before filming, give Maiko–as–Ms. Hemlock a run for her money.

"I knew you'd like that shit," Dave said conspiratorially, and Adrian bear-hugged him as the crowd around the table whooped.

By the time filming rolled back around a couple of days later, Adrian had come down off the residual effects of the drinking and coke, and was back to popping Adderall. He didn't have a problem. He was fine.

11

Maiko wanted answers. Adrian had been acting a little cagey lately, jittery sometimes, with restless legs and fidgety hands. She slipped into his trailer on the set of *Atomic Crusader 2* while he was off getting hair and makeup done.

Running her hand on the smooth surface of the miniature kitchen counter of the trailer, she began opening drawers one by one, trying to find . . . *something*. Nothing was in the kitchen but spatulas and an egg whisk. She moved to the little bedroom area of the trailer and went through the tiny closet. There were extra pairs of boxer briefs and white undershirts but nothing that would alarm her.

It wasn't until she went to the miniature couch in front of the miniature television set that she found something. Digging into the cushions, she found a baggie of loose pills. She pulled one out and examined it. Blue, oval. She returned the pill and its bag to the original spot. She sat there, thinking.

So. Adrian took pills. And he hadn't told her. Maybe they were antidepressants. Maybe they were workout enhancers.

Maybe they were vitamins. She downplayed the pills' effects because the possibility that he was into recreational drugs scared her.

When Maiko had been with Charlie, she forgave all manner of sins. She believed she couldn't do better than Charlie, and Charlie was content to let her think that. If she brought up the pills to Adrian, maybe he'd be so upset as to leave her.

She should talk to Christine about this. But she was worried. Christine had the shortest fuse about what was tolerable in a relationship and what wasn't, and drug use was one of her dealbreakers. What if Christine told Maiko to leave Adrian? Maiko *loved* him.

She just didn't *trust* him one hundred percent.

"What are you doing in here?"

Maiko was glad she'd tucked the pills back into their original position because there was Adrian, fresh from hair and makeup, returning to the trailer. He seemed defensive rather than excited to see her, and Maiko's heart sank. But she turned her body toward him and gave him a wide smile, as if everything was all right.

"Wanted to surprise you," she said.

His expression changed from discomfort to delight. "Oh!" Defensiveness gone, he crossed the tiny trailer and sat down next to her. She tilted her face up for a kiss.

"We shouldn't, though," he said huskily, eyes already filled with want. "We're short on time and you have your hair done for production already."

"We can go fast." Maiko slid onto his lap, straddling him. She undid the button on his pants. "What's the point of working on the same set if we can't play a little?" she said teasingly.

"You're right, of course." He grasped her hips with both hands.

"And that's what touchups are for," she murmured.

She'd deal with this problem tomorrow.

But she didn't. And the first time Maiko realized that Adrian might have a bigger problem than just pills was when they were dancing at Dublin's after *Atomic Crusader 2* had wrapped and he got a nosebleed, all down the front of his shirt. He didn't seem to notice and continued to dance, but Maiko pinched his nose with her forefinger and thumb. He immediately stopped moving and looked at her with surprise. "You're bleeding," she shouted over the din.

Adrian caught his nose with his fingers, and she let go. She gestured at his shirt, and he looked down at the bloody mess that had sprung from his fountain of a nose. "Fuck," he said.

Maiko disappeared from the dance floor and when she returned, she grabbed him by the arm and pulled him toward the door. She'd called a cab and when the cab driver saw the blood, he balked. "Oh hell naw," he said. "No coked-out bros in *my* car."

"He's not—" Maiko said, and then she turned to look at Adrian. She realized, in that moment, that he had come back from the bathroom right before the nosebleed. "Were you doing coke?" she whispered, trying to keep her voice low.

Adrian mumbled something in response, probably because he was embarrassed. There were onlookers and paparazzi starting to pay attention to the two, and the cab pulled away from the curb. "Let's go back inside," Adrian said, and Maiko had to agree, because the cameras were an onslaught of flashes and noise, and the only way to get peace was to be in the bar. She'd sober up and drive them home, she decided.

When they were back at the condo, however, she didn't confront him. She figured that he'd just blown off a little steam. She set his bloodied shirt on a hanger in the garage with a note for their housekeeper to take it in for cleaning. She snuggled into him on their bed, watching his face grow slack as he fell deeper into sleep.

The next day, she asked, "When did you start using coke?"

Adrian balked. "What are you talking about?" he hedged.

"Adrian. Do you think I'm stupid? That was a cocaine nosebleed yesterday."

"You mean, you don't think it was a change in air pressure?" he joked, but when he saw her expression, he stopped himself. "You're right. I don't use it! I swear. A guy in the bathroom offered me some and I was having such a good time, I thought, *Why not?*"

Maiko didn't believe this lie. "A person thinks *why not?* and takes what's being offered in a bathroom if it's a free tampon, *not* coke," she pointed out. "Since when have you been laissez-faire about drugs?"

"Since when have you been so uptight about them?"

Maiko didn't back down. "This isn't about *me*. This is about *you* right now. And I'm asking you, when did you start using?"

"This is ridiculous," he fumed. "I don't have to answer your interrogation." And he left the apartment, spinning his car out of the garage.

After he left, Maiko sat on the blue suede couch in their living room and weighed her options. She could leave him. She couldn't be with a drug addict—or could she? Or she could give him another chance. Maybe it was a one-off, just like he'd said. That's probably what it was. A one-off.

By the time Adrian came back to the apartment, Maiko had made up her mind. "Adrian, you have to stop," she said.

"Mai, it was only once—"

"Maybe it was only once, but it can't happen again. Okay?"

He nodded, took a few steps forward, and hugged her close. "Okay." He spoke into her hair. "I'll be better."

"I love you," she reminded him.

"I love you too," he said.

And it seemed resolved.

Until the next time it happened.

TMZ
ADRIAN HIGHTOWER: COKE BRO?!

Witnesses at Dublin's say that they saw Adrian High-tower snorting cocaine in the bathroom. Hightower, who was with his girlfriend, Valentina Posh and high-fashion model Maiko Fox, was later seen with a nosebleed that got all over his shirt. We think he might have a problem . . .

12

2006

With *Atomic Crusader 2* wrapped, it was on to the next thing. Both Maiko and Adrian were hungry for new projects, especially one that they could star in together. Even before *AC2* had started its publicity ramp-up, the people on the internet were chattering about Madrian and how they couldn't wait to see them together in the movie. It was shaping up to be a success if the online discourse was to be believed.

They set their sights on *Helix Felix*, about a government spy and his reluctant accomplice. Barbara was a role almost as substantial as Lindsey Wilton, and Maiko auditioned for it with jittery nerves, wanting so desperately to grow her movie repertoire. Adrian had already auditioned for, and won, the role of Simon.

"Plan the wedding, maybe? So you don't wear a hole in the carpet," Adrian suggested, when he caught her pacing in the condo. The couple had set a date: March 10, 2007. Filming for their upcoming project should be done by then, and with time to spare for all the fussy little last touches that weddings always seem to have. Not that Maiko had ever planned a wedding before, but she assumed. That gave Maiko and Adrian over a year to get used to the idea of becoming Mr. and Mrs. Fox-Hightower.

"If it's *our* wedding, shouldn't we plan it *together*?" she asked.

"You know I'm not good for that kind of stuff. Flowers and cake decorations and cummerbunds."

"At least help me narrow down the theme," she insisted. They had hired a planner named Pauline, who asked them for their dream wedding ideas. Maiko was irked that Adrian didn't want to contribute his thoughts.

"Weddings have themes? Why isn't it 'Hey, we're getting married'?"

In the end, Maiko chose a theme of pink and gray with gold chevron stripes. The venue was a giant villa with a green lawn, where the guests would sit during the ceremony, and the colors didn't matter very much. She went dress shopping with Helen, who watched with a dour expression as Maiko tried on frock after frock at a couture shop, and Christine, who used some of her vacation days to fly in from Roanoke. She clasped her hands excitedly whenever Maiko presented a new gown, while Helen took large gulps of the complimentary champagne. Maiko finally decided she didn't want anything less than a Balenciaga-designed dress.

"That'll cost you, you know," Helen said, eyeing the ten-thousand-dollar gown that Maiko was handing back to the proprietor. "Like ten times as much as these."

"I don't care. I'll only get married *once*."

Christine said enthusiastically, "That's right! Get what you want."

They had plans to get Mexican food after shopping, but Adrian didn't show up when he was supposed to. Maiko tried not to show that she was upset. The three women had a nice meal, Maiko chalked up his absence to his forgetfulness, and they parted ways. Helen lit a cigarette as they were waving their goodbyes, and Christine wrinkled her nose. Helen looked at the cigarette, then back at Christine, and carefully ground it out in a nearby ashtray.

After Maiko arrived back home, she found the condo deserted. She turned a half circle, expecting to see Adrian somewhere, but the rooms were still. Then she heard a door slam. Adrian arrived from the front door, hair disheveled, nose reddened. Maiko was immediately on the alert. "Where were you?"

"Out with the guys."

The guys were Dave and Tim. Maiko didn't know that Dave was the person who got Adrian started on the pills, but she knew that he wasn't the best influence. Every time Adrian came back from hanging with Dave, he was jittery and aloof.

"You were supposed to meet us for lunch. And now it's three in the afternoon. Were you doing drugs again?" She knew she sounded accusatory but she didn't like this side of him.

"Okay, *Mom*," he sniped defensively, and Maiko knew that whatever she said next would be grounds for a fight. She didn't *want* to bicker. She breathed in and out deeply and let the subject go.

"What do you want for dinner?" she said brightly, changing the subject, and Adrian gave a one-shoulder shrug. Moody as a teenage boy when on coke, he stalked off to the fridge and grabbed a bottled water, drinking in long gulps.

Maiko softened even more. "I think I want to ask a designer to make my wedding dress custom," she said.

Adrian wiped the water from his lips. "Whatever you want," he said gallantly. Whenever the topic of the wedding came up, he was more generous, as if trying to remind Maiko that he was still the same guy underneath his new facade.

"I'll make some calls," she said, more to herself than to Adrian.

Instead of looking up information on how to contact Balenciaga, she found herself calling Christine. "I think I have a problem," she whispered.

"What?" Christine whispered back.

"I think Adrian is on something. Like, drugs. Habitually."

"Oh *no*." Christine was as straight-laced as they came; to her, even beer was dangerous. Maiko wasn't sure why she was discussing this with her most ascetic friend. She knew the next words out of Christine's mouth would be very negative.

"I saw some stuff in the tabloids but figured it was just speculation. But if it's true . . . don't suffer fools, Mai," Christine said warningly.

"I love him," Maiko said. "Maybe I can give him an ultimatum? Make him choose between drugs or me?"

"When has that ever gone well for you?"

Christine was referencing, of course, prior boyfriends with their own issues. Men Maiko had tried to change. Men who never altered their own sense of self but forced Maiko to bend against her will.

Christine sighed. "You sure do pick 'em."

Maiko sighed too. "I don't know what to do. The wedding is in fourteen months. We already have the venue booked."

"That's still early!" Christine insisted. "You can lose the deposit. Break up with him, Mai. You don't need a druggie in your life. Trust me."

Maiko bit her lip. "*Druggie* is such a loaded word . . ."

"Listen, I was supportive when I thought he made you happy. But there's nothing but tears from here."

"I don't know," Maiko said. "He hasn't raised his voice. He hasn't manipulated me. He's just a little snippy and cagey. I can live with that. He's a good man, underneath it all."

"You're making concessions *now* but think about how you'll feel in five years! Ten!"

Maiko paced the floor of the bedroom, peeking over her shoulder to make sure Adrian couldn't overhear her conversation. "I'll think about it," she promised.

"Don't suffer fools," Christine repeated.

13

Maiko had grown up not knowing much about money, just that her parents had a lot of it. She hadn't concerned herself with the pricing of typical goods and services, and had had a credit card by age thirteen that she could use for "emergencies"—aka, spa treatments and nail salons. She hadn't known that credit cards weren't endless sources of money, and had spent lavishly throughout her teens, in the way that young people who have no concept of a hard day's work at $7.25 an hour will do.

It was a hard adjustment when her parents cut her off and she had to take responsibility for herself. Modeling, at the start, is not lucrative. It's grueling and involves long hours and very little pay. She was lucky not to go hungry, and had Helen to cover her a few times when her half of the rent was due. Maiko became more aware of bills, and even after she got paid hundreds of thousands of dollars for her modeling and she loosened up a little bit about money, she still had a niggling thought in the back of her mind that it would all come crashing down one day. She was never 100 percent *comfortable.*

And that came to a head when she got her offer for *Helix Felix*. Her agent, Jen, called her with the news. "You were offered the part of Barbara for *Helix Felix*."

"That's great!" Maiko said.

"But bad news. They're offering you a lot less than what we asked for."

Maiko caught her breath. "How much less?"

"Fifty percent less than Adrian."

Fifty percent of a payday was a lot of money to leave on the table. "Did they say why?"

"They say you're still a model, not an actress, and that you will be paid accordingly for your experience. And . . ." Jen hesitated.

"What?"

"They wanted someone Caucasian for the role. They're offering you less because you're not white."

"Oh." Maiko felt a heaviness in her stomach. "I need to think about this."

Adrian was lying on the couch, one arm draped across his eyes. She had been fine with being paid less than Adrian during *Atomic Crusader 2* but now, with equal billing, she was still relegated to less.

Even though she had not yet proven herself in the box office, she didn't want *less*. She wanted to earn just as much as Adrian.

"Adrian," she said, "did you know that you're being paid way more than me?"

"Huh?"

"Your check for *Helix Felix*. It's way more."

"It's not up to me to negotiate your paycheck, Mai." He turned over on the couch, showing her his back.

She sat heavily on the corner of the couch, her stomach clenching. She looked at the wall opposite her—the wall with all of Adrian's *Atomic Crusader* merchandise. A framed poster of Adrian as the superhero. An assortment of action figures in different poses. A lunchbox with Adrian's picture on it. Beside that was a Valentina Posh shrine for Maiko. One of her blown-up print ads where she lounged in a black lace demi bra and panties set was framed next to Adrian as Atomic Crusader. There, too, was a framed Polaroid of the two of them on set of *Atomic Crusader 2:* Adrian laughing, one arm slung around Maiko's shoulders. They were a *team*; they worked together, not against each other. If he had gotten a big payday, he should have fought for her to get one, too, as a matter of principle. And what's worse, he didn't even seem to realize that this was how she felt.

"Did you know that they wanted someone non-Asian?" she cried out. "It's like I have to prove my worth twice as much because I'm a minority."

If they weren't on the same page about *this*, the most fundamental building block of their relationship, how could she be sure about *anything* else? How could she marry someone like this?

"It's fine, Mai, just think of my money as *our* money. It will be soon enough, anyway."

"That's not *the point*," she said.

"It's not like you're hurting for money here," he murmured.

"Damn it! That's not what this is *about*, Adrian!"

And then she left the room to tell Jen she wasn't going to settle for *less* anymore.

ADRIAN WAS STILL contracted for *Helix Felix*, but Maiko saw the role float away into the ether. She had asked for more money. The producers told her, in no uncertain terms, to fuck herself.

"Who do they think I am?" Maiko said to herself repeatedly. "*Who do they think I am?* To devalue me so much?"

A few weeks later, she learned that the part of Barbara had gone to model-actress Ava Mears, and Maiko could do nothing about it.

The wedding planner, Pauline, wanted to continue conversations with Maiko, get her opinions on cake flavors and flower arrangements, and Maiko had to admit that the wedding planning didn't appeal to her anymore. Christine's words reverberated in her mind: *don't suffer fools.* Would Maiko be the fool if she stayed with Adrian? Maybe they were just too different now. For all the talk they had had together about their big dreams and wishes, Adrian was now holding her back, even if he didn't realize it.

Maiko thought that he was her partner. But maybe he was just a stepping-stone on her way to better things, bigger greatness.

Out of desperation, she called Helen for advice.

"What do you want my thoughts for? Dump him," Helen said in the same breath.

"But . . . *should* I?"

"He said he supported your dreams but then took a paycheck twice as much as yours and *then told you not to worry about it?* Yeah, fuck that guy."

"He thinks his money will be *our* money," Maiko said, feeling a little defensive toward Adrian now.

"Naw. You should be earning the same, based on your screentime and talent. I mean, what do I know, right? I'm just a model. Never been in the movies. But if he's supposed to be your equal, that means in everything. Money included."

"You're right," Maiko murmured.

"Hey, you'd be honored to know I took your words to heart and stopped smoking."

Maiko was too distracted to say anything substantial to that. "Oh. Good."

"Anyway, you know I'm right."

But before Maiko did anything, she called Christine.

"I'm thinking of breaking up with Adrian," she said hesitantly.

"Do you want me to be supportive or do you need me to just listen?" Christine asked. This was why she was Maiko's best friend.

"I need you to just listen."

"Okay. I can do that."

"He's using drugs more. I think. He got a cocaine nosebleed a while ago and I thought it was a one-off but I think he's using it more and more. And I don't know if I can be with someone who is damaging themselves that way."

"Mm-hmm." Christine paused, then added: "But you're usually okay with damaged men. What else is it?"

Maiko sighed. "It's this money thing."

"Tell me about it?"

"He didn't stand up for me when my contract was less than what he was making. He didn't understand why it's a big deal to me. He still doesn't understand."

"That's awful."

"Yes. So it's just these compounding issues. And I can ask him to go to rehab, but I want him to be honest with me—and with himself—first. He doesn't think he has a problem. He has to want to go for himself." She felt tears welling up and her throat was tight. "I'm afraid that if I offer an ultimatum he'll choose . . . whatever is not me. And I don't know if I can deal with that."

"I hear you. If you're going to do this, do it quick. Like ripping off a Band-Aid. I know you, Mai. You let things fester. I bet this has been eating away at you for weeks and you're *just now* telling me about it."

"Yeah." Maiko rubbed her eyebrow. She *did* have a habit of letting things bother her for far too long before she acted on them. Charlie had been a shithead for months before she finally ended it. "I need a nice guy," she said.

"Your next boyfriend will be nice," Christine promised.

THE DAY BEFORE *Helix Felix* began principal photography, Maiko arranged to have a moving truck downstairs.

"Adrian, I'm leaving you," she said.

"You're leaving? You're going out? Where?" he asked, not getting it.

"No. I'm leaving." She took off the engagement ring and placed it on the coffee table. "I don't think this is working. I'm moving out."

He had been lying on the couch, legs hanging off the edge, as he always did when he took a nap, but this got his attention. He swung his feet down onto the ground and sat up. "You don't think this is *working*?" he repeated incredulously, face slack.

"I'm leaving," she repeated.

"Goddamn it, Mai, you can't just *say* shit like that and expect me to—I don't know—to *understand*? What about us doesn't work anymore? Please explain it to me."

"I don't think you support me," she said quietly.

"What's that?" He leaned forward on his fists, one ear cocked. "You don't think I support you? I've *been* supporting you! And we're going to have a joint account when we get married! My money is your money!"

"It's not the same," she insisted. "I want to be taken seriously as an actress, and you're undermining me by not supporting my equal pay!"

"I am not the studio, Mai! You don't even have a proven track record with movies yet. Yes, *Atomic Crusader 2* is going to be huge, but the studio just doesn't know it yet. Just be patient." Now standing up and pacing back and forth in front of the coffee table, he threw his arms out to both sides of his body in a show of frustration. "I'm not able to control this stuff!"

"But you could *insist* on pay parity! You have that power, as a star."

"Listen," he said, pleading now entering his tone, "I don't know about that. I'm just some guy. Some really, really lucky guy. I got lucky with my career and I got lucky when I found you. And I love you. Please, don't do this."

Maiko hitched her purse higher up on her shoulder and looked down at her feet. She shook her head. "I'm sorry," she whispered. "I can't."

"You *can't*? Why didn't you *talk* to me, Mai?"

"I *did*! You were just too high to listen!"

She walked downstairs and he followed, barefoot, and the full realization of what was happening seemed to hit him when he saw the movers parked out in front of the condo. "You're moving out? Right this second?"

She didn't answer. It was obvious what was happening and she didn't think she needed to say anything.

"Mai, this is nuts!" he argued. "Please, come back upstairs and we'll talk it out."

But she wouldn't move. She told the movers, "There's a second bedroom full of boxes." They disappeared upstairs.

"How did you pack all of those boxes without me knowing?"

"I don't know," she shot back. "Where have you been every night this week? Out with Dave and Tim? When you come home, what do you do?"

"Okay," he said, running his hands through his hair repeatedly, "okay. I get it. I'll get clean for you. I will. Just don't do this, Mai. Please." He was crying. "Please."

"I can't trust you, Adrian," she said quietly. "You said you'd stop using drugs before. But you didn't stop. This is your own damn fault."

She looked over her shoulder. Of course, there were photographers; she could see the light hitting their lenses as they took their shots. She pursed her lips into a line and looked at Adrian as if to tell him, *Get it together. We're not alone.* He was too distraught to understand.

It was too little, too late.

Part 2

Collaboration
(2007–2014)

Atomic Crusader 2: Rise of Hemlock Is a Bona Fide Blockbuster Hit!

We watched them sizzle together on a yacht in the Bahamas, and now we can watch them in high definition as they sizzle on-screen as John Jackson and Lindsey Wilton—Atomic Crusader and Ms. Hemlock, respectively. Adrian Hightower and Maiko Fox show that they left nothing behind in the bedroom as they lock eyes in the superhero caper.

It almost seems a pity that Madrian is no longer a thing, because they are *hot hot hot* in this movie. When Ms. Hemlock purrs, "I can wrap that in ice for you," referring to the—ahem—wound she's given Atomic Crusader, it's enough to melt the polar ice caps.

Will there be a third *Atomic Crusader*? Only time will tell. *Rise of Hemlock* is in theaters now and on track to gross $500 million in the first weekend.

Peachkiss5 (6:05 P.M.): I saw this opening night. This movie is my bisexual awakening, I swear to god.

LaZonaRosa (6:07 P.M.): How could they have broken up?? THEIR CHEMISTRY FFS.

LunaRocket78 (6:11 P.M.): Madrian is EVERYTHING. I'm so upset that they are no longer an item!!!!

08/04/07
WHAT A-LISTER IS A SECRET DRUG ABUSER?

Blind Item: We just learned that this A-lister who has superhero ties was recently in rehab after a coke binge. Rumor has it that this heartbroken man met a princess with her own demons while there, and now they're hooking up.

ANON378: A-lister, huh? It can only be a handful of ppl.

ANON901: I bet it's Adrian Hightower. Wasn't he just MIA for a couple of months after breaking up with Maiko Fox and now is hanging around Jess Marin?

ANON264: Ooh good guess.

14

2008

What do you think of making a baby?" Jess asked, her green eyes twinkling. She was lying on Adrian's bed—*their* bed—tracing one of her dainty feet up his calf. Adrian studied her for a moment: her sloping nose, her full mouth that she often filled in with bubble-gum pink. He considered what he should say. He couldn't imagine being with someone forever, anymore—Maiko had ruined that for him. But the idea of becoming a father was appealing. *That* was the type of forever he could get behind.

Even if he and Jess were temporary, a child's love would be enduring.

Adrian and Jess had met at Glorious Be rehab facility in 2007. He had been sitting at a cafeteria table drinking a pineapple juice when Jess, an attractive blonde, took the seat next to him. "I've seen you in group," she said, introducing herself.

"I know who you are," he'd replied. Jess Marin was a pop

sensation. She should've been touring Europe but had canceled the remaining dates because of "exhaustion."

"Surprise," she said, popping out both of her hands like he was a child. "Exhaustion is code-speak for drug addiction."

"For some reason, I'm not surprised."

"Why not?"

"Because you *have* to be on drugs to do what you do. Traveling and singing and performing and doing it all over again the next day. You couldn't pay me to do it."

"I hear you get paid pretty well these days," Jess said with a quirk of her eyebrow.

Adrian groaned. "What's in the rags now?"

"Just that your ex is pissed that you were offered twice as much as she was on your last project. I have to say, I'm on her side. That is bullshit, if you ask me."

"I *didn't* ask."

"I'm telling you anyway."

Adrian studied the woman next to him. She was bare-faced except for a little bit of black mascara. Even her eyebrows were dusty blond.

Adrian liked that she was telling him what she thought. It was refreshing, having someone who said what was on their mind before it became a problem. Maiko had let her feelings fester until she had no choice but to leave him. Jess was just telling it like it was. She smiled. "What?" she said. "Something on my nose?"

"I like you," he said. "If we were at a real café, I'd ask you out. But because we're at Glorious Be, I don't think I should."

She gave him a wink. "I'll see you on the other side, then."

Adrian mulled over what Jess had said to him. Maybe he *was* wrong. Maybe he should've been more insistent that Maiko get equal pay. After all, *Atomic Crusader 2* had come out with huge box office returns. Maiko would've commanded a great deal of attention if she had been in *Helix Felix*.

Adrian left rehab after two months, with a promise to be sober and a new outlook on life. He watched Jess Marin pick up the pace on her life from afar, checking out gossip rags' updates of her resumed tour. When she came back to Los Angeles, he was ready to ask her out. But how? They weren't allowed to have their cell phones with them at Glorious Be, and she never passed him her number. He had to do things the old-fashioned way, at least in Hollywood: he asked his publicist to contact *her* publicist and pass along his information. If she was still interested, she'd call.

Adrian heard from Jess the next day. "Hey, stranger," she said, her breathing deep and centered.

"Is this a bad time?" he asked, even though *she* had called *him*.

"I'm just finishing yoga and still in that deep-breath mindset, you know? How are you?"

"Great. Great, I'm great. Uh. I was wondering if you'd like to go out sometime." He felt supremely awkward, his ego having taken a small beating when Maiko had left him.

"Is *that* what you were wondering?" Jess's voice was sultry.

Adrian cleared his throat.

"Sure, let's go out," Jess said, peppier now. "No alcohol though."

"Of course. Coffee?"

They decided on dessert instead, going to a nice bakery that was known for its buttercream creations. Jess was a little worried about her figure, but not as intensely as Maiko had been, and Adrian found that refreshing, too: that she would eat a cupcake in front of him without fussing. Afterward, they'd fallen into bed quickly, and that was that. Adrian found Jess addicting in all the right ways; he abandoned his drug habit for her, at least for a little while.

They'd made their red-carpet debut as a couple at the 50th Annual Grammy Awards in early 2008. Jess had been up for an award for Best New Artist, though she didn't win. She went back to her notebook after the loss and wrote a new song about it, which Adrian thought was healthy. His new girlfriend, he noticed, did not let things chafe like his ex.

So Adrian thought nothing of it when Jess spent more and more time at his condo, and even encouraged her to give up her place so that they could live together. Late that fall, more than a year after they'd reconnected, they went to Greece on a luxurious vacation.

It was just the two of them and a hired photographer for *People* magazine—Jess wore a Jenny Packham gown that sparkled in the flickering sunset, and all was perfect. In the water off the Santorini coast, the lovebirds were photographed sipping Orangina and dipping their feet into the surf from the vantage point of a little boat that they had rented from the locals.

Adrian barely thought of Maiko on that vacation, instead focusing on his girlfriend, who was really quite extraordinary.

Jess sang him original songs every night while on the coast as she worked through what to put on her next album. "For my muse," she told him. The songs were happy, upbeat tunes about falling in love, and Adrian beamed when Jess sang a new tune for him. "I've never written as much as I have now. I'll have to keep you around forever."

It was only in the soft, glancing moments before falling deep into slumber that Adrian thought of Maiko: wondering how she was doing, if she was okay—maybe it was the lavender laundry soap used by the hotel, which smelled like her.

When they were on their way home from their little photo-ready vacation, sitting in the private airport waiting for their pilot to arrive, Jess and Adrian were subdued. They were lost in their own thoughts, Jess playing with her long blond hair and Adrian drinking a cup of coffee. Jess stood up abruptly and said she had to use the bathroom, and Adrian nodded; he looked at the side table strewn with Italian magazines and plucked one at random. There, looking up at him, on the arm of another man, was Maiko Fox.

She was almost unrecognizable without her long hair; she'd chopped it short and added blunt bangs that made her high cheekbones look like razors. Adrian absorbed this change in her appearance before switching his gaze to the man she was with. Thomas Whitley. Adrian knew him by virtue of being in the business—he was as well-known as Oliver Stone—but had never worked with him in person before.

Adrian felt a sharp stab of pain in his gut. He missed Maiko. He would never admit it to himself, or to his new girlfriend, but he wished Maiko were here with him. He wasn't at the point yet where he could look at their time together fondly and with nostalgia; it was still sharp and close to him, because he'd never had closure to begin with. Perhaps Maiko would always be a sore spot for Adrian.

"What's that?" Adrian heard a voice from behind him. Jess had returned from the bathroom and was now leaning over his shoulder. "Oh."

"Did you know about this?" Adrian asked, his temper flaring just slightly. He was on the defensive and didn't know why. It was just a picture. It was just his ex. He shouldn't—and didn't—have grounds to be upset. Yet he was.

"Of course I didn't know," Jess said. "Why would I know?"

"Because . . ." Adrian couldn't find the words. Because Jess had said *oh* in such a loaded way. A sad way. Like she didn't want Adrian to find out through an Italian rag.

"Look at it like this: she's moving on, and that's a good thing." Jess wrapped her arms around his shoulders, planting a kiss on the side of his head. "You don't want her miserable and at home all the time, right?"

But he did. He had been so blindsided by Maiko breaking up with him that he wished she'd be cursing her decision and feeling like he was the one that got away. He realized these feelings were petty and tried to let them go.

"You're right," he said. "It's good that she's found somebody new. Even if he's old enough to be her father," he added under his breath.

Jess laughed, a throaty sound. "Yes, he's not that age appropriate. Look at that gray hair," she said, and swiped at Adrian's reddish-brown hair as if to compare the two men. Adrian felt better. He was younger, more virile. He was exclusively with Jess Marin, one of the biggest pop stars in the world.

He had won.

And now, lounging in bed with Jess, he thought of his own childhood, going to his dad's car dealership, walking around touching the sleek bumpers and getting behind the wheel of a demo car just for fun. How his father would, when Adrian was younger, let him ride in his lap when they were moving the cars around in the parking lot, and his dad would touch the foot pedals but Adrian would be able to move the steering wheel. He enjoyed that.

What would the equivalent be for a movie star? he wondered. Maybe letting the kid sit in at craft services, eat all the fruit cups they wanted, while watching Dad emote. Or maybe they'd sit in the video village and watch their father there as he filmed, marveling at how their father looked so regal and somehow three-dimensional despite being on small screens. He knew he could be a good father; he'd had a great childhood and had a dad he could look up to.

Jess said. "We'd have to time it right. I don't want to have to cancel any dates for the Starstruck tour."

Adrian beamed. "Okay."

15

It may be true that some power couples, when they break up, fizzle when they strike out on their own.

That was not the case with Maiko Fox and Adrian Hightower. Maiko had anticipated a lull in her modeling when she thought she'd get the part of Barbara in *Helix Felix*, but when that didn't come to fruition, she booked as many campaigns as possible to keep herself busy. Her calendar was full for the next two years—she thrived on the catwalk, and recently she even had an ad with Sephora for which she clipped her locks to her chin, with bangs. She regretted letting the stylist cut her signature long hair, but what's done was done, and she walked her seventh Valentina Posh fashion show with her blunt bob.

It was at this fashion show that she met Thomas Whitley. He worked his way to the stage after the models had finished dressing—Maiko was, again, in the oversize sweatshirt she'd now stolen from Adrian that she just couldn't give up—and he asked for an introduction. Maiko had looked behind her and to her side before realizing that this distinguished gentleman was actually talking to *her*.

"Oh," she squeaked hesitantly, as she shook his hand. Then, louder: "I've seen all your movies."

"And I've seen *yours*," he said admiringly. "I was wondering if I could entice you to join me in a new venture." He gave her his business card.

"What kind of venture?" she asked.

"I'm producing a movie. I'd love to have you in it."

"It's not—it's not *porn*, is it?"

Thomas Whitley gave a hoarse bark of a laugh. His slate-gray eyes lit up with delight. "Oh, no!" he chortled. "It's called *Scout's Honor*. A movie with kids. About a Girl Scout troop that solves mysteries. I thought you'd be a great Erica. She's a troop leader." He shouted all of this over the chattering noise of other loud conversations and music blasting.

"I kind of . . . gave up on acting," she said regrettably, trying to hand back his card.

"What's that?" he said, not hearing. "Listen, call this number. We'll have lunch."

Maiko was left standing there after the show, holding the little piece of cardstock in her hand, and when she was back in LA, she dutifully called the number, planning to explain that she wasn't in the movie business.

But a lunch invitation became a dinner one, and Maiko, not wanting to be rude, accepted.

Thomas took her to Capo, an upscale restaurant in Santa Monica. He'd brought a car to her apartment to pick her up, riding in silence, storing up any small talk for the conversation over their dinner. The paparazzi were camped out at the restaurant, waiting for a scoop. What ran in the tabloids the next day were speculations about what twenty-six-year-old Maiko Fox was doing with a forty-eight-year-old like Thomas Whitley.

Thomas slipped off his blazer when he sat down, and Maiko let her gaze linger on him: He had big, strong hands and a Rolex on his left wrist. His face was obscured by the menu, so she looked at the top of his head. He still had all of his hair, which made her feel more tender toward him than if he'd been balding.

"The lamb is good here," Thomas said, and Maiko looked back down at her menu.

"Maybe just the grilled salmon?" she suggested, and the skin around his eyes crinkled as he smiled at her. It was a warm smile, full of promise.

"Sounds good," he said, and gestured to a waiter for service.

As she sipped her vodka tonic before the meal began, she said, "I want to thank you for your interest, but I'm not in movies anymore. Modeling is where my heart is."

"That's all well and good," Thomas said, steepling his fingers. "It's just, Maiko—can I call you by your first name?—I think you're missing an opportunity here. You are beautiful and young, but modeling is very fickle. Valentina Posh doesn't have anyone over thirty on their roster. You're going to want a backup plan for the coming years."

Maiko was silent for a moment, eyes cast down.

"I am offering you a chance to stay relevant in Hollywood," he continued. "You'll age wonderfully—I can tell already. And you had an amazing sense of timing and gravitas in *Atomic*

Crusader 2. I was mesmerized. The camera truly loves your face. I think you could have a very successful career in film."

Maiko thought. He had a point. Hadn't her father said that Hollywood types were fickle? And here was another man, who knew what he was talking about, telling her the same thing.

"I suppose," she said slowly.

"All I'm asking for is an audition."

Maiko wondered if she'd have to *do* anything at this audition that she didn't want to do. But Thomas had a kind face, and kind eyes, and he was looking at her over his glass of white wine, gauging her reaction. He seemed unhurried, letting her come to her own conclusion. The waiter arrived with their plates and Thomas pulled the cloth napkin onto his lap.

"All right," she said finally.

"Good." He began cutting into his lamb and she wondered what to ask next. Feeling a little toasty from her glass of vodka tonic, she said, "Tell me more about you."

Thomas leaned in closer over the candle. "Well, I've produced quite a few movies, like—"

"No, not your résumé. I don't know; tell me about your childhood."

"I remember . . ." He closed his eyes briefly as he thought. "I have a sister, Veronica, and I remember staying up late and watching for fireflies in our backyard when we were kids. We'd catch a few in old jelly jars and they were ugly bugs if you looked at them closely, but they emitted such a beautiful glow when they were roaming free among the tall grass in our yard."

"Where is Veronica now?" Maiko asked.

"She's still in North Carolina," he answered. "Works in insurance."

"Did the fireflies inspire you to become a producer?" she asked teasingly.

"No, I have my father to thank for that. He would take Veronica and me out to the movies every Saturday. I tried to be an actor at first—I joined the theater department at my school, auditioned for everything, got nothing." He chuckled ruefully. "I am terrible at pretending to be someone else, it turns out. My parents had a bit of extra money. We didn't grow up poor or anything. And they died when I was eighteen." He swallowed, Adam's apple bobbing under his beard. Maiko reached across the table and held his hand, which he squeezed back. "I decided in college that I was going to be a person who used my inheritance in a way to make the world better, not just for myself. I helped a friend produce a play, which went on to win a few awards. And I loved it. I decided to go bigger. I moved to LA and financed an indie film, which did well, and then the ball really started rolling."

"How did your parents pass away?" Maiko wanted to know.

"Car accident," he said, eyes sad behind his glasses.

"I'm sorry," she said.

"It was a long time ago. But thank you."

Maiko lived in terror that her parents would suddenly not *be* anymore. She tried to imagine her mother and father disappearing from the world one day, without warning, and her eyes pricked with tears. She loved them so much, despite the period of estrangement, and she couldn't imagine the pain he had gone through. She decided to change the subject. "Do you have any kids? I googled you," she admitted. "I know you're divorced."

"Tristan," he said through a bite.

"How old is he?"

"He's eighteen, a freshman at Brown. His mother—Georgia—wanted him away from Los Angeles and all the brownnosers that follow me around. But little does she know that the kids in Rhode Island are just as savvy as Californians and know who I am."

When Thomas dropped her off at her apartment, after going through another round of paparazzi as they left the restaurant, she said, "Thank you for a lovely evening."

"I didn't even tell you. You look stunning," Thomas said.

"Thank you for the compliment too." She laughed.

The dinner seemed to blur a line between professional interest and personal flattery. Maiko wasn't sure what the etiquette was. She wasn't going to *kiss* him, but she wanted to make sure she knew that she understood the gravity of his extended offer.

"I'll see you again soon, I hope," he said, and gave her a bisou on her cheek.

16

Adrian and Jess began trying—if *trying* was Jess forgoing birth control pills for the first time in a decade and approaching it with a laissez-faire attitude. If it happens, it happens, she seemed to suggest, and they enjoyed their lovemaking as they always had. When it still hadn't happened by the time they had to pause for the Starstruck tour, Jess seemed crushed but not defeated. "Maybe we should see a doctor?" she suggested.

She and Adrian didn't know how bad it would get—yet.

He was in the midst of preproduction flurry on his directorial debut, *The Sensation*. He'd finally finished his script and secured funding, hiring his old roommate Tim to be a light rigger on his project. He had courted a few producers for his film, but had given Thomas Whitley a wide berth, settling instead on Red Automatic Pictures.

Adrian was surprised, therefore, to arrive on his set at one point in 2009 and see Thomas Whitley there, holding two Styrofoam cups of craft services coffee.

"To what do I owe the pleasure?" Adrian asked, checking his watch.

"I wanted to see how the dollars are being used," Thomas said.

"But this isn't your production . . ." Adrian had a sudden streak of worry hit him.

"No, but I'm considering producing your next one."

Adrian chewed his lip. "I don't have a next one."

"But you will. Fellas like you always do."

"Does Mai know that you're doing this?" Adrian asked.

Thomas raised one of the cups of coffee to his lips. "*Mai*, eh?"

"Maiko," Adrian corrected himself.

"I haven't told her," Thomas admitted. "But she doesn't interfere with my job, and I don't interfere with hers."

You cast her as the lead in your movie, Adrian wanted to say. He knew that much, despite not Googling Maiko in the past year. News just filters back.

Thomas gestured with the second cup of coffee, and Adrian took it. "Let's watch you direct," Thomas said.

They walked together to the soundstage. "What are you working on next?"

"It's a story about a surfer on Hawaii's North Shore," Adrian said carefully. He hadn't rehearsed the pitch so it felt foreign coming off his tongue. He took a sip of the awful coffee to collect his thoughts. "He's trying to win the Pipeline competition. Needs the prize money, is a penniless orphan with a bad track record of keeping jobs. Has a girlfriend who's a waitress who supports him. I'm calling it *Surf City*."

"You come up with some godawful names, you know that,

Hightower?" Thomas chuckled, watching as Demarcus Jones walked past in costume. The set was crawling with busy crew members getting the scene perfect. "Brilliant idea, of course. We haven't seen one of these stories from an orphan's point of view."

"Exactly." Adrian nodded along, even though he wasn't sure if Thomas was right. It just seemed like a good idea to agree.

"I'd love to see an early read of it," Thomas said.

"Sure. I'm still working on the script, but when it's finished—"

"No, send me what you have. I'll give you my notes within a couple of weeks."

"That's really kind of you, but—"

"No buts. Just do it."

And so. Adrian finished filming *The Sensation*, and when the premiere rolled around, he invited Thomas Whitley. In return, Thomas invited Adrian and Jess to *Scout's Honor*'s premiere later that year.

Adrian wondered what it would be like to see Maiko again. They hadn't set eyes on each other since the premiere for *Atomic Crusader 2*. He and Maiko had danced around each other all night, standing on opposite ends of the group cast photos. Adrian had glanced her way every so often, but she was always looking in the opposite direction, and he had felt so lonely.

That was one reason that he was so keen to be with Jess. She was happy and flirty and *fun*, and she wanted to be with him. They had moved in together, but Jess wasn't interested in marriage, which gave Adrian some relief.

"If you're with me, you're with *me*," she had said, when they decided to be monogamous. "No one else."

And that was fine with Adrian. He had bedded so many women after Maiko had broken up with him—finding them at clubs while out with his friends, coming back to the condo, fingering them on his couch. Eating them out while muttering Maiko's name. A few went to the tabloids: *My Night with Adrian Hightower!*

Yes, he's an attentive lover . . .

One morning he woke up with the worst comedown he'd ever experienced. He was creaky and sore, his stomach was upset, and his nose was running like a faucet. Adrian was convinced he had the flu. Despite the sex from the night before, he was depressed; he didn't want to open his eyes because he knew he'd have to confront his life if he actually woke up.

The woman he'd brought home with him was long gone— the sheets were cold to the touch and Adrian realized he didn't even remember her name. He'd pulled himself into a sitting position and looked at his feet.

"Hightower, you're a mess," he'd told himself, and his voice was raspy and dry.

He had nearly been fired from *Helix Felix* for unprofessional behavior and it took his agent's finessing to keep him on. He missed Maiko something fierce, but the churning in his heart was replaced with the nausea in his gut. He barely made it to the toilet before he threw up. Maybe it was time to get his act together. He was tired of living like this.

And he'd met Jess, and he was clean, and they'd moved into a house in the Hills from his Sunset Strip condo. His life was back on track.

Except the fact that they couldn't seem to get pregnant.

He called his mother in Florida.

"Hi, Ma. Is Pop there with you?"

"No, sweetie," Betty said. "He's at the dealership again."

"*Still*? It's nearly nine over there, isn't it?"

"You know how your father is."

That Adrian did.

"I have a question. Maybe it's good that I have you alone."

"Oh? What is it?"

"Was it easy for you to get . . ." He didn't know how to say it without blushing. "Pregnant? With me? Or Leslie?"

"Oh, honey, no," Betty said faintly. "Well, getting pregnant was, for the most part, easy. *Keeping* babies was another matter entirely."

"You had a miscarriage?" he said hoarsely.

"Plural. Yes."

"I'm so sorry, Ma."

Betty sighed. "It's all right," she said. "I mean, it's not all right, but it's something I came to terms with a long time ago. My angel babies. Are you and Jess having a hard time?"

Adrian hadn't known how much he needed to talk to his mother until now. The story about the attempts to start a family, the negative pregnancy tests, the reliable periods, all came pouring out.

"It's hard, Adrian. Wanting to be a parent, and not having it happen—I don't envy the position you're in right now."

"It sucks," he said frankly. "But we're going to keep trying.

With modern medicine on our side, there has to be a better chance of it working. We're going to see a fertility doctor."

"And what if . . . " Betty said, then stopped herself.

"What if it doesn't work? I'm going to be an optimist and hope for the best."

"Of course. I didn't mean to upset you. I hope it works out too. Are you all moved in?"

Adrian felt drained. "Yeah, we're all moved in and settled. I set up a writing room." The script for *Surf City* was pouring out of his fingertips and he was making good progress.

"That's great, honey. And *The Sensation*? How's that coming along?"

"Great, Ma. I'll send you a screener when it's ready."

17

2010

She's only here because she's sleeping with the producer," Maiko heard someone murmur.

"No way!"

"Yeah, she's with Thomas Whitley . . ."

Maiko felt ashamed for the first time in her professional acting life. She'd always prided herself on being hired because of her merits, not because of who she was associated with. Though, now she thought about it, she was hired for *Atomic Crusader 2* only because of her association with Adrian. Maybe she wasn't a good actress, after all. Her confidence crumbled.

Because Thomas Whitley? He seemed to have wanted *her* because she was Maiko Fox, supermodel, and not because she was Maiko, blossoming actress. He saw the dollar signs after *Atomic Crusader 2* and pounced on them. And it was an equal-opportunity arrangement where Maiko got new roles under her belt—she signed a three-picture deal with Double-U Pictures for the security of it—and Thomas raked in cash, hand over fist, with his new ingenue.

Maiko wasn't sure how she and Thomas became an item. Their first dinner meeting had blurred the line between personal and professional. He'd called her after the paparazzi photos outside of Capo had gone viral and suggested another *meeting*. A box had appeared at her door around the same moment: a courier dropping off a gift. Maiko marveled when she opened it. It was a red sheath dress and a pair of black Louboutin heels with the signature red sole. She wore the outfit to the second dinner, pairing it with a bold red lip, and Thomas looked like he had won the lottery. "You look amazing," he'd said. "Although . . ."

"What?" she asked, spinning around to see if she'd sat in something horrid.

"You should grow your hair out. It looks better long."

Maiko accepted this tidbit, because she herself agreed. They'd eaten grilled mahi-mahi, and Thomas walked her to her door, holding the small of her back. Maiko had turned and looked at him. "This is more than just a movie, isn't it?" she said quietly.

And he had kissed her.

She didn't go weak at the knees; her heart didn't flutter. But she liked the attention. He seemed to be a good guy. She had him to credit for her return to movies. So she kissed him back—she felt like she owed him that.

With Thomas Whitley in her corner, Maiko felt poised to take over a new bit of Hollywood. She needed him. He wanted her. It was a fine arrangement.

Except when the crew pointed it out. She felt *dirty* somehow, like she had bought her way onto the set of *Scout's Honor*.

Thomas had asked her to join him at the premiere of *The Sensation*, Adrian's directorial debut. Maiko fretted about what to wear. It was silly, she thought, as she looked through racks of designer dresses with Nancy, her publicist, because she shouldn't care about what Adrian thought of her. He was with Jess, she was with Thomas. Madrian, no more.

She was weighing whether to move into Thomas's house, considering the trajectory of their relationship, and she wondered if she was thinking of it because she felt "behind" Adrian and his life goalposts. He had bought a house with Jess, and maybe *she* should do something similar? Just to show that she was completely and totally over him?

Nancy held up a blue glittering sheath against Maiko's side. "This one," she said grandly. It had a scoop neck and thin straps. The fabric was practically translucent but woven through with silvery threads. Showing off her body was part of her life, but Maiko wondered if showing off *so much of it* was the right choice for this premiere.

"Maybe something a little more . . . understated?" she hazarded, and Nancy passed the drape back to the stylist to place on the clothing rack.

"We'll take that one," Nancy said to the stylist, and then held Maiko's arm to draw her to a corner of the room. She said in a low voice, "This is just what we need right now. Show you're desirable and gorgeous and a little bit eye-catching. Trust me."

Maiko looked at the blue gown again, hanging on the rack, and silently nodded.

"Good," Nancy said.

So Maiko tried on the gown, staring at her reflection in the mirror as the tailor adjusted and pinned for alterations. She couldn't see how the fabric skimmed her body and hugged every curve; instead, she fretted about her weight, pinching at the little flesh on her upper arms.

"You look gorgeous," Nancy reassured her, and Maiko nodded again, contemplative. She could see her underwear through the dress. With flashbulbs going off on the red carpet, she would have to wear a matching thong and no bra.

On the night of the premiere, Maiko had her hair and makeup done, and then she slipped on the dress and a pair of heels. She had borrowed sapphire earrings from a prominent jeweler and they dripped from her lobes, catching the light. Her nails were pearly pink, nearly nude, and she held a sapphire clutch. When Thomas arrived at her door to pick her up, his eyes raked over her body in silent shock, and then he smiled. "I don't know why I'm surprised that you look divine," he said. "You're always beautiful, but tonight you look even more amazing than usual."

Maiko took his hand and they walked down to the limo. When she had settled against the leather seats, she accepted a glass of champagne from Thomas. His hand was on her knee and he drank in her perfume.

When they stepped out onto the red carpet, Maiko looked

around for Adrian without trying to be conspicuous. As she and Thomas were herded into the maelstrom of press and photographers, she caught sight of Adrian with Jess. Jess was wearing a pink gown with a small ruffled train that she had to kick into submission every time she changed direction.

They emerged on the other side of the photo ops and milled around inside the lobby of the theater. Maiko pointedly ignored Adrian, now that she knew where he was. As if summoned, he approached Thomas with an outstretched hand.

"It's good to see you," Adrian said, giving him a firm handshake. "Thanks for coming."

"I'm excited to see what you came up with," Thomas said. "How's work on your next project?"

"I'm revising it now. I'll have a new draft ready for you to look at in another month, maybe two."

"Excellent."

Thomas, a man of few words, stood in an awkward pause as Adrian turned to Maiko. He didn't proffer his hand. Instead, he looked at her in the eye, and very deliberately didn't examine her nearly translucent dress. "Maiko, I hope you're well," he said.

"I'm great. Thanks."

They held eye contact for a little longer than what was necessary, as if they were going to communicate more. Maiko felt a sudden ache as she remembered how he used to look at her, and how wrong it was now, as Adrian turned that gaze to his girlfriend, who was beside him.

"It's nice to meet you, Jess," Maiko managed to say.

Jess raised an eyebrow and looked her up and down. "Likewise. That's *some* dress."

"Thank you," Maiko said, though she wasn't sure if she'd been complimented.

"Let's grab our seats, shall we?" Thomas interjected, placing a hand on Maiko's arm and guiding her toward the inner sanctum of the theater.

Maiko could barely concentrate on the film. She could tell that it was well directed in that there were no jarring moments, but she didn't realize it had been so well received until the end, when people stood to applaud. She turned to Thomas and he was out of his seat, clapping enthusiastically. With a sinking heart, she realized that Thomas was going to offer on the next project.

She and Adrian were going to be dating the same producer, in a sense.

The low feeling didn't subside as she got into the limo to return home. Thomas chatted excitedly about the "extraordinary vision" of the film, the "impeccable eye" of Adrian, his interest for whatever would come next, in an uncharacteristic show of effusive enthusiasm.

Maiko stared at her pearl-pink fingernails and blurted out, "What if we move in together?"

Thomas trailed off. He looked at her, smiling. "You want to move in with me?"

"I do." Maiko felt herself sinking farther into the leather. She felt that she *could* love Thomas. That this was what she needed to move on.

———

DURING THE SUMMER holiday, Thomas's son, Tristan, was scheduled to return home from Brown, and Thomas was ready for Maiko to meet him. Whether the same was true for Maiko, she wasn't sure, but she took a deep breath and nodded when Thomas asked if they should schedule a get-together for Tristan's birthday.

"Since we've been together so long," Thomas said, "it'd be nice if you came to this celebration with my family."

When Maiko stepped through the door of Thomas's mansion, her host gesturing her inside with a smile, she found Tristan there, standing in the kitchen wrestling with a bottle of wine. With a yell, he pulled out the cork and brandished the bottle in victory. He caught sight of Maiko and smiled.

"I won't bite," said Tristan. Then under his breath he said, "Like Dad."

"Tristan," Thomas said warningly, and the young man ducked his head and strode out of the kitchen to the dining area, where there was a massive cake covered in gobs of blue icing, and presents in matching pastel paper stacked around a magnificent oak dining table. Tristan disappeared into the next room, gazing at an old photograph of himself and his father taken years prior that hung over the mantel.

Maiko walked tentatively into the living room and sat down on the edge of a couch cushion. She and Thomas had discussed her shacking up with him, but they had not made the commitment yet. Maiko sensed that it would happen soon. She looked at the back of Tristan's head as he pondered the photograph. Sandy brown hair, slightly mussed. A slight hunch in the shoulders. A discerning pinky lifted as he sipped his wine. Thomas entered the living room with his glass and one for Maiko.

"So you met Tristan," Thomas said, smiling. "Son, this is Maiko, my girlfriend."

"Nice to meet you," Tristan mumbled.

Thomas gave Maiko her glass, which she accepted with a murmured "Thanks." She held it without drinking. Thomas smiled jovially at his guest.

"We have an announcement," Thomas said, gesturing to Maiko to stand next to him. She did.

"Oh God, what," Tristan said in a flat tone.

"Maiko is moving in with me," Thomas said happily. "Right, Mai?"

"Right." She nodded.

"Congrats," Tristan said, with the same flat tone.

"Son," Thomas said with a slight warning in his voice.

Maiko wondered what Tristan had meant by his cutting remarks. Were the rumors about his anger true? Thomas had never laid a hand on her, but then again, why had she not met Thomas's ex-wife? Wouldn't they have to be on talking terms, if Thomas and Georgia had to parent their child together after the divorce?

Tristan, as if understanding her confusion, sat next to her on the couch when there was a lull in conversation and Thomas went to refill his wineglass in the kitchen. "If anything weird happens, you can tell me," he said in a low voice. "I've seen it all."

Maiko nodded politely but didn't say anything. Tristan, as

if frustrated with her, gave her a disgusted glance and slid to the easy chair opposite the sofa. He slurped at his wine, getting slightly sloppy with it.

Thomas came back to the room and said brightly, "Tristan, shall we open presents?"

18

I t took a lot to embarrass Adrian, but he was distinctly embarrassed now, standing in a cubicle with sexy magazines. *What's your pleasure?* he thought to himself as he looked at the covers, fumbling with the plastic cup that was supposed to hold his contribution for the fertility doctor. Adrian didn't like porn. He understood its point, but he wasn't sure if the actors were doing their job out of financial duress; he preferred to use his imagination, besides.

He and Jess had gone to the best fertility clinic in the city, and after they sat down to talk to the doctor for more than half an hour about their trials and failures, Dr. Retton, a cheery gray-haired woman in a lab coat, said, "Okay, Ms. Marin has already had blood drawn so those results will let us know a bit more about why you're having trouble conceiving. What I'd like to do now is get Ms. Marin in for a transvaginal ultrasound. Mr. Hightower, would you mind giving us a semen sample? You're welcome to bring it in later or do it now."

Adrian froze in his seat, and Jess turned to him smilingly. "You can just do it now, can't you?"

Talk about performance pressure. Adrian found himself in the cubicle fifteen minutes later, sweating slightly, as he knew they were waiting for him and his sample. He unbuckled his belt and squeezed his eyes shut and wondered what to think of. He thought of his girlfriend.

But after five minutes, nothing was happening—he was too nervous—so he resorted to the magazines. Even that didn't work. He pulled up his pants and re-zipped them with finality.

When he returned to the doctor's office, Jess was already back from her ultrasound, dressed, leafing through a *National Geographic* magazine. He'd taken that long. She glanced up and saw the empty cup with the orange lid. She raised a brow.

"I couldn't . . . " he began to say.

"That's all right," the doctor said cheerily. "We'll let you take the cup home with you and bring it back to us tomorrow morning, if you prefer. Here's a pamphlet with instructions." Dr. Retton gave him a slip of blue paper.

"Ms. Marin, your hormone levels are fine," Dr. Retton continued, glancing down at the paperwork in front of her. "You don't have any cysts, so we can probably rule out PCOS. We'd like to do a fasted blood draw and check all of your panel. You can both come back in tomorrow—for your blood draw and Mr. Hightower's sample. Be sure to make a follow-up appointment so we can discuss those results."

Thus dismissed, the two walked out of the office into the parking annex. Adrian glanced down at the orange-lidded cup, still in his hand, the blue pamphlet tucked into his palm behind it. *How strange,* he thought. *To be reduced to blood panels and semen samples. A puzzle to be reconstructed.*

"That went well," Jess was saying, as they walked to their car in the highly secured parking garage. This office was known to cater to celebrities and appreciated for its confidentiality. No paparazzi were there to out them. Adrian dug into his pants pocket and hit the fob to unlock the car.

"Hopefully we'll have answers soon," he said.

DR. RETTON WASN'T sure what was the cause of Adrian and Jess's infertility issue. All of Jess's test results came back normal and Adrian's semen sample was considered "robust."

"Unfortunately, I can't tell you what is to blame for your troubles," the doctor said to them during the follow-up appointment. "It could be cervical mucus. It could be a hormone imbalance that isn't consistent."

Jess visibly deflated. "What do we do now?" she asked.

"My recommendation is an IUI. If it's the mucus that's the problem, we'll bypass it."

"Whatever it takes," Jess said, nodding. She looked at Adrian. "Right?"

"Right." He grasped her hand. "Anything you think will work, Doctor."

Adrian hated seeing Jess depressed about this. They'd moved into their new house, which had extra rooms, and he wanted to fill them with laughing babies and toddlers with wobbly legs. He could see his family growing up in the house, his teenage kids giving him shit while he sat outside by the gated pool. His parents coming to visit—Grandma and Pop-pop—staying in one of the guest bedrooms across the hall. Everybody eating pancakes and eggs in one big sunny kitchen.

Never mind that Adrian's father wouldn't leave his dealership for more than a day. He never took the full weekend off; there was always something to do.

As Dr. Retton outlined the specifics for getting Jess ready for an intrauterine insemination, Jess held Adrian's hand tighter and tighter, cutting off blood flow to his fingers. But he held on.

19

Betty texted Adrian: You should come home.

Adrian had been on the other line when his mother had called. Double-U Pictures, with Thomas Whitley at the helm, wanted Maiko to play Amanda in *Surf City* opposite of Adrian. Adrian had been chewing on his lip wondering how to tell them that it was a terrible idea when the studio heads said, "Of course, this is just a courtesy call. She's locked in a three-picture contract with us. She'll have to say yes. We know you two have a history. I'm hoping you can put that aside and play nice with each other."

Thomas, who was in on the conference call, said, "Of course, she'll say yes."

Adrian was still thinking about this conundrum when he called his mother back. Betty said, "Your father is in the hospital. When can you get here?"

"We have an appointment with our fertility doctor tomorrow that I really don't want to miss—is it urgent? What happened?" Adrian felt a sudden streak of panic in his chest. "Is he all right?"

"He was complaining about his shoulder hurting, and then

he couldn't seem to catch his breath . . ." Betty's voice was coming from far away. "I drove him to the hospital in a rush. He collapsed on the floor walking into the ER. It was the scariest thing. Doctors are running tests now, but it looks like a cardiac event."

"I'll be right there," Adrian promised. Jess found him twenty minutes later, throwing things into a suitcase, which lay open on their bed.

"What's going on, babe?" Jess asked.

"My dad had a heart attack," he said. "I need to go to Florida."

"You're leaving? When?"

"I just booked a flight out for tomorrow morning."

"Wait a second. I just went to Dr. Retton this week and injected myself with Ovidrel already! We have our insemination at noon and you're *leaving*?"

Barely pausing, Adrian said, "I know this is terrible timing, but it can't be helped. I can't leave my mom all alone while Dad is in the hospital." He tossed a bunch of socks into the case and returned to the walk-in closet for underwear.

Jess closed the suitcase and sat on it. Adrian had a handful of boxer briefs that he clutched to his chest and he stopped to look at her. "*Thank you*," she said dramatically, as he finally gave her the attention she wanted. "Listen, I know this is awful, but you can't just go. We went through so much this cycle. We paid so much money and you're going to throw it away to go see your father, who barely even speaks to you when you call home?"

This stung. Adrian knew his dad was busy; it was his busyness that probably contributed to the heart attack in the first place.

"Wait a day," she pleaded. "Come with me to the IUI."

"You don't need me," he said. "You'll have my deposit."

"You don't want to be there while I'm getting inseminated?" she asked softly.

"It's not necessary," he said, though he felt bad expressing it. "Jess, if it were any other situation, I would be there, but this is my *parents*."

"And this is *me*. They have Leslie. Your sister can hold down the fort until you get there on Friday."

"I already booked the plane."

"So change plans!"

"The answer is no," he said with finality. "I'm sorry."

Jess huffed and got up from the suitcase. Adrian flipped the lid open and stuffed the underwear into its depths.

That night, when he got into bed, Jess was already on her side of the mattress with her back turned toward him. He carefully spooned her and placed an arm over her hip. She pretended to sleep but he knew she was awake and still upset. He gave her a kiss on the back of her neck. "I really am sorry," he whispered into her hair. She stiffened and deepened her breaths, ignoring him. He turned away and shifted to his side of the bed, where he slept until four thirty, when he had to get ready to get to LAX.

THE SUN WAS different in Tallahassee. It seemed much more oppressively hot and the humidity sank through Adrian's clothes as he strode to his hired car. Leslie had offered to pick him up at the airport, but he demurred, opting instead to have a manned service zip him around in an SUV with tinted windows.

When he arrived at his parents' house to drop off his bags, Betty was not there; she was at the hospital with Jerome. Using his old key to let himself in, Adrian set his suitcase on the futon he would be sleeping on and looked around at his old bedroom: an exercise bike sat in a corner, full bookcases crowded the perimeter, and the curtains had been changed from his old blue shade to something lilac. It would've made more sense to stay at a hotel, he realized belatedly, but he also knew that his mother would want him there.

His driver took him to the hospital, where he donned a pair of sunglasses and a baseball cap and inquired where he could find Jerome Hightower. After getting turned around a few times, he found himself in a small room filled with blinking machines and his mother and sister sitting in corner chairs.

"Adrian," Betty said, standing and giving him a hug.

"Hi, Ma." He removed his sunglasses.

"I'm sorry for making you come out all this way," she said, patting him on the cheek.

"What happened? For real?"

"He had a heart attack. He's had a couple of stents inserted. He'll be fine." Betty said this quietly, holding Adrian's clammy palm.

Jerome, in fact, was sitting up in the hospital bed, an IV snaking out from the back of his hand, and looking crabby. "I'm in the hospital," he barked. "It's serious!"

"He's just annoyed he can't be at the dealership," Leslie whispered.

"There is a mountain of paperwork I need to do! I shouldn't be here."

Adrian had to laugh weakly. His father was just the same as he had always been; Adrian had worried that Jerome would have changed behavior after his emergency episode, become meek or something. The man sitting a few feet from him had the same frenetic energy he'd always had, made wilder by his required commitment to staying in bed. Jerome's untethered hand shook with impatience. He wanted to get out of there.

Adrian nodded. Relieved, he turned toward his father and said, "No more Taco Bell, right, Dad?"

Jerome waved his hand dismissively. "I haven't had Taco Bell in years now."

"I'm not sure that's true," Betty said.

Jerome huffed.

Betty brightened a little as she said, "Did you go by the house first? Is everything all right? I know we got rid of your bed a few years ago . . . Will the futon be comfortable enough for you? Or did you want to check into a hotel?"

"Don't worry about me, Ma, I'll be fine."

She patted his arm. "I know. I knew I could count on you to come. I hope Jess is all right?"

Adrian checked the clock above his father's head for the time. There was three hours' difference between Florida and California. Jess would just be getting ready to go to Dr. Retton.

"She'll be okay," he said.

Jerome was discharged a couple of hours later and they all went back to the house. Betty made veggie burgers with whole-wheat buns for dinner and Jerome grumbled but ate his without daring to issue a complaint. Adrian had to wrangle his father to sit on the couch instead of going in to the dealership at nine o'clock to check on the mound of paperwork he was sure waited for him.

"How's your girlfriend?" Adrian's father asked, his fingers subtly rubbing on his other arm as if to make sure that his pulse was still strong.

"She's fine. I should call her, actually."

But Adrian made no move to call at that moment. He was suddenly exhausted. It was only six P.M. to his body, but he was so tired, he felt like it was midnight. He excused himself to go to his bedroom.

Adrian thought about everything he'd left in LA—not only his girlfriend, but everything going on with *Surf City*. He would have to call Thomas Whitley, too, to explain where he was and what he was doing instead of finalizing the script for his movie.

He suddenly thought of Maiko and how she was doing. She *would* be perfect for the role of the main character's girl-friend. Amanda was a lithe, athletic type; she looked like a ballet dancer. Mai was a little tall, but she would work. Adrian chewed his lower lip, wondering if she would be okay with the casting. He knew she could use the work, but at the same time, it would be opposite *him*.

When his mind turned to Maiko, it also turned to the era in which they had been together. He craved a bump. He knew it was because he was stressed and wanted to blow off some steam, but the craving existed nonetheless. He slapped both of his cheeks with his hands, turning instead to his phone and calling Jess. She would steer him right.

"How did it go?" he asked.

"Fine." Jess was short with him, but at least she'd picked up the call.

"Jess, I'm sorry. I'll be home tomorrow."

"No, it's okay." She seemed to soften just slightly. "I know how important your parents are. I just . . . I could've used your support today."

"I know. I'll make it up to you."

"You better." There was a small smile in her voice now.

He closed his eyes and swiped a hand across his brows, trying to loosen the tension there. "I miss you, babe."

"Miss you too. And hey, maybe in a few weeks we'll be future parents. Won't that be cool?"

"The best," he said, grinning.

He didn't need drugs. All he needed was right here.

"Listen. The role of Amanda in *Surf City*." He rubbed his brow again. "The studio wants it to be Maiko."

"What?" The smile was gone from her voice.

"They think she'd be perfect for it."

"Is this just a way for you to get back together with your ex?"

"Jess. *No*. Not at all. I think they're hoping that it'll be box office dynamite."

"The tabloids will have a field day," she said.

"Jess, there's not much I can do . . . and I would never . . ."

"I know, I know, 'I would never . . .' I got it."

"Seriously! I would never!"

"I *got* it. I'm sure you're happy about this, Adrian. After all, it's your movie." And she hung up on him.

January 2011

In Touch Weekly

MADRIAN REUNITED! The former lovebirds are working together on a new film, *Surf City*, penned by Adrian Hightower and directed by Elsie Taye. Maiko Fox has been tapped to play Amanda, Hightower's girlfriend, in the Oahu-set story. We are hoping for a reunion of our favorite high-profile celebrity couple!

20

2011

Maiko was surprised when she was offered the role of
Amanda in *Surf City*. Thomas came to her with the offer and she had to look twice at it to understand correctly: this
was her ex's movie, and this was her current beau telling her
to take the role.

Madness.

The studio enclosed a note with a photocopy of the monetary part of Adrian's contract for starring as David in *Surf
City*, and wrote that they "hoped she would strongly consider
the role of Amanda." Her paycheck would be equal to his.
How could she not take the role after someone—she had her
suspicions—had fought for her to get parity?

After a long hesitation, she called Adrian. It was the first time
they had spoken since they'd seen each other at *The Sensation*
premiere.

"Hi," he said.

"Hi."

After an awkward pause, she continued, "About this movie . . ."

"*Surf City.*"

"You're going to have to tell me more about it."

"We're going to film on Hawaii's North Shore. It's about a surfer who is down on his luck until he makes it to the Pipe Masters. Amanda is his girlfriend. It's a meaty role. The studio heads were really gunning for you to accept it."

"I read the script," she said. "It's great. But . . . do we . . . have to kiss?"

Adrian was quiet on his end of the line. "If it makes you uncomfortable, we can do without it," he said.

"If you take out the kiss, I'll do it. It's just . . ." She didn't know how vulnerable she wanted to be around Adrian, but she really needed to put up boundaries now if she was going to go through with this. "I can't kiss you. There's too much history."

"Understood. Welcome to the team, Amanda," he said, then clicked off. Maiko felt a slight disappointment that he didn't even stick around to ask her how she was doing or how things were with Thomas. She then realized that it was probably good that he was being professional; fewer lines to cross that way.

Thomas toasted her with champagne. "Back to the big screen," Thomas said, wielding his flute with a smile.

She and Thomas were doing well. She'd warmed up to him in the past year; she had taught him a few new things about their lovemaking that made him a better lover, and he always seemed to appreciate her. She had moved into Thomas's place, once again eschewing her own apartment. Thomas had given her a spare bedroom to house all of her shoes.

Perhaps, she thought, kindness and empathy were what made a relationship good.

"It means moving to Hawaii for six months," she said to Thomas, sipping from her glass.

"I'll be right there with you," he promised.

"Really?"

"Well, for part of it. I'll be back and forth from the office in LA."

Maiko nodded.

She fretted on the six-hour plane ride from LAX to HNL about meeting Adrian again. Thomas had to work in LA, so she was alone in first class, sipping a vodka soda to relax her nerves. When she arrived at the resort where the cast and crew would be staying during filming, she bumped into Adrian at the front desk. Expecting him to act a little weird around her, Maiko cringed, but Adrian was nothing but smiles.

"Maiko!" he said enthusiastically. "I hope your flight went well."

"It was very nice, thank you," she said, cautiously feeling out the situation. Was he going to be hot, cold, effusive, taciturn? He surprised her by giving her a side hug, one that was very friendly but nothing more than that. His body was warm against her hip and he patted her lightly on the opposite shoulder before he let her go.

"Good to see you," he said, smiling. "Get settled in and I'll see you first thing tomorrow."

"Okay," she said softly, and watched him go. The front desk attendant waited for Maiko patiently while she sorted her feelings—confusion, with her cheeks reddening, then relief—and helped her with her room card.

Once in her room, Maiko stepped out onto the lanai and watched the surf. The role of David's girlfriend wouldn't be too difficult; she had read the script and noticed a lot of similarities between Amanda and herself. Sure, Amanda had been a former ballerina, not a model, but they both were half-Asian, grew up rich but got cut off from their parents, and were madly in love with Adrian/David. Because she was playing his girlfriend, she would have all of her scenes with Adrian, but the main story was about David's surfing, so there wouldn't be any intimate scenes filmed. The script had an ending kiss when David won the Pipe Masters, but she'd had that stricken, and they would finish the movie with a hug instead. A hug was doable. Maiko picked at her nails. He'd just hugged her now, right? And it had been fine.

She didn't want to admit that her heart had skipped a beat when she'd seen him leaning across the front desk. Residual chemistry from when they'd last been together, she thought. Nothing more than that.

She was with Thomas now. And Adrian was in a relationship too. She wouldn't do anything to jeopardize either.

Even though the smallest part of her wondered.

THE NEXT MORNING, Maiko woke up to her cell ringing. She blearily looked at the caller ID, and it was Christine.

"What's wrong?" she asked, worry filling her tone.

Christine was crying. "Derek and I—we broke up," she sobbed.

"Oh, honey. I'm so sorry." Maiko yawned and looked at the bedside clock. It was barely five A.M., which meant Christine had waited until almost ten in her time zone to call. "Was it him?"

"No! That's the crazy part," Christine said. "It was me."

This was unexpected. Christine had been head over heels for Derek, had even moved to Virginia for him. "What happened?" she wanted to know.

"He wanted to get married, and I . . ." Christine took a big gulp. "I'm not ready."

"You've been together for, like, a decade," Maiko said, not understanding. "Wouldn't you *want* to get married? Start the next chapter of your lives together?"

"Have you ever thought—no, you probably haven't. But maybe . . . Have you ever thought that there might be someone else? No one in particular, but the *idea* of someone else?"

"Not really . . ." Maiko said uncomfortably.

"Yeah, it's hard to say." Christine was silent for a moment. "I just feel like . . . like I am supposed to love more than just Derek. That there's love in me for more than just him."

"Like polyamory?"

"No, like . . . like . . ." And her voice lowered. "Mai, I think about . . . *women*."

"*Oh.*" Maiko was surprised. She wondered why that was her first reaction, but maybe it was because of Christine's upbringing. Christine had never mentioned women before. She never flirted with Maiko unnecessarily like Helen did, even though Maiko knew that she wasn't Helen's type. "That's okay too," she said, after a pause. "You're allowed to like women."

"Am I? Am I really? Because you know how I grew up, Mai. I still go to church every Sunday. I'm worried about my soul."

"Listen, Christine, this is fine. You are fine. Your soul will be okay. I love you."

Christine was crying again. "I love you too."

"This sounds like something you need to sort out on your own. Without Derek. Do you want to come home?"

Christine mewed a yes, and Maiko tried her best to comfort her, offering to help her look for an apartment when she got back to the mainland.

When she got off the phone, the sun was peeking over the waves and Maiko needed a coffee. She went downstairs to the dining area of the resort and got a steaming cup. Adrian was there, too, and stepped toward Maiko with his coffee in hand. "Want to watch the sun rise?" he asked. She gave a little nod, and they gravitated toward the giant patio outside. They stood quietly, watching and listening to the surf slide sibilantly in and out.

Maiko spoke. "I guess I owe you a congratulations."

"About what?" he asked.

She fixed her eyes on him then. "The Oscar nomination, of course."

"Ah." He gazed out onto the water and nodded. Took a sip of coffee. "Thanks."

"Best Director for *The Sensation*. Sounds good."

"I'm not going to win it," Adrian said dismissively. "*The Social Network* is going to get it. I guarantee you."

Maiko shook her head. "I can see *The King's Speech* sweeping, but a movie about Facebook? Really?"

"When Fincher wins, I'll say I told you so."

He spoke wryly, without ego.

"I'll take that bet," she said lightly. She finished her coffee and crushed the disposable cup in her hand.

"Five bucks," Adrian said.

"Big spender."

"You know it."

"You're up early," she said after a pause, changing the subject.

"Excited," he responded. "Couldn't sleep anymore. I can't wait to get started on this production."

Already, other cast and crew were filtering onto the patio while Adrian and Maiko chitchatted, coffee in hands. They greeted Adrian, and as he was familiar with almost everyone on the crew, he greeted them back, stepping away from Maiko imperceptibly, as if to widen their small circle and let new people in. But no one took him up on it, either because they were too intimidated to stay and chat with the star or because they didn't want to interrupt what he was saying to Mai.

"Where's Jess?" Maiko asked.

"Sleeping. She's working on a new album and the muse keeps her up late. She'll probably come down around ten to watch the filming."

"Are you ready?" she asked, and Adrian chuckled.

"I've been taking surfing lessons in LA for the past three weeks. I can paddle. I can pop up on the board. I can even hang on for a few seconds. But Pipeline? I'm going to need that stunt double to make me look good."

Half of the movie would be taking place in the water around Waimea Bay; the other half, around inner Oahu, in and around houses secured as sets. Maiko's wardrobe was tank tops and bikinis, cutoff shorts and thong sandals. Adrian would be wearing little else besides swim trunks.

Maiko nodded. She felt a little weird to be standing next to him without Thomas's or Jess's supervision. But it wasn't like they were going to *do* anything. They were adults—adults in relationships. Besides, they were going to have to get used to it. They were going to be working together as a pair for the near future.

21

Working in the surf was unpredictable. Water has its own mind; it crashes and eddies. A number of crew were locals who understood that water would not do what it was "supposed" to do and tried to lightly lecture Elsie Taye, the director, about lengthening the time constraints for each shot, but the shoot was soon days behind, even in the first week of production.

When, after a long day at the end of a long week, Adrian slipped to the sand near the foot of the resort and found his buddy Tim partaking in some weed, he didn't find himself somewhere else to go. He stayed with his friend and toked a little too. He needed to take the edge off. Just because Thomas Whitley was dating one of the stars didn't mean that he wouldn't be pissed about the shoot going awry. And even though Adrian wasn't the director, it *was* his script, and that made him feel responsible somehow, that he'd chosen this location for the film and it was fucking up takes with every shot.

Tim gave him a side hug and said, "I won't let you get into anything else, buddy. I swear it. But I know you need this."

They stared out at the surf and let the smoke dissipate above their heads. Passing the joint back and forth with Tim, Adrian relaxed. He dug his feet into the sand, which was still residually warm from the sun, and reasoned: He'd been good for so many years. Why not let this happen once? It didn't mean anything.

But when he stole his way into his room, Jess could smell it on him. She was outraged. She stage-whispered, "Did you smoke?"

". . . yeah." He sat down on the side of the bed.

"Adrian!" she uttered, climbing into the bed behind him.

"It's nothing, just weed."

"You were sober for how many months . . . *years* . . . and now . . ."

"I set the clock back to zero. It's okay, babe. I just needed to relax. Whitley is coming into town tomorrow and is going to ask why the production is behind schedule. I was a liability on *Helix Felix*; he'll blame me for slowing things down."

"I can't *believe* you," she said, standing up and pacing the floor. "We worked *so* hard to stay sober and here you are, one week into shooting this movie with Maiko, and you're already back to your old habits."

"One, Maiko has nothing to do with this. Two, weed isn't cocaine."

"I see how you rushed to defend her," she said, riled up.

"Babe, chill."

"*Chill?* I'll chill when you're not knocking your sobriety off 'to *relax*.'" Then, sighing, she wrapped her arms around his shoulders, settling her stomach against his back. He leaned into her and she bit his earlobe. She murmured, "Tell him what you told me. That it's impossible to do these stunts safely without the right conditions. He'll understand."

"Let's hope." He twisted around and looked at her. Jess had been sad, lately. He knew she was writing—the notebook with its messy sheets and her curled handwriting was open on the hotel desk—and Adrian wondered if she was channeling her sadness about the failed IUI into her songwriting. He gave a small wish to the universe that it would be cathartic for her.

"I'm going back to LA," she told him.

"What?"

"I'm going to start all the hormones for IVF."

They had discussed this as a possibility, but hadn't come to a conclusion about it.

"Won't you want me there?" he asked.

"Yes, but your work is here."

"Can't it wait? Until the shoot is over?" He knew he was asking a lot of her. She felt her biological clock ticking; she was already in her thirties and neither of them was getting any younger. She shook her head.

"I'm going to do this with or without you," she said. It was the first time she had declared this thought, and Adrian was taken aback. They'd always been a team—hadn't they? It wasn't exactly fair that Adrian had gone to Florida to be with his parents during the insemination but that had been extenuating circumstances. This was just . . . work. Couldn't she wait? Couldn't he be a part of this experience with her?

"Please," he said, and turned around fully to look at her in the eye. "I want to be there for you. I know this is way more intensive than the IUI. Won't you want my emotional support?"

Jess studied him. "The production is already running behind."

"Whitley is going to whip us into shape. I swear." He held her hands. "Don't leave me here." Wildly, he wondered what would happen if he and Maiko were left alone together and hated himself for it.

Jess sighed. "I'll reschedule."

He gave her a kiss on the forehead. "Great," he said, relieved in more ways than one.

THE 2011 ACADEMY Awards were reason enough for production to pause for the weekend—Adrian had been working longer hours to make up for lost time—and he and Jess flew back to Los Angeles for the ceremony. *Scout's Honor* hadn't been nominated for anything, but Thomas Whitley joined the throng of celebrities on the red carpet, Maiko at his side.

She was already tanned from her days outdoors on the beach, with subtle highlights along her collarbone where her bikini's string had been tied. She wore a strapless white dress with a cascading skirt and miniature train, and it was vaguely bridal. Gossip rags began wondering if it was a sign that an engagement was to come.

Adrian was wound up. His typical centering exercises didn't work for him here; he had *told* people that he wouldn't win

Best Director, yet a small part of him wondered *what if?* He had his list of people to thank tucked into the inside pocket of his suit jacket, just in case. He patted at it nervously while standing on the red carpet with Jess. She held his other hand and he gripped it, white-knuckled, as he tried to make his hand stop shaking.

As Anne Hathaway and James Franco started the ceremony, Adrian shifted in his seat and stared hard at his hands. He craved—no, he *needed*—a hit. He'd blown his sobriety, over a thousand days' worth, just last week when he toked with Tim. Now he wheedled in his mind, what's another reset when he'd been sober for a mere six days?

As if she understood his feelings, Jess reached over and grasped one of his palms. He tightened his fist around hers. She leaned over and said, "Just relax. If it happens, it happens."

This had the opposite reaction than she had intended. How could she say *that* to him, after the years of Adrian saying the same thing about their forays into baby-making, and her being hurt by his laissez-faire attitude? He tensed up even more and excused himself to go to the bathroom. They were still hours away from the Best Director award and he was wound too tight.

He didn't have anything on him, but he hoped that there would be some younger actors in the bathroom making their own merriment. Just as he expected, some twenty-somethings were passing around a joint in the toilets. "Hey man," Adrian said, "can I . . . ?" His fingers were already outreached.

"Sure, man."

Adrian took the proffered joint, sucked in a deep breath, and held it until his lungs started to burn. He passed it back to its owner and leaned against the wall of the bathroom.

"You okay, man? You don't look so great."

"I'm just nervous," Adrian chuckled.

"Oh shit! You're up for an award tonight?"

Adrian wanted to nod but his head was swimming. "Yeah," he breathed.

"Good luck, dude, rootin' for you."

Adrian returned to his seat feeling a bit more mellow. Jess, bored by the forced banter between the two hosts, was sitting with one hand idly playing with her bracelet, and she looked up when he sat down. The puff of air from his deflating seat carried the scent of pot toward her and she stopped messing with her jewelry. "What did you do?" she whispered.

"Nothing," he said sullenly.

Jess pressed her lips together so they were a thin line and turned back to the stage. They kept silent until Hilary Swank introduced Kathryn Bigelow to read off the nominees for Best Director. Jess clutched his arm. Adrian stared very hard at Kathryn as a cameraman focused on his potential reaction.

"And the Oscar goes to . . . Tom Hooper for *The King's Speech*."

Adrian settled back in his seat and clapped. Not Fincher, then, but not him, either. And he had to be okay with that. He'd owe Maiko five bucks.

The cameraman disappeared down the aisle to record the

next nominee and Jess leaned in to Adrian. "Sorry, babe," she said mournfully.

Adrian shrugged. So it goes. He would roll with it.

MAIKO AND ADRIAN didn't speak at the Oscars, or even at the *Vanity Fair* after-party, which they both attended, socializing in different circles. They flew separate flights back to Oahu for *Surf City* filming and didn't talk to each other again until they were on the sand at Waimea Bay. There they stood, in their bathing suits surrounded by cameras and crew, setting up the shot. Maiko dug a toe into the sand. "Sorry you didn't win," she said.

"I have your five dollars somewhere," he said wryly.

"Keep it."

"A bet is a bet," Adrian insisted.

"You said Fincher would win. You were wrong. Let's just call it neutral, okay?"

He and Jess had gotten into an argument in the car on the way to the after-party. "I can't believe you," she'd said, once they were in the privacy of their limo with the driver's partition up. "Smoking out at the *Oscars*, I mean!"

"It was just one toke," he'd said.

"I'm not trying to be shrill, Adrian, it's just . . . we are sober people. We take it one day at a time. But you're not, lately, and I'm worried you derailing yourself will derail *me*."

Adrian had known that Jess's concern reached farther than just for himself, but he'd bristled at her declaration. Why couldn't Jess be responsible for *herself*? Just like he was responsible for *himself*?

"I don't want to go to this party," he'd said.

"They're expecting us to show up."

Adrian had sighed.

When they got to the party, they put their amiable faces on and went to mingle. But they barely spoke to each other when they got back to their giant house, and Adrian fell asleep before Jess was even out of the shower.

Now, staring at Maiko in the gorgeous Hawaiian sunshine, he regretted his decision to smoke. Not because it had displeased his girlfriend, but because it reminded him of the drug problem he'd had when he was with Maiko and how it had cost him that relationship.

"Maiko," he said.

"Hmm?"

"I just want you to know that I thought a lot about what you said, before . . . um. And that I'm glad you took this role."

She was quiet for a minute, looking out at the surf instead of at him. "I figured you were the one fighting for me to get equal pay," she admitted. His heart rose in his chest. Her eyes flicked over to him. "Thank you."

The scene that was up next was the non-kiss of David and Amanda. Adrian was confident that it would be easy: one shot, boom, done. The crew huddled on the sand and the director of photography placed his eye on the viewfinder.

The moment called for Maiko and Adrian to step toward each other in the light of the setting sun. Maiko looked nervous but stood on her mark, and when the director, Elsie, yelled "Rolling!" she turned on her smile and waded toward Adrian in the shallow water. The hem of her maxi skirt dragged in the surf, as it was supposed to, and Adrian abandoned his surf- board to run toward her. She leapt into his arms, hugging him around the neck, and as he put her down, he grasped the back of her head, smoothing her hair. They placed their noses and foreheads tip to tip and closed their eyes, breathing. To Adrian, it was just another day at work.

"We're still rolling, but let's try that again," said Elsie. "Reset!"

Each time, they got closer and closer, until their stomachs were flat against each other, her cheek against his. And as they continued to hug, Adrian felt something growing in his stom- ach. It was *Maiko*, and she smelled like coconut sun lotion, and his hands were buried in her hair, and he wanted to kiss her— maybe because he felt the scene would work better for it, but maybe because he just wanted to kiss her anyway. Familiarity.

He pressed his forehead against hers. Really breathed her in. And then the impossible: Maiko's lips found his.

Adrian reciprocated, pressing his mouth against hers. His heart soared for just a moment as he believed in the kiss, be- lieved in the love.

"And cut," Elsie said. "Finally. It looks good, you two."

Adrian untangled his limbs from Maiko's and took a step back. "Sorry," Maiko said, seemingly embarrassed. "The scene just seemed to call for it. It was in the script originally, after all."

"You made the right call," Adrian replied. He flashed her a quick smile. His stomach was still doing somersaults from the kiss and he told himself to calm down.

Later that night, as he lay awake in the bed that he shared with Jess, he thought about the kiss. He had expected a kiss with Maiko to feel loaded and heavy; instead, it was light and *happy*. Was it because they'd been acting? Or was it because life with Mai had just seemed so much easier than the life he was living now?

22

Maiko tried not to remember the times she and Adrian were filming and he'd had to act like he was her devoted boyfriend. It wasn't a stretch of the imagination to fall right back into that mindset, of him looking at her from under those red-tinged eyelashes with those brown eyes, his lips tugging at the corners as he confided something to Maiko. There was one scene where he held the back of her head and leaned in like he was about to kiss her—it was, in fact, the part in the script where Amanda and David had kissed, before it was rewritten—and as they pressed their foreheads together, Maiko had the urge to kiss him. So she had. She didn't think, she just acted; she was Amanda at that moment, swept up in the joy of being with David.

Maiko had to sigh. It had been nice to get lost in Adrian's eyes again. She had felt the pull between the two of them when they filmed that scene. His mouth had tasted of mint, of him. Then Elsie Taye had shouted, "Cut!" It took a moment for her to remember where she was, what she was doing. The camera moved away from them and Adrian dropped his hand from where he'd touched her. He turned and began setting up the next shot, discussing it with the director of photography. She'd sat bewilderingly wondering about her feelings and glad that Thomas was in LA at the time.

Then Adrian had caught her eye. He'd given her a crooked smile and turned back to the DP. Maiko suddenly knew that Adrian had felt it too—but it didn't mean anything. Residual feelings from long ago.

"What the hell was that?" Thomas asked, when he watched the dailies. He was on the phone with Maiko, one of their evening calls, and the jealousy was apparent in his voice. "You signed a contract saying you would *not* kiss. And yet you did? Were you pressured? Did you discuss it beforehand? Elsie says *you* initiated the kiss, is that true? It sure looks like it from the playback."

"No, no, and umm?" Maiko was flustered.

"I have to say, Mai, this is unusual for you. You specified that you wouldn't kiss. But you did anyway. It looks good, unfortunately. The other producers want to keep it in. We're using the shot."

Maiko was silent, tracing a finger on the white sheets of her hotel bed. "I'm sorry," she said finally. "But I'm glad it's actually going to be used."

"Don't be sorry. Do better."

"I'll be good now, I promise," she said.

Thomas hung up.

Maiko was careful after that to show no interest in Adrian. They wrapped filming without any other incidents and she was sure to keep herself farther away from him than what was strictly necessary, so that the on-set producers wouldn't report back to Thomas about her philandering ways.

MAIKO TOOK CARE of Christine from Oahu: bought her a plane ticket, helped her with the deposit on her new rental. When filming had wrapped and Maiko was back in Los Angeles, she went out with Christine for lunch downtown.

"How have you been doing?" Maiko asked, carefully biting into a forkful of spinach.

"Fine, I guess." Christine wasn't very talkative, and Maiko wasn't either. Maiko decided to tell Christine about what happened in Hawaii, including Thomas's angry phone call after he saw the dailies.

Christine softened slightly. "Hmm. I wish I had a life as interesting as yours. Although I guess my conundrum is pretty bad."

"So you think you like . . . women?" Maiko asked. She knew she should tread softly, because Christine would be like a scared rabbit discussing this out in the open where other diners could hear.

"I loved Derek. Still do. But I keep thinking about what I'm missing out on. That I haven't explored everything, and that includes women." Christine sipped her iced tea. "I can't believe I'm talking about this."

"No, no, this is good." Maiko speared a spinach leaf. "Do you want to . . . explore?"

Christine started giggling. "I've never been interested in

you, Mai," she said. "You're my best friend. Your roommate Helen, however . . ."

"She is a Glamazon," Maiko agreed, and thought about how Helen had been interested in Christine years ago. She wondered if Helen still carried a torch for her best friend.

"I don't know." Christine chewed the inside of her lip. "But I think my heart isn't ready to settle down. Derek didn't want to share me, and I didn't want to cheat."

Maiko's cheeks flushed and she felt defensive, but then realized that she had nothing to be ashamed about. She'd felt a little something for Adrian while they were pretending to be a couple on a movie set—what was so bad about that? It was *Method*. She'd gone home to Thomas Whitley in LA and everything had been normal.

"I think," she said slowly, "Thomas wants to get married."

Christine threw her another look, this one slightly alarmed. "And *you're* ready for that?"

"I don't know. Maybe."

"Are you sure you want to get married to this guy? He told you to 'do better.' Isn't that faintly dad-like?"

"He's so normally not like that. It was weird."

"Maiko." Christine's voice held a note of warning. "You don't choose the best guys. Adrian was the nicest one and he was a *drug addict*. I'm just saying, watch out for red flags."

"Okay, okay."

They finished their lunches and hugged each other goodbye. Maiko returned to Thomas's house in Malibu, where she slipped off her flats and padded into her dedicated shoe room. She was putting them away when Thomas stood outlined in the doorway, leaning on the jamb. "Where were you?" he asked, a slight smile on his face.

"Out with Christine."

"You look too nice to have gone out with one of your girl-friends. Where were you really?"

Maiko was confused. "With Christine," she repeated.

"Are those the Tory Burch flats I got you?" he asked, coming forward and pulling them from their dedicated shelf space.

"Ye-es?"

"Why waste Tory on a lunch with Christine?" he said, his voice still very pleasant, but something hard was beneath his tone. Disbelief.

"They're comfortable?"

"Why do you keep answering me with questions?"

"Why do you keep asking me weird questions?" she shot back.

He bristled. "What, is it weird for me to want to know where my girlfriend is?"

"No, not at all. I just . . ." Maiko's mind whirled. "I don't know why you'd think I'd lie about being with my friend. We were just having lunch. We went to a café downtown. We had salads. She told me about breaking up with her boyfriend and I—" She didn't finish her sentence.

"I'd rather you would have guests come to the house instead," he said, the pleasant note back in his voice. "We can order in. Fewer paparazzi to hound you."

"They weren't that bad—"

He glanced down his nose at her. "Fewer paparazzi," he said again.

"Okay. Whatever you think is best," she said.

"Good."

He replaced the flats on their shelf and walked out of the glorified shoe closet. Maiko wondered what the hell had just happened.

Surf City has been panned by critics, who call it a "misogynistic remake of *Blue Crush*." Despite the 32% score on Rotten Tomatoes, the film, starring Adrian Hightower alongside old flame and muse Maiko Fox, has had a robust premiere, raking in a projected $90 million against its production cost of $60 million on its first weekend.

Forum Post: <u>Maiko Fox and Adrian Hightower reunite as lovebirds in the film *Surf City*.</u>

2cool4u (5:15 P.M.): I'm one of the people who went to see this movie on opening night. It was nothing special but it was beautiful. Made me want to visit Hawaii.

Goose-and-gander (5:17 P.M.): I also saw it and it was a snoozefest EXCEPT when Madrian was onscreen together. God they have the most intense chemistry.

tacotaacotaco (5:21 P.M.): i don't buy that they're not having an affair off-camera. just the chemistry in the trailer alone made me squirm. their partners must be on edge watching them nearly make out on screen.

Fashionhound (5:23 P.M.): taco, just because they can fake chemistry with each other doesn't mean that they are actually fucking. Did you see them on the red carpet? They barely even acknowledged each other.

tacotaacotaco (5:25 P.M.): no, I didn't see that. was there a post on here? link?

Fashionhound (5:26 P.M.): <u>Link</u>

Mandolinectarine99 (5:31 P.M.): Wow, they really stood as far apart as they could on that red carpet.

tacotaacotaco (5:32 P.M.): i don't buy it. if i were sleeping with my costar, i'd do the exact same thing and pretend they didn't exist during the movie promo.

2cool4u (5:34 P.M.): I'm with taco on this one. It would've been less obvious if they just acted buddy-buddy during the premiere. The way they played it, it looks like they have something to hide.

Pajumachoo (5:37 P.M.): Gosh I can't get enough of Madrian. I need them to be a real couple again. They give me LIFE.

October 5, 2011

<u>*It's been four years—why haven't Jess Marin*</u>
<u>*and Adrian Hightower had a baby?*</u>

Sources tell us that all is not copacetic with Jess and Adrian. They are constantly fighting about having children. She wants them—he doesn't! And why should he? He's been pining after his long-lost love Maiko Fox ever since she dumped him five years ago. Sources close to the former flames tell us that their chemistry on the set of *Surf City* was so intense, Jess threatened to leave him.

23

Adrian. There's a great offer for you. It's called *Pandora*."
There was a lot of wind noise, like Adrian's agent was
driving with the top down on his convertible while talking.

"Jason, I didn't audition for anything." Adrian shifted the
phone to his other ear.

"That's the beauty of it. Double-U Pictures wants you back.
You and Maiko. You don't *have* to audition. This is it, buddy.
This is what we've been waiting for. Your star is shining so
bright, you don't have to do anything but show up." Adrian
could imagine Jason with his Bluetooth earpiece in, so his
hands could be free to gesticulate wildly while driving.

"I don't know. Doing *Surf City* with Mai already put some
strain on my relationship."

"But it's a sure-fire hit, Adrian. You and Maiko *print* money."

"That's good for the studio, but what about for us? We have
lives, too, you know." Jess had been upset the last time he'd

starred with Maiko. Adrian loved Jess, but he wasn't sure if her jealousy could withstand another on-location film.

"I'm going to pretend that you didn't just take that tone with me. They'll pay you well. They'll pay *both* of you very well. Equal pay, right? We can do that. Just sign on to *Pandora*."

After the conversation with Jason, Adrian wiped his face with a sweaty palm and texted Tim. *Can u hang?*

My place? came the reply.

Forget being sober. He needed *something*. The last time he and Maiko had been in a movie together, they had kissed. It had awakened something dormant in him, some old memory, with a tinge of newness that made him want to be with her again. Plus he hadn't been ignorant of the online chatter. *Madrian, Madrian.* If they were going to get shoved together in another film . . . he would need reinforcements.

He stepped into the kitchen, where he found Jess sipping a homemade decaf latte from their Italian espresso machine and flicking idly through a fertility pamphlet given to them by Dr. Retton.

"Ready for our next round?" she said, holding it up.

"Are you sure you can do it while on tour? You heard what Dr. Retton said; it's not just a lot of injections, it's a lot of blood draws to check on your hormone levels too. And then you'll have to fly back at a moment's notice to get the implantation done."

"I know. I just really want this to happen."

"Maybe we should wait," Adrian said, wrapping his hands

around hers. "Wait until the tour is over, then do the whole cycle. I think you'd be a lot more comfortable."

"I don't want to wait anymore," she said quietly. "I waited for you to finish *Surf City*, I recorded the whole damn *All Aboard* album because my producer wanted me to strike while the iron was hot, and now I have to go on tour, and I'm tired of waiting."

"But Dr. Retton said you had to be on bed rest for some of the days after the procedures. What if you overexert yourself and make yourself sick? That's not good for anyone."

Jess didn't say anything. She sniffled. Adrian turned and hugged her. "Maybe you're right," she said finally.

"Finish the tour. Then we get pregnant. It's a great plan. I'll carve out time too."

"You mean it?" she asked.

He let her snuggle into him even harder and he said, "You bet." He didn't tell her about *Pandora*. He didn't tell her about Maiko being tapped to play the titular character. She would find out soon enough and he didn't want to add to her upset now. "I'm going over to Tim's," he said.

She stiffened in his arms. "And do *what*, exactly?"

"Just hang."

Jess pulled back and gave him a wary look. "I'm worried about you," she said sadly. "If you're using again—"

"I'm not. I swear I'm not."

"Because I can't be with you if you are. It's too damn hard for me to navigate this for myself."

"Babe." Adrian felt ashamed at what he had been meaning to do at Tim's place. Pink spots appeared high on his cheekbones and he cleared his throat. "I'll tell you if something is wrong," he promised.

"Okay." And she let go of him.

24

Maiko did as Thomas asked and ordered in Thai food when she next saw Christine. Her friend came shuffling up the expansive drive and looked at the towering house over the beach. "Wow," she said.

"Come on in," Maiko invited, and the two women walked through the bright, airy foyer and into the living room, where there was a soft and comfortable pair of couches sitting across from each other, a coffee table in between them. The women chose to sit on one couch together and curl up with their feet under them.

"How are things?" Christine asked when they were settled. Maiko poured her some fizzy water.

"Fine. I just found out that Double-U Pictures wants me to do another movie with Adrian, though."

"That's like the third one, isn't it? How do you feel about that?"

"Weird." Maiko drew lines in the condensation of her glass with her finger. "But the studio insists. It's the last film in my contract. Thomas, well . . ."

"He feels strongly against it, but who listens to the director, right?" Thomas's voice interrupted them. He had strode into the room and stood behind their couch.

"Yes, that's basically what's happened," Maiko finished. "He objected, wanted Chris Evans for the lead, but no one listened."

"I was told that Maiko and Adrian print money," Thomas said, crossing over to the other couch and sitting down. He poured himself a glass of the carbonated water and took a deep gulp. "They won't listen to me, even though I'm the other producing partner. But I'll be on the set." *Making sure nothing happens* was the added but unsaid threat.

Christine turned toward Maiko with question marks in her eyes. "I see," she said. She was obviously thrown by Thomas's intrusion into their conversation but couldn't say anything aloud.

The doorbell rang and Maiko said, "That'll be the food."

"I got it," Thomas said, hopping to his feet, and he walked to the front door. Christine gave Maiko a *look*, and Maiko shrugged her shoulders. She didn't know why he had popped in.

"He's just saying hi," she whispered.

When Thomas returned, he put out the pallet of Thai on the coffee table and passed each of them a pair of disposable chopsticks. But instead of leaving, he opened the cartons and peeked inside. "Do you mind if I join you?" he asked. "This looks delicious."

"Sure," Maiko said hesitantly.

"Fine," Christine said faintly.

The two women didn't want to discuss anything intimate after that. They kept to the weather and books they'd read and movies they'd watched. Thomas munched on his spring rolls contentedly and hung around even after they were finished with their meal.

"Want a tour of the house?" Maiko asked, and Christine nodded. So they got up, put their dishes in the trash, and Maiko took her on a meandering path around the kitchen to the gardens outside.

"What was that about?" Christine asked.

"I don't know," Maiko admitted.

"It was weird. Like he was checking up on us."

"I got that feeling too." Maiko plucked a flower from its stem and started tearing off its petals one by one. "He's not usually like that. But I think he's worried about the impending movie with Adrian."

"No offense, because he seems like a friendly, if misguided, guy, but I came to see *you* and talk to *you* and not Maiko-and-Thomas. If that makes sense."

"Yeah. I'm sorry. Next time, we'll meet up without him."

Christine nodded. "I can't always drive to Malibu, you know. It takes me like two hours to get here with the traffic."

When Christine left, Thomas guided her out the door. "This was nice," he said. "Come back and visit us again soon."

Maiko hugged Christine at the top of the driveway and watched her pad her way down the concrete. Maiko whirled around and said, "What was that about?"

"What was what about?" Thomas asked, feigning ignorance.

"Why did you . . . I don't know, stick around?"

"The food looked good and I haven't been social lately. I wanted to have a little conversation with my Thai."

"You barely spoke after the food got delivered and yet you hung around for two hours? Why couldn't you let me have a friend over for a private conversation?"

"Aren't we a team?" he asked, sounding wounded. "What do you have to say that I can't hear?"

"Nothing," she said. "Nothing about me, anyway. But Christine barely knows you. She wasn't about to tell me anything personal with you right there."

"Is it wrong to want to be friends with your friends too?" he asked, but Maiko felt as though it was an empty question.

"I just . . . I wanted to see my friend. And have a nice conversation. And you being in the room wouldn't let that happen. It frustrates me."

Thomas placed his hands on Maiko's shoulders. They were big hands, and she realized just how giant they were when they were on her. He pushed her back and forth slightly so that she wobbled on her feet, as he said, "I need you to respect my boundaries, which are that I'm not comfortable with you spending time with people I don't know without me there."

What's that supposed to mean? Maiko wanted to ask, but she was frozen. His hands on her didn't feel friendly. They didn't feel *threatening*, but they didn't feel like the hands of someone who was happy or doing the motion out of love.

He was the first to leave the room, stealing back upstairs for a phone meeting, and she stood rooted to the spot, wondering what he meant by his remark. The places where he'd held her shoulders felt cold.

February 3, 2013
Madrian Reunite for New Film

Maiko Fox and Adrian Hightower are again pairing up in a Double-U Pictures production, *Pandora*. Fox will play the titular role of an enchantress who wishes to end the world as we know it; Hightower will play Sean, an ordinary guy who happens to learn of Pandora's plans and tries to save the Earth—without falling in love during the process. Principal photography will begin in April 2013 in Romania.

25

2013

Jess found out about the casting from Deadline.

"Were you going to tell me you were going to Romania with your ex before, or after, I left for the tour?" she asked, holding up her iPhone. Adrian was riding his exercise bike in their home gym and slowed down, panting.

"I swear, I was going to tell you . . ." He wiped his face with a towel.

"Which is it, Adrian? Because it looks like you weren't planning to tell me at all."

He took a long drink of water. "It slipped my mind."

"We *live* together." She said this accusingly. "You couldn't have thought of it at some point?"

"You're at rehearsals all day, I'm learning lines. It's an impossible situation. But you're right. I should've told you."

"Damn straight." She put her phone down and massaged her temples. Adrian got off his bike and placed his palms gently on her cheeks. "I'm sorry," he said.

"Listen, it's going to be a long stretch with you abroad and me on tour," Jess said. "I need to know that I can trust you."

"Sweetheart. You can trust me. Have I ever given you a reason not to?"

She looked him in the eyes and then relaxed, smiling slightly. She clasped his hand that was on her cheek with her own. "No, you've always been good about that."

"Damn straight," he parroted back.

"Okay. It's just . . ." She twisted her hands together. "Are you sure you want to be with me?"

Adrian started. "What kind of question is that?"

"An honest one. Do you?"

"Of course I want to be with you." Adrian's heart thumped loudly in his ears.

Jess cracked a wan smile. "Okay. Try not to keep big news from me in the future. Don't disappoint me."

"You got it, babe."

Soon, Jess was off on her All Aboard tour and Adrian was getting ready to film *Pandora* in Romania. When he arrived on the set, he found his way to his trailer in the block reserved for cast and crew and swept the window curtains open. He felt low, kind of bad about himself. He was under self-induced stress to make a better movie than *Surf City*, and being here, in a foreign country with no one he knew except for Maiko, didn't help. He knew she was in a nearby trailer and his palms started to sweat. He craved a hit.

A PA stood at the trailer door, listening to his headset. He relayed, "Table read is in an hour. Let me know if you need anything else."

"Yeah, about that." Adrian didn't know how else to ask. "Is there any *green* around here?"

The PA didn't even hesitate. "I'll put you in touch with someone who can help."

"Thanks." Adrian palmed off a few bills of Romanian leu into the guy's hand and watched him go. It was like ordering room service. Within forty-five minutes, Adrian had whatever he wanted on his coffee table. He left the drugs there in plain view, because who was going to come up to his trailer anyway? He could have Adderall for breakfast, pot with dinner. He cracked the slanted window in the en suite bathroom when he smoked out of a hospitality apple he'd hollowed out, blowing his shaky breath out into the world. It helped take the edge off.

Adrian was self-conscious about having to see Maiko again. They had not seen each other since the *Surf City* premiere a year prior. As the main stars settling in for the first table read of the film, they found themselves assigned to sit next to each other, and Adrian wished he could avoid her. Not because he was feeling any sort of way about her that was inappropriate, but because he was worried she would see he was high. She was just as observant as Jess, and he knew that she knew the signs of when he was using.

When he slid into the seat next to her, he pulled his baseball cap down low on his forehead and looked straight at the script in front of him. He didn't even utter a hello.

She glanced at him and then, after a pause, looked at him fully, like she was unsure of what she was seeing.

"Adrian," she said, and it was as if they were the only two people in the room, even though the conference table was filling up with the cast, and the crew sat and stood at different levels behind them.

"Hmm?"

"What's up?" she said carefully, looking at his bloodshot eyes.

Adrian didn't like the attention. "Just . . . getting ready for this reading."

She stared him a little longer.

"All right, everyone," Thomas said loudly, and the chattering among the cast and crew died down. "I'm so excited to see all of you here. Let's make a fucking great film. Are you ready?"

Maiko relented, busying herself with her script.

RELAPSE. ADRIAN KNEW he had fucked up, but at the moment, he didn't care. His head swam pleasantly, like it was soft water buffeted by moss. He just needed to get through this table read without thinking about the woman beside him—Maiko.

Thomas was chattering on, describing the vision for the film, and Adrian snuck a glance at Maiko. Her long hair was back, flowing in a curtain between them.

"Open in an enchanted wood, otherworldly," said a crew member, narrating the script. Adrian wouldn't be in the story until a quarter of the way in, when Pandora met him on Earth. He settled into his chair, sliding low in the seat and sipping a bottle of water leisurely. His throat was parched from smoking. As the script wound on and on, Maiko listlessly stating her lines, Adrian wondered if she was happy with Thomas.

Or happy in general.

He hadn't thought of Maiko's happiness in a while. Not since he had spent time in Santorini with Jess and the laundry there smelled like lavender, Maiko's scent. He glanced at Thomas Whitley from under the brim of his hat and saw him studying Maiko, and then his eyes landed on Adrian too. That gaze was piercing. Adrian felt like he'd done something wrong, had been sent to the principal's office, in that flickering gaze alone. Then Thomas moved his eyes back over to Maiko and the heat evaporated off Adrian's shoulders.

Could she be happy with Thomas? He seemed so . . . old. And austere. And he had a reputation for being kind of a jerk. He had produced *Surf City* and Adrian had seen sides of him he hadn't liked.

"The humans will rue the day they crossed me, *Pandora*," Maiko said, imbuing, for once, a hint of grandeur in her voice.

Pandora disappears into a whirlpool of smoke. She appears on Earth in the middle of a cave. Under the flickering light of a candle, she incants . . .

"Domino dee, domino doe, watch me rule over the ruins of this world," Maiko cackled. Her trustworthy sidekick, a wolf named Gaius, gave a howl of delight.

Twenty-five minutes had passed, and Adrian's character of Sean joined the chorus of voices now.

"Who's down there?" he demanded. "This is private property!"

*Sean is a regular guy, the salt of the earth. He is wearing jeans and
a flannel shirt and holding a flashlight. When he sees Pandora in the
cave, he stops short. She's beautiful—mesmerizing.*

"What are you doing here?" Adrian asked. "No one has
been on my family's farm in ages, not if they know what's good
for them."

"I'll make you a deal," Maiko said. "Don't bother me while
I stay here and I'll spare your life."

"Spare *my*—? Lady, you're weirding me out. And besides, if
you need a place to stay, I have a barn. Much more comfortable."

Adrian gave Maiko a half grin, one that looked like a smirk.
He knew he was still high and he hoped no one else noticed.
She glanced at him and, off-book already, said her next line. "I
will be sacrificing your cow, then."

The two shared a silent smile together, knowing this was
the funniest line in the film. Adrian snuck another glance at
Thomas, who looked at them disapprovingly from under his
director's visor.

Adrian and Maiko had always had a good time—hadn't
they? Before the rift? This didn't have to be awkward. They
could be friends and work together. Thomas and Jess had nothing to worry about.

But there was a churning in Adrian's stomach. He wasn't 100
percent sure.

———

Maiko, even at the best of her ability, was not the most gifted actress. She had been hired on as part of Madrian at the start of her career, and the rest she had been gifted by Thomas Whitley. Adrian watched her during the third week of filming as she struggled to keep up with all of the other actors. Even the wolf-dog playing Gaius was a seasoned actor by now, trained to stop on a dime.

This was the first time Maiko had had to carry a film. She'd been relegated to girlfriend roles in the past, but in *Pandora* she *was* Pandora: all-encompassing, all-angry, all-wrathful enchantress. The lens was trained on her solely for many shots, and Thomas Whitley seemed to get irritated behind the camera as he realized just how bad Maiko was at emoting.

"You're supposed to be *angry*, Mai," he said. "Wrathful. Godlike. This is a world that is unfriendly to you and your magical beings. Show me how *mad* you are. Scream with me."

"Argh!" Maiko screamed.

"Harder!" he yelled.

"*Argh!!!*"

"You can do better than that!"

Adrian could tell she felt self-conscious and was holding back tears. Thomas steered her to the side of the set.

"This isn't hard," he said, annoyance plain on his face.

"I'm *trying.*"

"No, you're not, Mai. But I guess you can't do any better than this."

"If you gave me better direction—" she started, but he cut her off.

"This isn't my fault," he said sternly. "If you were a better actress, this would be easy. I knew we should've hired Ava Mears."

That got Maiko's hackles up. Ava had replaced Maiko on *Helix Felix* and Thomas knew that that was a sore spot for her. "Listen—" she began, but he cut her off again.

"No, you listen. This film is a two-hundred-million-dollar production and you are screwing it up. Every time you have to do another take, you're taking up precious little time we have to get this right. So you go back on the set, *fucking emote*, do your *fucking* job, and we'll be fine. Got it?"

It was obvious that Maiko had never heard him talk that way before. She'd never been on one of his sets when he was a director before, though. She'd perhaps heard rumors of his temper, but thought they were just that: rumors. Adrian could see the effect his words had on her: running down her back, making her veins run cold.

"Fine," she shouted.

"Yes, that energy! Good. Go!" And he slapped her on her ass, but it wasn't the playful smack of a boyfriend encouraging his significant other to do well. Rather, it was the slap of a director who was tired of his actor of being obstinate. Adrian was stunned.

Maiko ran to the trailers.

With a furious glance at Thomas, Adrian followed.

"Maiko! Wait up!"

She was wiping tears off her face as she stumbled toward her trailer. "What do you want, Adrian?" she cried, sounding frustrated.

"Let me help you."

He held her by the elbow and steered her to the nearest door, which was his. He sank her down on the soft couch and she wept quietly for a few minutes. Adrian waited for her tears to subside before he reached out with a small pack of tissues. She grabbed one and dabbed at her nose.

"I've never been on one of his sets before," she said. "It's stupid, but his personality has changed so much."

"I don't know if it *changed* so much as *revealed itself*," Adrian said.

Maiko laughed tearfully. "You're probably right."

Adrian gazed at her. The thing was, he *missed* Maiko. He hadn't seen his girlfriend in weeks, and Maiko smelled just as amazing as she always had—some semblance of lavender and sandalwood and the inherent *Maiko-ness* that she exuded from her pores. Crying seemed to have exacerbated the scent. To keep himself from getting too comfortable, he grabbed a hard-back chair and flipped it backward, his legs splayed on either side of the chair back.

"I can help, if you let me," he said.

She crumpled the used tissue in her hand and looked at him directly. She was quiet, but then: a nod. "Okay," she whispered.

"You're doing great as Pandora," he said. "Truly. But there's something that makes me feel like you're holding back. I've been watching you work and watching the dailies, and it's like you're . . . *wary* or something. You look at my character like we're not close. These two have a spiritual connection to each other. Remember, she wants to destroy the world as we know it, but the only thing standing in her way is Sean." He gestured with his hands. "She is an all-powerful being, and he's just a random guy. But they have a connection."

Maiko nodded, leaning in, drinking in his words. She looked so serious, so focused, that Adrian wondered what she was thinking. If she was considering more than just the words he was saying, but picturing the scenes as they *should* have been, in her head. How she could've done them differently.

"Right," she said. "I understand that. I guess I just . . . have trouble right now."

"You can talk to me," he said.

"I can talk to you as my costar, but can I talk to you as my ex-boyfriend?" Her words were so soft, it was hard for him to hear.

"Maiko. You can talk to me in any way that makes this film better. *That's* what I care about. I don't want to make a bomb." And the thing that he didn't say: *I care about you too.*

She paused and gazed directly at him, sizing up whether she could trust him with her words. "It's just . . . ," she said slowly, "I feel like we're not even *friends*. And so it's hard to pretend to care about you that deeply when we're just pros *acting*. I'm not an actress. I'm just a model who lucked into this because people want to see me with *you.*"

Adrian chewed on the inside of his cheek. "I don't think that's true," he protested, but he knew that her worries had some validity. She'd gotten the part for *Atomic Crusader 2* because she had been dating him at the time.

"I've taken acting classes," she continued, looking down and picking at her cuticles. "I've been in more movies, not always with you. But I know that I need to *believe* that we're *something* in order to make it work. Method, if you want to call it that. Right now, all I get from you is . . . *Adrian*."

There was too much history there. It would be so, so easy to put a hand behind Maiko's head and draw her closer to him. It would be so, so easy to smell her sweet breath, place his lips on hers. Adrian considered it for just a moment, in that hesitation of gazing deep into her eyes, and knew she was contemplating it too. Maiko pulled closer to him, her sight never leaving his, parting her mouth as if she were to say something more.

She leaned forward, and so did he. Her hand reached out and touched his cheek. He sucked in his breath.

Her eyes slid to his mouth, and she moved even closer.

Adrian remembered that he was not single.

He pulled back, and just like that, the moment was over. Maiko looked down at her hands, examining the nail beds, as if she hadn't just been caressing his face.

"I'm sorry," he said. "I can't do this to Jess."

"I know," she whispered. "I didn't mean it."

Damn, he wanted to, though. He knew how to love Maiko. Knew her body and knew her sounds and if he wasn't in a monogamous relationship, he would've crossed that line without hesitation, no thoughts in his head. But that was another life.

Her gaze moved to the coffee table, where the assortment of drugs brought in by Adrian's PA sat in plain sight. She didn't get closer to them, but she pored over the baggies with her eyes and then re-met his gaze. He chose to pretend that the stuff wasn't there.

"Moment forgotten," he said. "But I'd love to be your friend again."

"Is it just that easy?" she asked incredulously.

"Sure. Friendship is a matter of choice."

"I think it goes deeper than that, but." She licked her dry lips and flicked her eyes back to the coffee table. "Reciprocity. You can start by helping me with acting. And I can start by helping *you*."

"What do you mean?" he said, feigning ignorance.

"Adrian." Her voice held a note of warning.

"It's not what you think," he argued, but he knew that it was a lost cause. She'd known him when he was a user, and she could see the telltale signs in him now.

"What, am I supposed to think that some *friend* just left this here for safekeeping?" she asked. Adrian scratched the back of his neck and stood up. He no longer wanted to kiss Maiko; he wanted to tell her to leave. "I can help you, if you want," she said.

"I don't want your help," he snapped, then felt remorse for his tone. "Sorry. I just . . . I don't have a problem. It's fine."

"I'm not an expert on these things," she said carefully, "but I know that a person who was sober wouldn't have this stuff just hanging out in his trailer. I *know* you, Adrian. I know when you're using. Don't insult me by playing dumb."

Adrian chewed on the inside of his cheek. Would he relent? Would he admit that he was in just a little too deep?

"Let me be your friend," Maiko said, and Adrian felt his resolve crack.

He missed Maiko. Not just in a sexual way, but in a way that had her more than just peripherally in his life. He remembered that she was sharp-witted. That she was a good conversationalist. That she'd been there for him, until he hadn't reciprocated, and that's when she left.

Adrian set his mouth in a firm line. "Jess can't know," he said.

"Can't know about . . . ?"

"That you're helping me. That I've been . . ." He gestured with his hand toward the coffee table.

"I don't talk to your girlfriend, Adrian." Maiko scraped her index finger with her thumb, thinking. "But are you sure *you* don't want to tell her about it?"

"She can't know," he insisted.

Maiko clasped her hands to her knees. "Okay," she said. "Well, I won't tell her. So it'd be up to you to keep it from Jess, all right?"

Adrian nodded. "Okay." He shoved his hands deep in his pockets and hunched forward a little, pondering. Did he have it in him to fight his demons again? *While* working on a production? In a foreign country?

As if she knew what he was thinking, Maiko said, "Take it day by day, right?" And, making a decision, she swept all the drugs into her hands and walked over to the en suite bathroom.

Adrian listened to her empty the bags into the toilet and flush. He stood rooted to the spot, hands still in his pocket, thinking, *If I need more, I can just ask the PA again . . .*

But he knew he had to try. He brushed his nose with his thumb and sighed.

26

When Maiko left Adrian's trailer, still feeling a little shaky, Thomas was waiting in hers. "Who let you in here?" she griped, unsure of what he wanted.

"Mai, I just want to apologize. I can be kind of a bear when it comes to directing." Thomas looked chastised and had his hands folded behind him, as if to show that he wasn't about to raise his palms again. "I know it's not my strongest suit. I just want this production to do well. But I realize now that yelling at you doesn't help either of us get what we want."

"That's kind of you, Thomas. Thank you for the apology," Maiko said stiffly.

"Can I take you out for a nice dinner?" he asked. "To make up for it?"

"I'd rather just go back to the hotel. I'm tired and I'm pretty sure I have another five o'clock wakeup call. Unless you replaced me?" This she said with a slight smile, testing whether he'd be up for a bit of teasing. He smiled back at her, and it was the warm grin she was used to from Thomas.

"Nonsense. You're doing great."

Even though these words were hollow, Maiko took them to heart. She had what she needed from Adrian, and with that friendship rekindled, she felt that she could probably perform better.

"I got you this," Thomas said, and produced a pudding cup from behind his back. Maiko stared at it, not sure what she was supposed to do with it.

"I'm on a strict diet," she said finally.

"I won't tell if you don't," he said, winking.

She accepted the chocolate pudding but didn't open it. She knew it was just from craft services and that she wouldn't eat it. She placed it on the little kitchenette counter and reconsidered his request. "Actually, a dinner out sounds great."

"I know a little spot nearby. Sound good?"

"Sure."

He gestured for her to leave the trailer and pressed his hand against the small of her back as she exited. He drove her in a production vehicle outside of their little trailer village, and all the while, Maiko wondered what she was doing with this guy. She knew she liked him. She knew she respected him. But did she love him?

There had been a moment in Adrian's trailer when she'd wanted to kiss him. How could she be in love with Thomas if she didn't want to stay true to him?

Maiko sat down at the proffered table, aware that people were looking at them. Phones were pointed in their direction, and these were just *diners*. There were no paparazzi that she could see.

After a while, Thomas cleared his throat and pushed his napkin onto the table. Maiko was still chewing on her sea bass and gulped her bite hurriedly, worried that he wanted to leave. But he gestured to her to stay seated, and she put down her fork, wondering if perhaps he was going to the restroom.

"Maiko," he said, standing.

"Um. Yes?"

"I wanted to do this right. I don't want it to seem like I'm doing this just because we fought earlier. I've been carrying this thing around for two months."

Maiko's curiosity was piqued. She then realized that he was digging into his pocket for something.

"I'm not one for public displays of affection, but I want this whole restaurant to know how much I love this woman." He turned in a circle, shouting the last sentence to all the diners around. The onlookers smiled and nodded, as if in encouragement, even though they didn't seem to understand English. Then he knelt down on one knee. The ring he displayed in the tiny velvet box was sparkling and clear.

"Maiko, you're the most amazing woman I've ever met. You're kind, beautiful, talented, and you make me a better man. Would you consent to be my wife?"

Maiko froze, and in that moment, she sized up the crowd, all with their phones recording the proposal, and, for a split second, wondered how he would take a refusal. The humiliation that would spread across his face. Her packing her bags and leaving the hotel block, leaving *Pandora*, to go where? She considered it all for just a second before she nodded and smiled widely. "Yes," she said.

Thomas grinned. He placed the ring on her finger. She stood as he did, and kissed him lightly on the mouth.

And isn't this what she was supposed to be doing, getting on with her life? She was thirty-two and not getting any younger. If she wanted a family, why not with Thomas? He had the means. And he wasn't *awful*. He'd apologized, right? Maybe he was worth taking a risk on.

Wedding Bells For Whitley

Director-producer Thomas Whitley and actress Maiko Fox are set to tie the knot in the summer of next year. Sources tell us that the two got engaged while filming on location outside of Bucharest, Romania. Whitley is directing and Fox is starring in *Pandora*, due to be in theaters next fall.

MAIKO DIDN'T SAY anything when she arrived on set the next day. She didn't wear the ring to work, not knowing where she'd stow a six-carat diamond safely. She kept mum the entire workday, but at wrap, craft services wheeled in a sheet cake with "Congratulations" written on it in icing. Thomas stood beside Maiko, shaking hands with crew members who were wishing them well. Adrian approached the couple.

"It all makes sense now. Congrats."

"It was a surprise," she said with a hint of a smile. "We hadn't discussed it or anything."

"That's great, Maiko. I'm happy for you," he said. Whether he meant it was another story.

Maiko was shrugging on a sweater and picking up her purse. She would, of course, forgo any cake. "Ready?" she asked.

"For . . . ?"

"The *meeting*," she said in a low voice.

"Oh. That. I guess . . ."

"Come on, I'll drive you." And she made to leave the set. Adrian took one look at the giant cake and Thomas being patted on the back by various crew members, and took off. Thomas didn't seem to notice them leaving, which was fortunate.

Adrian climbed into the borrowed production vehicle. "Do you know where you're going?"

"Of course. Just need to fiddle with this GPS here . . . aha." She turned the device on and it greeted her with a *bună ziua!* "Oh, shoot. This entire thing is in Romanian." She fiddled with it, trying to change the language to English.

"Does *Thomas* know where we're going?"

"No, does that bother you? I thought you wanted to be discreet about this." The GPS startled to *good afternoon!*

"Thanks."

"Okay," she said, inputting the address. Then: "I'm taking you to an expat meeting. I found it online."

It was quiet for a few minutes as she rolled out of the lot.

Adrian wondered what else to say. "Good job today. You did a lot better."

"Yes, Thomas didn't have anything negative to say, did he?" Maiko said with a grin.

"I imagine it's because he's happy for another reason."

"Probably." She laughed.

"Tell me how it all happened." Perhaps it was masochistic of him, but he wanted to know.

So as she navigated the highway, she told him about the hidden gem of a restaurant and the proposal and the ring and the phones recording them. "I'm surprised you didn't know already, based on the number of phones taking pictures of it happening."

"I don't read the rags," he responded, looking out the window.

"I try not to too."

They made idle chitchat about the workday and before Adrian realized it, they were outside a nondescript building. "It's in here," she said. "I think it's best if I don't go in with you, though. I'll just hide out here."

"I appreciate it," Adrian said. "Listen, you don't have to wait. I'll catch a cab back." Adrian suddenly didn't want her there to see his failures or for paparazzi to catch wind of any of it.

"Are you sure?"

"I don't want anyone to see, you know . . ."

"And it'll be way obvious if I'm waiting outside of an NA meeting that I know someone inside. I got it. Okay. I'll see you on set tomorrow. But I am going to watch you go inside."

"I'll go in. I promised, didn't I?"

"You got this."

Ears burning, Adrian got out of the car and looked back at her as he climbed the steps. She waved at him from behind the tinted glass. He gave her a nod and disappeared inside.

BY THE TIME Maiko had returned to the hotel in Bucharest, she was dead on her feet. It was past nine and she'd been up since five. All she wanted was a hot shower and some baked chicken, but Thomas met her at the hotel room door.

"Where have you been? I've been worried sick. I turned around for a second and you were gone, and for hours. I tried calling you."

"I don't have my phone on while here. It doesn't work."

"What were you *doing*?"

"I was out with a friend."

"Who could you possibly be out with? This is a small set in a foreign country." His expression changed. "You weren't with *him*, were you?"

"If you must know, I was with Adrian, yes." She kept her voice casual, but inside, she quavered. She wondered if he was going to be upset about this.

"How could you?"

"How could I *what*? I was helping a friend."

"You were out with your ex while I was waiting at the hotel like an idiot. Mai, doesn't our engagement mean *anything* to you?"

"Of course it means a lot to me," she said, annoyed. "I wasn't doing anything wrong. He had to go somewhere and I gave him a ride. I dropped him off and came home."

"Where did you get a car?"

Maiko sighed. She was tired of being grilled. She walked into the suite and slipped off her shoes; Thomas followed her, hands in his pockets, shoulders hunched angrily. She'd shower tomorrow after her workout. And she didn't need any chicken. She needed respite.

She began taking off her stage makeup and applying moisturizer to her face. Thomas stood next to her. "Well? I'm waiting," he snapped, staring at her in the mirror.

Maiko looked at him in the reflection. He had a furrow between his eyebrows that aged him. His mouth was turned down in a grumpy frown. She remembered his kind smile when they'd first met. It was a far cry from the look he was giving her now.

"Nothing happened. That's all you need to know."

He turned to her and grabbed her shoulders. He did the same wobbling shake he'd given her before. "Mai," he said, his voice low.

"Get your hands off me," she said, flinty.

He lifted his palms and said, "I care about you deeply. You can see why this behavior concerns me."

"And you trust me, right? It was nothing. Now let me brush my teeth. I have an early morning. And so do you."

And they didn't speak for the rest of the night.

27

Pandora wrapped a couple of weeks later, and so did Jess Marin's All Aboard tour. The cast and crew of *Pandora* wearily packed up and left Romania, their jobs done. Jess's final tour stop was Los Angeles, and Adrian met her backstage when her very full bus finally cruised into town.

She threw her arms around him, and he held her at the waist, and they breathed together. "I missed you so much," he said into her hair, and she squeezed him tighter. She felt frailer than she had before the tour began, and he knew it was because she was rehearsing and dancing for hours a day. She'd come home and he'd feed her, he decided.

"You ready for the concert of a lifetime?" she asked when they finally parted, and she raised an eyebrow. Her bubble-gum-pink signature lip color was on, and Adrian got the sense that she'd put a shield up so that her crew couldn't see how vulnerable she felt around him.

"Totally ready," he said, playing along, and she handed him off to a crew member who would show him to the VIP section of the stadium. Adrian waited with a few other celebrities for the lights to go down and the spotlight to emerge.

Jess was a revelation. She must have been tired after her months of touring, but she didn't show it. She pranced across the stage, she swung her hair, she shook her ass along with her backup dancers. She changed outfits five times, and each showed off her hard-won physique—high-cut thighs, nipped-in waists, sleeveless for her toned arms.

When at last the show was over, Jess bowed to her screaming audience and took the hydraulic elevator from the stage, disappearing from view. Adrian found her backstage again, peeling off her fake eyelashes and flicking them onto the floor.

"Great show, babe," he said, and she looked up at him, her expression suddenly exhausted. She was no longer *Jess Marin*, superstar, but just Jess.

"Thanks. I'm ready to go home and shower."

"No after-party?" he asked.

"We've been *after-partying* all tour. I'm ready for my own bed." She shifted her jaw worriedly. "I'm ready for the next step in our *lives.* Ready to take this tour, take it out back, and put it out of its misery."

If she'd hated performing, Adrian wouldn't have known it from the concert experience he'd just had, but he said nothing about it. "I'll drive you home," he promised.

JESS WAS READY for something else: the in vitro fertilization process. She went back to Dr. Retton daily for ultrasounds and blood tests, and started giving herself shots of hormones to pre-pare for the egg retrieval. Soon, Adrian and Jess were at the office with Jess strapped in and sedated for the procedure.

Adrian was given another cup and told to make his contri-bution. When he got back, the egg harvest was about to be underway, and he stood at Jess's head while the doctors poked and prodded her swollen ovaries, siphoning eggs.

The two left the office, Jess sore, Adrian tired, but with a good feeling between them. "We might've just made a baby," Jess said. "A petri dish baby."

"A blastocyst," Adrian replied, and for some reason the word, technical as it was, was so funny that they dissolved into laughter. Jess went straight to the couch after they got home to rest with a bottle of Gatorade, and Adrian puttered around the house, gaug-ing which room to turn into a nursery.

A few days later, Jess and Adrian went back to Dr. Retton's for the embryo transfer.

"Look, here are your embryos," Dr. Retton said, showing them a picture of little gray blobs against an equally gray back-ground. Jess and Adrian held hands, squeezing hard. "I advise freezing these three but transferring this one."

"Just one? Don't we want to transfer more so that there's a higher chance of them sticking?" Jess asked.

"That depends. Do you want triplets?"

Jess and Adrian caught each other's eyes. Jess looked some-what hopeful. Adrian shook his head no. "Just one is great, Doc," he said.

"We can save the others for you to use in the future," Dr.

Retton said, the implication clear: if this didn't work, there'd be a backup plan.

So Jess and Adrian watched on a screen as a magnified version of their embryo got sucked into a needle and placed in Jess's uterus. It was over pretty quickly, and as Jess got dressed again, she was leaking tears.

ADRIAN MET OPHELIA in 1999, when they were both auditioning for a mayonnaise commercial. "Realistic couples preferred" said the posting, but each had gone to the casting anyway, hoping that they'd get paired up with someone. They took a look at each other in the waiting room, sized each other up, and silently communicated with their eyes: *You in?*

Yeah, you?

Adrian moved seats and sat next to the woman, who was about twenty and had dyed black hair with fair skin. The dark hair was a little harsh on her, but it made her blue eyes pop.

Though they didn't get chosen for the commercial, they got happy hour drinks after, and Adrian idly asked her for her story. Like Adrian, Ophelia had come out to Hollywood right after high school, which had been in Grand Rapids. "I just, you know, didn't want to go to college?" she said, in an affected Valley Girl accent. "I'm only gonna be young once. Might as well make money off of my face."

If Adrian had to be truthful, Ophelia was not a natural beauty. Her cheeks were full, and she used too much blush. She had hooded eyes, which were not in vogue at the time. She held her weight in her hips, so she had thin arms and a thin torso; but no matter how much she dieted, she was always a size six, and in numbers-obsessed Hollywood, she couldn't get momentum to get her career going.

But she was really nice, and she and Adrian hit it off. Drinks became fast-food sushi, became a leisurely drive down Sunset to Malibu to see the waves, and finally, to bed. Adrian didn't feel bad about sleeping with Ophelia the same day he met her. It wasn't unusual for that to happen.

Ophelia sticking around was different than the other girls, though. She made him eggs in the morning (whites only for her, thanks). She borrowed his fleece sweatpants at night. She starved herself and still the bookings wouldn't come.

Then she got pregnant, and he had to listen to her rant about how this would've never happened with her ex, and Adrian took her to the clinic to get it taken care of—and things were fine, maybe, not too altered, but she was resentful that she'd had to get the procedure done in the first place. She had berated him about his chances to make it in Hollywood—specifically about a big, fame-fulfilling role like *Atomic Crusader*—and that was the last straw. Yes, he could be verbally abused about his character, his personality, and even his crooked lateral incisor, but he drew the line at his *hope*. He may have had the smallest snowball's chance in hell of getting a role like that of the superhero, but he wasn't about to let Ophelia tell him he was *less than*.

When he'd met Maiko the second time, on the *Evergreen* shoot, he was drawn to her immediately. Her effortless cool, her bite when he offered her his number. She was feisty. He still remembered the first time they slept together, after her Valentina Posh show. He had hiked one of her legs up from under the knee with his forearm and pushed himself deeper into her, so deep that she looked straight into his eyes as she moaned. It was a moment of connection he would never forget. She was beautiful, and she was perfect, and she had been all his.

And now. Now he was with Jess, and he loved Jess—truly—but something about being with her felt *sluggish*, like he had to work much harder at it to feel so good. Adrian assumed it was that he was growing and maturing, and relationships took effort, and not everything would be as perfect as the woman he'd fallen head over heels in love with at twenty-two.

But some part of him wondered.

28

2014

Maiko adjusted her veil and gazed into the floor-length mirror. "You look amazing," Christine said, voice awed. Maiko saw her in the reflection, and there were tears in Christine's eyes.

"Don't cry," Maiko warned, "or *I'll* cry, and I just had my makeup done."

Maiko turned around to hug her friend. Christine grasped the back of Maiko's couture gown and accidentally tugged on the cascading veil. "Careful," Maiko said, releasing one of her arms to secure the veil comb in her hair.

"Sorry, sorry," Christine said, laughing through her tears, as she helped Maiko with the comb. "So I know I shouldn't mention it, but . . ."

"Hmm?"

"You didn't invite Adrian, right? Even though you've been in movies together three times now?"

Maiko readjusted her veil in the mirror and made a non-committal sound. She had not invited Adrian. It would've been weird, she thought, having her ex there on her wedding day. Plus, Thomas would've blown a gasket.

Maiko knew that the subject of Adrian was one of Thomas's little hairpin triggers. They'd fought about him enough that Maiko wouldn't want to talk about him, anyway, much less have Adrian attend their wedding.

"Why even bring him up?" Maiko's mother said now, fluffing her daughter's gown. It was custom-made by Christian Dior—a huge, puffy thing that weighed more than ten pounds and looked like an upside-down cupcake, but Maiko loved the heft of it, swinging the skirt from side to side, prancing around in her Louboutin heels. Michiyo was striking in an emerald-green mother-of-the-bride dress with extensive beading around the neckline.

They had booked a hotel ballroom that could accommodate their guest list of four hundred, and during cocktail hour on the balconies the room would flip for the reception. There would be canapés, pink uplighting, a photo booth, and lemon buttercream cake. Maiko would even change into a reception dress, a slinky number she'd found in a vintage shop, with a side slit that would allow her legs some freedom to dance.

She was ready.

Helen was there as a bridesmaid; she stood biting her thumbnail in the corner of the room as Christine and Maiko embraced. The photographer and videographer were there, too, crouching and hovering, snapping and filming.

Christine turned Maiko to look at her and grasped her hands. "Are you sure you want to do this?"

Maiko swept her irritation away. Christine was just being overprotective. Thomas had a little bit of a temper, yes, but he was still a good man. And Maiko was *happy*.

The coordinator came to the door and preened with excitement. "You look amazing," she flattered; and then, all business after that, said, "It's almost time for the ceremony to begin. Here are your bouquets . . . Dr. Nakamoto-Fox, let me give you your corsage."

"How does Thomas look?" Maiko asked, a flash of anxiety making a sudden appearance.

"He's doing great. The guys are ready and just got their boutonnieres on."

"Okay." Maiko nodded to herself and grasped her bouquet.

"We're really going for it?" Christine asked.

"Yes," Maiko said, extending an arm. Helen joined the other three women in the huddle and Maiko gave them a group hug. "Let's do this."

THE CEREMONY WENT off without a hitch, and after photos and dinner, Maiko felt herself relaxing at the head table. She and Thomas had made their rounds during the meal to each of the forty tables, greeting their guests, and she slipped off her shoes now, feet aching.

The DJ was cueing up for toasts, and Maiko accepted a new glass of champagne from a passing waiter. Thomas sat next to her, turned in the other direction, chatting with his best man.

As the toasts began, Maiko glanced at her new husband out

of the corner of her eye. He was studying his best man with a fierce look, and Maiko wondered what Jay might say that he was worried about. Jay's toast was all flattering, about growing up together after Thomas had moved to LA, and complimentary things about Maiko, all of which centered on her looks, not her capability, but that was to be expected when one was a model, she supposed.

Guests clapped and Jay sat down. Christine was next. Maiko held her breath, hoping that her maid of honor wouldn't say anything rash.

"For those of you who don't know me, I'm Christine, and I've been Maiko's friend for more than twenty years," Christine said, holding the microphone aloft with one hand and reading off her phone with the other. "I am so pleased to be here as her maid of honor. We've been through so much together. And yet we still find ourselves gravitating toward each other even in the very different spheres we are in now.

"As you know, Maiko is a model-actress, and has been in quite a few blockbusters of our time." Polite claps. "But before that, she was just a nice seven-year-old who made friends with a shy Black girl in elementary school."

Christine went on about their meeting on the school bus and their awkward junior prom. Maiko glanced at Helen, who sat enraptured at learning all these little details about Christine's previous lives, and Maiko realized: Helen still wanted to be with Christine. Maybe this could be the moment when it happened.

"Maiko is special. I've known it the entire time I've known her. And so it takes a special guy to be with her." Christine held up her glass. "I hope it's you, Thomas."

Maiko felt puzzled by Christine's comment. It was received by the guests as a compliment, based on all the glasses that were held aloft and clinking, but Maiko knew her friend too well. Christine didn't like Thomas. Maiko felt a sinking feeling as she glanced at her husband again, and his face, though smiling tightly, betrayed his understanding of Christine's words. *Shit.*

Maiko barely had time to feel upset about Christine's speech, however, because Tristan grabbed the mic. The applause from the guests died down and Tristan, swaying slightly, said, "I'll make it quick since I know everyone gets antsy right around the time the cake is supposed to get cut. But I wanted to shout out to my dad and his beautiful new bride! Maiko, good luck, you're gonna need it." He laughed tipsily. "Oh, he's a handful. He's a great father, don't get me wrong, but a perfectionist and control freak, and not just on the movie set." Tristan gave a theatrical wink in Maiko's direction. "If you know what I mean."

Thomas was gesturing to Jay, who got out of his chair and tried to rescue the microphone from Tristan. The DJ got to Tristan before that, though, so there was a convergence of men on the dance floor wrestling for control of the mic.

The DJ said smoothly, "And now, the newlyweds will have their first dance."

Thomas had a tight jaw as he guided Maiko's elbow with his hand and led her to the dance floor. Her slinky reception dress contoured to the shape of her hips, which Thomas grasped possessively as they swayed to Etta James. The flashes from the photographers popped across her vision.

The music segued into Bruno Mars's "Marry You" and the couple separated slightly, holding each other's hands and bopping along to the beat. Others started to stream onto the floor, dancing, and Maiko watched Helen dance toward Christine across the crowded floor. Christine seemed pleased with the attention and boogied with Maiko's old roommate, and Maiko grinned.

Every time Maiko stopped and looked for Christine, Helen was there with her. *Interesting.* And then, suddenly, neither woman was to be found. As Maiko swept her way past the guests shaking hand-held fireworks in the direction of the newlyweds, grasping her new husband's hand tightly as they climbed into the limo, she hoped that Helen was about to treat Christine really, really right.

29

The first embryo didn't take but late that spring the second one did.

Jess was shaking, holding out a positive pregnancy test toward Adrian. They'd never seen two pink lines on one before.

"Babe!" he breathed, and gathered her in his arms.

For a week, they were happy. There was a new light in Jess, and Adrian marveled at the change in his girlfriend. She had been bedraggled and on the verge of tears by the end of her tour, but now even her *hair* seemed to glow.

He caught sight of his girlfriend holding her stomach while looking in the mirror, caressing her concave belly with a tender look on her face.

"C'mere," he said from the bed, and, unable to hold back his joy, laughed as she joined him in the sheets. They snuggled and Adrian lay a gentle hand on top of Jess's midsection. He was awed that there was a baby growing in there. He couldn't believe it was finally happening. After so many years of trying, and science had stepped in where nature had not.

Jess buried her face in his neck and breathed in deeply. She gave a sigh of contentment. Then Adrian's phone rang. He checked the caller ID.

"Hi, Ma," he answered. "Whoa, whoa, Les, slow down. What's wrong?"

His sister was talking very fast. Adrian had a horrible feeling that washed over his entire body, turning his stomach over. The fact that Leslie was calling from his mother's phone meant that she was with their parents, but the news couldn't be good.

"It's Dad, you need to come right away." Leslie gulped.

"Is he okay? What happened?"

Jess loosened her arms from around Adrian's neck and sat up in the bed. She was listening to his side of the conversation, and obviously disturbed by what she could hear.

"He's in the hospital—" Leslie was practically screaming now. "He had a heart attack, I saw him, he was blue—ambulance took him away—"

"I'm on the way," he said, already standing up, pulling his jeans onto one leg while holding the phone to his ear with his other hand.

"It might be too late by the time you get here," Leslie said, suddenly somber.

"I'll be on the next flight out. Tell Ma I'm coming." He ended the call and looked at Jess. She was gripping her hands tightly with a frown on her face.

"Do you want me to join you?" she asked, but Adrian shook his head.

"I don't want *anything* disturbing this little embryo," he said, touching her stomach gently. "I don't want to stress you out at all. It sounds bad."

"Keep me in the loop," she said, as he packed an overnight bag with three sets of clothes and his toothbrush. He shouldered the bag, kissed his girlfriend on the forehead, and was out the door.

IF ADRIAN COULD erase the first half of 2014, he would. When he arrived at the hospital in Florida, he saw, to his relief, that his mother was sitting quietly in the surgery waiting room with Leslie by her side—hunched over, sure—but she was not weeping. Leslie stood up to greet him, and he pulled her in close. She began talking while her face was pressed up against his shoulder, her voice muffled: "He's gone."

Adrian stiffened against the words, convinced that he'd heard wrong. "What?"

"It was too late."

He leaned away from his sister and jammed his hands into his jeans pockets. He was wearing sunglasses and a baseball cap to avoid being photographed, but wished he could take them off because he suddenly felt ridiculous.

"But after his stent—he must've been doing better," Adrian stammered.

Leslie shook her head, face somber. "He wasn't listening to the doctor. Didn't exercise, didn't even go for walks. Ate poorly. His arteries couldn't take it."

Adrian felt cold inside. His mind raced with possibilities—

had his father just done *this* or just done *that*, he would still be here. But it was all for naught. He glanced at his mother, who was holding her hands very carefully in her lap, not moving, and realized she was not doing well. He swiftly walked over to her and sat next to her, grasping her icy palms in his. He was worried that Betty was about to break down.

Adrian couldn't remember much about the rest of that day, just that they went home after waiting an impossibly long time for hospital staff to come talk to them. That his father's body was released to a morgue. That he and his sister were relegated to the task of preparing for a funeral. And all the while, he held this secret, that if he told his mother would likely make her look up with more than just a blank expression on her face, but he didn't want to jinx it. The announcement that he and Jess were pregnant would have to wait.

JESS JOINED THE Hightower family for Adrian's father's funeral. They'd had Jerome cremated, so when Adrian sat down at the service, he saw just a little gilded box on a table and felt curiously empty about the whole thing. His father couldn't possibly fit into such a small box. Jerome was somewhere else—at the dealership, maybe. That's where he always was.

So the words of the eulogizers fell on his ears in a soft, snowfall kind of way. Jess stroked his hand lightly, and as he glanced over at her in her black dress with bare lips he was comforted by the fact that she was pregnant. The baby was something to look forward to when the rest of the world seemed so bleak.

As he sat there, he formulated a plan that would give him a break from work for a while. The funeral ended and Adrian had concocted all of his plans for the future. He would turn down new engagements, at least for a little while, as he and Jess nested. He'd support her through the first year of motherhood.

Betty didn't want to spread the ashes yet, so the funeral attendees went straight from the service to the Hightowers' house for the reception. Adrian loosened his tie and busied himself in the kitchen, making sure that the finger foods were in abundance.

Jess was nowhere to be seen. He realized that she'd been missing from the whirlpool of people in the living room for a while now, and he swept through the house looking for her. The guest bathroom was clear, but when he made his way to the second floor, where Adrian and Leslie had shared a bathroom as teenagers, that door was locked. He waited for a minute or two, but when no one emerged, he tapped on the jamb.

"Jess? Are you in there?"

"Yeah," came a tiny voice.

"Are you okay?"

"I don't think so."

"What's wrong?"

"Is anyone else out there with you?"

"No, why?"

Jess unlocked the door and opened it a crack. She made sure Adrian had been telling the truth by checking behind him, then she let him in and locked the door again. She had been crying; her mascara had run little rivulets down her cheeks and hadn't dried yet.

"I'm bleeding," she whispered.

Adrian was in disbelief. "You're what?" he asked, not sure if he had heard right. "Is that normal for . . ."

"No. It's not normal. Not *this much* blood."

"Do you think . . . is the baby . . ."

She shook her head, tears beginning anew. "I think I'm losing the baby," she wept.

"Can you walk?" he asked.

"What?"

"Let's get you out of here."

"It's going to happen no matter where I am. I don't want to disturb your dad's funeral!"

"It's basically over," he said with firmness. "Leslie can give out hors d'oeuvres to the people. I can take you to the hospital."

"No." She was shaky. "If you don't mind . . . can you have Leslie come up here?"

"You want *Les*?"

"Adrian." Her voice had a bit more flint in it. "I am not going to a hospital in Florida, where people can write up an exposé on me. I'll call Dr. Retton. But I could use another woman's help. Get Leslie."

Adrian nodded, feeling baffled, and went downstairs to relay the message to his sister. He watched helplessly as Leslie left the living room and disappeared upstairs.

Numbly, Adrian walked outside into the humid air and sat

down on a decrepit swing set left over from his youth. He creaked back and forth on it, hoping no one would come outside and try to talk to him. He was blindsided by this bad news, which, on top of everything, was happening at the funeral for his father. Life could not be any more bitter.

He closed his eyes and breathed out slowly. He and Jess would rally. They'd transfer the remaining embryos. They'd be fine.

But as he creaked on the swing, he had the feeling that there was no coming back from this. His life was now irrevocably changed.

He didn't know if he was being pessimistic or prophetic.

Part 3

Sparrow

(2014–2016)

30

2014

Adrian sleepwalked through *Pandora* edits and publicity meetings. When it was finally time for the movie's premiere in fall 2014, he arrived on the red carpet feeling subdued. As he glanced over at Jess, he was surprised to find her glaring at the photographers hired to take her photos. She was even baring her teeth a little.

Though it *shouldn't* have surprised him. Jess had been distant and withdrawn ever since losing the baby. The two barely cuddled at night, even though Adrian ached for a hug. He missed his father—his voice on the telephone, even when he was an argumentative, stubborn ass.

When Maiko smiled at him—a friendly but noncommittal smile—at the *Pandora* premiere, Adrian frowned in return. *She doesn't know*, he thought. Should he tell Maiko about it? During the premiere? Would it bring a somber touch to what should be a cheerful event?

They all filed into the theater to watch the movie, yet the

film couldn't hold Adrian's attention. He needed to find another project, and fast. He felt his girlfriend receding from him like the tide, too wrapped up in her own grief to acknowledge his. He needed something to grab on to. He needed a friend.

In the darkness of the theater, he glanced over at Maiko. She was sitting a few seats away in the same row, the blue light of the screen reflecting on her serene face. She wasn't absorbed in the movie—she was leaning toward Thomas Whitley, who was next to her and whispering in her ear, and nodding. She couldn't feel Adrian's gaze, however, and Adrian slumped a little in his seat.

He would tell Maiko about his father at the after-party.

But Jess had other ideas. When the film was over and everyone was dispersing, she turned to Adrian and spoke to him for the first time during the entire event. "Home?"

"You don't want to go to the party?" he hedged.

Jess shook her head. "I'm tired."

It was barely nine o'clock. "Take the limo," Adrian urged. "Go home. Get some rest."

"And you're going to go to the party?"

"I'm the *lead*. I should be there."

"Fine. See you later." She leaned forward imperceptibly and he gave her a peck on the cheek. As he watched her walk away, swaying her hips slightly as she balanced on sky-high heels, he felt curiously empty. Shouldn't something like what they'd been through draw them closer together? Or maybe Adrian was too wrapped up in his own grief to exude tenderness at the moment. Maybe it was both of their faults, if blame had to be given.

He caught up with the Whitley-Foxes as their limo drew closer. "Can I bum a ride?"

Thomas raised both of his eyebrows in surprise but gallantly swept a hand in a gesture of *go ahead*. Adrian ducked into the limousine after Maiko, where she settled down in a mountain of emerald-colored taffeta. Thomas joined them and, before the car even began moving, poured a finger of scotch from the bar and offered it to Adrian, who shook his head. Thomas took a long sip.

"I just want you to know my dad died," Adrian blurted. He felt like he should say it in front of Thomas, too, so that he wasn't trying to get Maiko by herself at the party.

"That's awful. I'm sorry," Thomas said.

"I'm so sorry, Adrian," Maiko said.

Adrian cleared his throat and looked at his shoes, realizing. "Oh. You knew, though," he said quietly.

"We knew," Thomas admitted. "You were so spacey during the *Pandora* edits that we knew something was wrong. Some online rag reported on it. We sent a flower arrangement, but I'm guessing it got lost in the chaos?"

"No, I'm sure you did . . . and it's fine." Adrian squirmed. "I know you knew about my troubles. Before. Thank you for not telling Jess."

"What are you talking about?" Thomas said.

"Oh. I . . . in Romania. I had fallen back into drugs, a bit. Maiko took me to a meeting out there."

Thomas's eyebrows shot up, but he said calmly, "I wasn't aware."

"I didn't say anything," Maiko told Adrian. "I didn't know if it was my information to give."

"Oh. I hope it didn't cause any problems," Adrian said apologetically. He felt sweaty all of a sudden. "I wouldn't have minded if you shared."

Maiko shrugged with one shoulder, which made Adrian think that it *had* caused problems. He didn't like that feeling at all.

"Well, I could use a distraction, to keep me occupied," Adrian said. He had cleared his schedule, thinking he'd be caring for an infant. Instead, he was battling an empty house with an even emptier Jess. "Anything on your radar?"

"I'll let you know if anything opens up," Thomas said.

Adrian nodded and leaned back in the sideways seat as the limo meandered the LA streets. He wouldn't tell them about the miscarriage. That was too much to share.

A FEW WEEKS later, Adrian arrived home to find Jess's car in the driveway. He stepped into the house and she was standing next to their stereo. "It's done," she said, by way of greeting, and Adrian stopped there in the foyer that opened up into their living room, still in his shoes, and gave her a nod.

Jess bit her lip and pressed the play button. The master CD spun up and the glossy pop tunes he expected were more melancholic. Adrian crossed over to the couch, sat down on it, and folded his hands together to listen.

It was a mourning album. And it wasn't just one song—no, it was the entire thing. Adrian chewed on the inside of his cheek as he absorbed the songs of loss and depression. Jess never sat; she stood in her bare feet through the entire sixty-four minutes of the album. When it ended, she turned her back to Adrian and busied herself with pulling the CD out of the stereo and putting it back into the plastic case.

"I see," Adrian said, filling the silence. How had they gotten to this point? He felt constricted, like he was wearing a too-tight acrylic sweater. Itchy and uncomfortable.

"It affected me more than I expected," Jess said in a whisper, her back still to Adrian. He stood up and walked toward her, hugging her from behind, but instead of melting into his embrace she stiffened. And that's when Adrian knew that the next words wouldn't be good.

"I think I should move out," she said.

"You want . . . to what? Break up?"

"No, not in public. But see other people." Her voice was barely above a murmur.

"Jess, this is . . ." He sought out words. "It doesn't make sense. I've gotten women pregnant before. It's not *me*. You're not going to find a—"

"You're saying *I'm* the problem?"

"Well, no, but—" He unwrapped his arms from around her, stepped back.

"That's what you're saying. That I am the problem. That my body is malfunctioning. That I'll never be a mother."

"That's not what I'm saying. I'm telling you that an open relationship isn't the answer."

"What I'm getting from you isn't enough," she insisted. "I'm not just talking about sex and pregnancy and all that. You're gone all the time, working on your projects. You never have time for me anymore."

"That's just not true!"

"I want more *emotional connection*," she emphasized, and finally turned around to face him, though her gaze was off to the side. She clasped her hands in front of her and spoke to them instead. "All I get from you nowadays is scraps."

"I'll try harder," he said, already knowing that he would break that promise. The next project, if it materialized, would be more grueling hours, prep, and working out, and if he had been neglecting her before filming even started, it would be even worse once he was on a filming schedule. But Jess was shaking her head.

"No, not this time. Listen, that means you can get out too," she said, as if it made life easier. "Find some cute young thing, have sex with her."

"I—"

Jess shook her head, cutting him off. "I'm sorry. All this has made me . . . fall less in love with you. I can't help it. I hoped it would make our bond stronger, but you're not *here*. You're not *present* with me. You're always working. And I'm lonely. So, so lonely in this relationship."

"We'll find our way back to each other!" Adrian said desperately. "That is what we *do*! Relationships are made of ebbs and flows. Sure, we lose touch sometimes, but we can always reconnect."

But he could tell that he couldn't argue his way past her defenses. She was already mentally halfway gone.

"I'm tired of living like this. I want to be able to *dream* again."

And how could Adrian deny her that? She was depressed, she needed an escape. "Okay." He sighed, resigned.

"Okay." She was nodding, surprised, it seemed, that he had agreed.

31

Maiko held a secret: she was late.

The possibility that she was pregnant thrilled her, but she hesitated in telling Thomas. Would he want another baby, so long after having Tristan? They'd discussed getting pregnant in vague terms, a sort of "one day" kind of dreaming. That it had happened so quickly after the wedding seemed like a fluke.

Maiko sat at her vanity in the bedroom she shared with Thomas and looked at the pregnancy test. Two pink lines. This was the second test she'd taken because she didn't believe the first.

Unsure of what to do, she called Christine. Christine and Helen had started dating after the wedding—tiny steps, Helen had told Maiko. Christine was still a little timid about exploring her sexuality, and Helen had to be patient. "Not that I mind," Helen had said to Maiko when they were back on the set of a Balenciaga shoot. (Fashion eyewear had to be updated every year, after all.) "It's nice, teaching her things."

"That's my best friend," Maiko said, laughing. "I don't need to hear it."

Helen had grinned wickedly and brought her mouth close to Maiko's ear. "Teaching her *naughty* things."

"*Stop.*" Maiko had giggled.

Now, as Christine answered the phone, she wasn't surprised to hear Helen's voice in the background, screaming, "*Hi, Maiko!*"

"Just put me on speaker," Maiko said, sighing theatrically. She shuffled into her bedroom closet, which was the size of a small apartment. Half of the wardrobe was Thomas's—he dressed well, too—and there was even space for a red velvet chair, onto which Maiko had tossed a handful of dry cleaning on hangers. Sliding the clothes off to make room to sit, Maiko listened as Christine fumbled with the phone, trying to get the speaker to work.

"Okay, we're here now," Helen said loudly, and Maiko tapped the volume button down so that Thomas couldn't hear if he was roaming around the bedroom outside the closet.

"I have some news. I'm pregnant," Maiko announced, heart fluttering wildly.

"Oh my gosh!" Christine shouted.

"Congratulations?" Helen said, with a puzzled note in her voice.

"It's a good thing," Maiko explained. "But I haven't told Thomas yet."

"Why not?" Christine demanded, at the same time Helen said, "Ooh, yikes."

"Why 'yikes'?" Maiko asked.

"Well, obviously, to *me,* it seems like you don't want to tell him because you still want an out," came Helen's voice.

"I'm married. I'm happy," Maiko said, though she wondered if that was true. She'd been over the moon when she'd been with Adrian, until he broke her heart by using. She'd never come close to that same feeling of ecstasy with Thomas, but she was *secure.* Thomas was a slightly neurotic, slightly controlling man, but what successful businessman wasn't?

"Okay," Helen said, and Maiko thought she sounded unconvinced.

Christine wanted to know how far along Maiko was, and Maiko could say only that it was still early, that things could still go wrong. "Maybe that's why I don't want to tell him yet. In case something happens and it crushes him?" But Maiko knew that wasn't the reason, either.

Deep down, she mourned the child that *could have been.* The one she knew she'd had no business having, and made the correct decision about all those years ago—Adrian's. And something about this new possibility made her think of the old what-could-have-beens, and she had to sit with that for a while.

The three women chatted a little longer, and when Maiko hung up, she really wanted her mother.

Michiyo and Maiko had gotten along a little better since their reconciliation: Maiko had included her parents in her wedding, and Michiyo had been happy to join in. Michiyo hadn't been there when Maiko bought her dress, but she and Mark had chipped in monetarily for the wedding venue, despite Maiko's repeated declarations that their contribution wasn't needed. They attended the rehearsal dinner, and Mark had given a stoic toast; Michiyo had chided him for being a little too serious on the eve of his daughter's wedding.

Pulling on a pair of jeans, Maiko crept out of the closet and down the stairs to the garage. She pulled out her little Porsche, which Thomas had bought her, and drove to Calabasas. She hadn't called her parents in advance; she made a split-second decision when exiting the freeway to go to her mother's pediatric office instead of to the Fox house.

When she pulled into the parking garage, she wondered what she was going to say to her mother. She walked past the children with their parents in the waiting room, past Teresa, the receptionist, into the bowels of the offices and sat in her mother's desk chair. Michiyo would return shortly, Maiko knew. She always stopped in her office to drink from her bottle of cold oolong tea before seeing a new patient.

"Maiko-chan? Is that you?"

Michiyo seemed surprised to see her daughter sitting in her office chair. She stood in the doorway, stethoscope around her neck. She wore crepe-soled shoes and a pair of lavender scrubs under her white coat.

Maiko twirled the chair around and placed her hands on the desk. "Hi, Mom," she said.

"I have patients," Michiyo said, but she didn't sound irritated. "Is everything okay?"

"Everything's fine," Maiko assured her.

Michiyo came closer to the desk and pulled a few manila folders off it. "Can it wait?"

"Sure," Maiko said, and she felt a strange sense of comfort wash over her. She hadn't spent a lot of time in her mother's office when she was young, but she *had* spent *some* time there, and it was the same as it always was: high, molded ceilings with Grecian-like pillars in the lobby that bookended an aquarium full of rainbow fish, large windows letting in natural light (on Maiko's father's insistence), calm Muzak over speakers.

"If you get bored, talk to Teresa," Michiyo said and, with a smile, walked out of the room.

Maiko waited, and as she did, she felt herself revert back to her childhood self. She swung her knees back and forth in the swiveling office chair. She counted dots on the ceiling tiles. She tried to make pencils stand on their pointy ends. And as she played, she thought about how she was going to love her child, whoever they turned out to be. She grew more and more excited, so when Michiyo walked back into the office, she burst out with, "Mom, I'm pregnant."

"Ala!" her mother said, Japanese for *oh my!* "You should have waited to tell your father and me at the same time."

"Right. Sorry," Maiko said, feeling slightly abashed. "But I wanted to tell you first."

Michiyo lit up at this. Maiko knew that she had a favorite parent, and it wasn't because she didn't like her father—no, he was a fine man, but also slightly neurotic and slightly controlling, just like her husband—and she really just wanted to be with her mother.

"Should we get dinner and tell him together?" Michiyo said.

Maiko smiled. "I'd love that."

32

Ever since Adrian's father had passed, he'd felt a wave of emotion inside that roiled and rocked him. When he thought of Jerome, he sensed a great emptiness, like an echoing room with no walls or doors. Then when he thought of Jess's miscarriage, he felt that room tighten around him like a boa constrictor. He wanted alcohol to dull the ache, he wanted drugs to make him forget. But he tried to take each day one at a time, existing but not really *living* as he sleepwalked through his pain.

Jess's album and her subsequent change in their relationship only made things worse.

A new project never materialized; Thomas Whitley had not called, and Adrian, in the throes of his low moods, had not sought out anything else. What he did was go on the rebound. It was like his breakup with Maiko all over again, this time sans drugs. Erin, Paula, nameless women he met at Whole Foods and bedded.

He met Alanna on the set of a commercial for car insurance. (It was easy money and it let him do *something* with his time.) She was a brunette with big hazel eyes who stared at him hungrily as he glanced up from reviewing his lines.

"Hey," he said, when she approached him, as if she were trying to get closer to a wild animal on a safari. She looked dazed, as if she didn't know what to say or do, just that she was compelled to join him near the talent's chair.

"Hi?" She pulled out a compact of setting powder and a makeup brush. "Can I reduce some shine?"

"Sure." He sat and let her sweep him with the brush. "What's your name?"

"Oh. Alanna."

"Hi, Alanna. I'm Adrian."

She gave a short burst of laughter and said, "I know!"

Adrian felt his lips curl into a wry smile. "I know you know, but it's polite to introduce oneself, isn't it?"

"I guess so." She carried herself uncertainly, and Adrian suddenly wondered if she was too young for him.

"Um, Alanna, how old are you?"

She batted her lashes self-consciously. "Twenty-four."

That wasn't too bad. He was in his mid-thirties. Adrian tried not to think about the age difference. "What're you doing after wrap?" he asked.

"Umm. Going out with my friends?"

"Wrong. Going home with me."

It was bold, and she did a double-take. "Aren't you *taken*?" she whispered, like people were listening—which, some were, but it didn't matter.

"We're splitting up," he said.

"Oh, I'm so sorry to hear that," Alanna said, putting one of her dainty hands on his.

"Meet me at my car when today wraps," he said. She nodded absentmindedly.

At the end of the day, Alanna wandered over to Adrian and his car in the parking lot. "Follow me to my house," he said, and as he drove to his and Jess's house, he wondered if this was a smart idea. Jess wouldn't be there, and he had security, but *still*.

But they were barely in the front door when he turned and mashed his lips on hers. She breathed in with surprise, but wrapped her arms around him and that seemed like enough consent for him to grasp her ass.

Adrian knew he was moving on too fast, and too hastily, but Alanna was already stepping out of her underwear under her denim skirt. She knew exactly what this was and was as eager to get a notch on her belt as he was to fuck her. So he obliged. He thought of nothing while he put the condom on, and tuned out the noises she was making. All he could consider were his urges, what turned *him* on and what made *him* want to get off. He barely cared if she did, too, but toward the end he refocused and carried her to her bliss.

"I wasn't expecting that," she said, laying on the leather couch, the same couch that Jess had bought after weeks of searching for the perfect camel shade. Adrian winced at the memory.

"Yes, you were," he responded. "You knew what you wanted." She giggled. "I guess I did."

He re-zipped his pants and swept a hand through his hair, even though he knew he should run them under soap and water.

"Can I see you again?" she asked hopefully.

"Um. Okay," he said, not sure how he should respond. He didn't know if he wanted to.

"Here's my number," she said, pulling out an old CVS receipt from her purse and scribbling it down. Adjusting her skirt, she stood up and smiled benignly at him.

He held the front door open for her. "Talk to you later."

THE COMMERCIAL SHOOT required some pick-up shots, so Adrian went back later that week. Alanna flirted with him shamelessly on the set. Because Adrian was the star, the crew didn't say anything and let it be. They knew he was having an affair with a makeup stylist but they kept it mum, gossiping about it among themselves but not disclosing it anywhere else. That was the code of crew.

They met at his house after wrap, and Adrian fucked her again.

"What does the end of the commercial shoot mean for us?" she asked, head lolling to one side in postorgasmic bliss.

Adrian didn't know what to say. *Adios?* He was not that cold-hearted. He knew that Alanna wanted more. He just wasn't sure if he could give that to her.

"I don't know," he said truthfully. "But I'll call you."

She nodded absentmindedly and pulled her clothes on. She left him with a lingering kiss at the door. He scratched his head as he watched her go.

He wanted to talk to someone. Not just anyone. *Maiko.*

He texted: *Hi.* He bit his thumbnail, waiting for her reply. It came soon after.

M: Hi.

A: How are things with Whitley?

M: Fine. How are things with Jess?

A: Not so great.

M: What's wrong?

A: She's not happy.

M: Oh. I'm sorry.

A: It's my fault, probably

A: She says I'm not around enough to emotionally support her.

A: What does that even mean

M: I suppose it means that you're not there for her in more ways than one. Is anything big happening in your life besides, you know, your dad . . . ?

A: No

M: Okay. Well, I'm sorry to hear that it's not going well.

A: Jess wants us to see other people.

M: Somehow I doubt that.

A: For real. I don't understand it but Jess wants me to date.

A: I suppose she has her reasons. I heard through the grapevine that she's shacking up with this guy, Michael.

A: Worked on one of her albums, apparently. I've never met him.

M: How does that make you feel?

A: Like shit.

There was a long pause.

M: I should get going.

A: Yeah, don't want to keep Whitley waiting.

Adrian felt awful. Talking to Maiko hadn't been productive. He wanted to hold her hand. He wanted to touch her face. He closed his eyes, phone in his hands, and remembered that first glimpse of Maiko after he'd told her about *Atomic Crusader*. How she'd glanced behind at him, her long hair swirling around her face, her lips parted in a huge smile. He missed her. But she was happy with Thomas, so he knew he couldn't ask her to come over.

He had Alanna's phone number. He could call her. If they went out, the cat would be out of the bag. For now, his relationship with Alanna had been constrained to the darkness of his house. No one else knew about it. But maybe he needed to show Jess that he was doing what she asked. Publicly.

Before he lost his nerve, he dialed, listening to the ring with his eyes closed.

"Hey, it's me. Adrian. Do you want to go out tonight?"

April 6, 2015
Adrian Hightower Spotted with Mystery Woman!

Adrian and a mystery woman were seen having dinner at Nobu. More pictures below. Speculation on who she is . . . starts now.

FrostyFrouFrou (10:15 P.M.): Who is this woman and why is she clutching his arm like he's her property? Where is Jess Marin??? You know, his GIRLFRIEND OF 7 YEARS????

Boba89 (10:17 P.M.): i hate how if someone is with a person of the opposite sex, we immediately think they're fucking . . . but did you see the pictures of them in his car??? that lady leaned in for a kiss!

OhNoWow (10:18 P.M.): If I were Jess I would be *devastated* . . . anyone see her most recent instagram post?

FrostyFrouFrou (10:21 P.M.): If Adrian cheated on Jess while she was dealing with his miscarriage, I will never forgive him.

PearlyPinkPolish (10:22 P.M.): I kinda expected adrian to cheat but I figured it'd be with maiko not with some rando. She's not even cute

33

Have you heard this?" Thomas asked, placing a pair of earbuds in Maiko's ears. The music playing was new to her, and very melancholy. Maiko listened for a few moments then shook her head.

"What is it?" she asked, pulling out one bud.

"It's Jess Marin's newest album."

"*That's* Jess Marin?"

"I know." Thomas looked giddy to share the news. "It's nothing like her old stuff. If you listen closely, she's talking about loss a lot. So I went and looked at her Instagram. Take a look."

Maiko swiped open the app on her phone and checked Jess's feed. There was a block of text accompanying Jess in a mirror selfie, her hair hiding half of her face:

I don't talk a lot about my personal life here but I wanted to let you know something. I have been dealing with infertility. My partner and I have taken steps with medical help to conceive, and had it worked, we would have had a happy post to share with you all. But instead, it's just another picture of me, this time mourning the loss of a soul we will never meet. I wrote this album for you, little one.

"Oh . . ." Maiko suddenly felt cold in her stomach. Poor Adrian. They must have lost a pregnancy.

Should she say something to Adrian? Text him, maybe? *Sorry about your miscarriage . . .*

Were they close enough that she could bring this up? No. Let him come to her, if he wanted.

Maiko found it hard to believe that Jess would want Adrian to see someone else, especially during this trying time. And what was he *thinking*, going out with Alanna in public? It looked heinously bad, especially now that Jess had exposed this private piece of their life.

"Did you ever . . . you know?" Thomas asked.

Maiko was confused. "I don't know?"

"Get pregnant with him."

It was not something that Maiko had ever discussed with her husband. Somehow, it didn't feel . . . *safe* to talk about. She realized then that she'd always known this about Thomas: that he wasn't someone to be comfortable around enough to tell him about her health. She somehow knew that if she said something about it to Thomas, he would be weird about it. Consider it like Adrian had marked his territory. That he'd feel even more possessive.

"No," she said simply.

"Do you want to get pregnant with me?" he asked, acting coy.

Maiko swallowed. She hadn't told him yet, but she knew

she was going to carry this baby to term—health willing—and what was she waiting for?

"About that . . ." she said, drawing it out.

Thomas looked at her more sharply, and then glanced down at her midsection. "Really?"

Maiko nodded, smiling. Her lips felt molded from wax. "I was waiting to tell you."

Thomas let out a giant guffaw. "Well, what do you know," he said as if in awe. "Wait, how long have you known?"

"A week?"

"You kept this to yourself for a whole week?" A look passed over his face, something like a cloud. Then he smiled at Maiko. "Wow!"

"Yeah," she said.

A: I fucked up bad.

M: I saw the Instagram post. And the tabloids.

A: Alanna's great, but—I don't know what I'm doing with her.

M: I know.

A: And Jess is pissed, because this whole arrangement was supposed to be discreet. She's out banging Michael Porter but because it's not splashed on Page Six it's fine, I guess?

M: I can imagine.

A: What am I supposed to do?

M: I don't know, Adrian. Maybe break it off with Alanna and do some damage control with Jess?

A: Yeah, but J doesn't want much to do with me at the moment. I think she secretly enjoys having people hate me.

M: Do you think maybe this relationship isn't good for either of you? Maybe it'd be better to split up?

A: I can't break up with her—not so soon after she aired that thing about the . . .

Maiko understood. He'd be seen as even more heartless than before. *Sorry, Adrian.*

Jess Says "He's Still My Man"!!!!

Jess Marin says that Adrian is still her man, even after her long-time boyfriend was caught taking a mystery brunette out on the town. A publicist for the power couple claims that the woman was a collaborator for his commercial for Allstate; nothing more.

My Night with Adrian Hightower!

Well, I wouldn't call it a *night*. We had multiple en-
counters in his trailer when I was on set for his most
recent commercial . . .

So Adrian was out playing games. Any lingering thought
that Adrian would want to be with Maiko flitted away. She resolved then to work on her relationship with Thomas. To grow
to love him harder, to be a good wife. She berated herself for
considering leaving her husband. Yes, Thomas had a temper;
yes, he was a little bit . . . *off*. But his possessiveness could be
seen as a positive, maybe.

She went out shopping and found some lingerie. Pink,
strappy things. She slipped them on and put on a glossy fuchsia
lip and dark eyeliner, then added a silky robe on top of the
ensemble and left it untied.

Walking down the stairs to Thomas's home office, Maiko
grew more excited at the thought of surprising him. She
knocked on the door lightly, and when she heard his *come in*,
she pranced inside.

The reaction was not what she'd expected to receive. Thomas
looked up from his laptop and barely made any acknowledgment of Maiko's presence. She swept the robe open and struck
a pose.

"What do you want, Maiko?" he asked, feigning oblivious-
ness.

"To surprise you," she purred, and walked toward his desk. He slapped the laptop shut. But instead of smiling and welcoming her onto his lap, he glanced at her over the rims of his glasses and made a noncommittal sound.

"What?" she asked.

"I'm working," he said.

"But you can take a break," she said, coming closer and tracing a finger along his jawline.

"I guess I can," he said, letting her straddle his hips. "Growing, are we?" he said, hand smoothing over her small belly.

"She's getting bigger," Maiko joked, and started unbuttoning his shirt.

"Forget the shirt, Mai."

He fucked her while still wearing it. She kissed his neck but he didn't kiss hers back. Maiko had the distinct feeling of being *used*. She didn't even finish before he grunted, hands still grasping her hips, and pulled out of her. Maiko tamped down her sadness. Ever since getting pregnant she'd been so *needy*, like her body craved orgasms. But her husband was a disappointment.

Thomas wiped his forehead with a hand. "Mai?" he said.

"Yes?" she said hopefully, like he was going to offer something else to help her come.

"Pink isn't really your color."

She didn't know what to say to that. He'd always loved her in everything she'd ever worn, including pink. She strode toward the stairs and, as soon as she was in their bedroom, stripped off the lingerie. She wiped the makeup off with a tissue and it streaked on her face. What did it matter when he didn't seem to care what Maiko looked like?

At dinner that night, they sat across from each other at their long table and ate their macrobiotic meal. "What's this?" he asked, glancing at her.

She was barefaced and in jeans and a T-shirt. "What's what?"

"Just because you're married now doesn't mean you can be lazy. Where did my wife go?"

"You mean, the woman who wore makeup and seduced you this afternoon? Where did *she* go?" Maiko snapped. "What's with you?"

"Nothing's 'with' me! Respect my boundaries, Maiko. I need you to not look like a sloppy woman while I eat."

"Sloppy. Your *boundaries*." She repeated the words, veins turning to ice. She pushed back her chair and left the table, leaving her plate for him to collect.

She slept in the guest room that night, unable to share a bed with this strange man. She didn't know who he was, why he was being this way. She had been trying so hard to love him. Maybe this baby was a bad idea. What had Tristan said again? That Thomas was a bear to be with?

The next day, Thomas came to her with a wrapped package, long and thin. "I'm sorry," he said. "I don't know what came over me. I shouldn't have been so snappy."

Maiko chewed the inside of her mouth. "Why were you being so . . ." She didn't know how to finish her sentence, and he shrugged, holding the back of his neck with his free hand.

"I'm just stressed, I guess," he said, and handed her the box. It was obviously jewelry, and she opened it to find a necklace with a pink gemstone pendant. "You look nice in pink," he whispered.

She accepted his apology, but didn't trust him quite the same way again.

34

Maiko began to avoid her home—though that's not what she told herself when she was in her Porsche heading to Calabasas again and again throughout the week. She spent time with her mother in her office and, after Michiyo had completed seeing her patients, followed her to the architectural monstrosity that was her childhood home. There, she and Michiyo would do things with their hands, like prepare traditional Japanese dishes, and talk.

Maiko was surprised at how much she could now talk to her mother. It was like the estrangement had bottled up all sorts of emotions and thoughts, and it was time for the discussion to be let out. She wanted to know everything there was to know about motherhood—what to expect, what was blown out of proportion, what surprises were in store for her. And Michiyo was happy to chat. Indeed, it seemed as though Maiko's mother was overjoyed to have her daughter back again and talked even more than she ever had when Maiko was growing up, as if to anchor her there at the Nakamoto-Fox house.

Maiko was still three months away from her due date, sitting is it about bad news that becomes like a sixth sense? "What happened?" she asked, feeling like the bottom was falling out of her stomach.

"She . . . I don't know. She was fine, and then the next, she was . . . gone. I called 911, they came, they think it was an aneurysm . . . She had been complaining of a headache earlier, but we thought nothing of it . . ."

Maiko felt like throwing up. She had the strange thought that her reaction should be more volatile than this. Instead, she was just quiet while her father sniffed on the speaker. *I will always remember this moment,* she realized. *My dad crying while I learned of my mother's death.*

Death. She didn't know how to reconcile this idea.

She'd never hear her mother say "Maiko-chan" again. *Why is this the first thing I thought of?* Surely, there were other, more important things she would miss. But not hearing Michiyo's voice ever again would tear Maiko's insides apart more than anything else in her life.

"I should've come home more often," she mewed. "I should've been there to see her more."

"No, no," Mark said, still teary. "You were doing what you had to do. I'm just sorry I had to tell you this when your daughter will never get to meet her."

Suzume. She would never meet her grandmother. The thought registered, but it didn't make sense. A world without Michiyo?

She hadn't even told her mother she loved her when she left that evening. Maiko had said goodbye to her parents and just walked out the front door like it was nothing. Didn't look back, didn't wave when she snaked her car around in the long driveway, just drove off like she was going to see Michiyo the next day, and the day after that. The thought made her sick.

Thomas emerged from the shower with a towel wrapped around his waist. He saw Maiko's expression and gently took the phone from her. "She'll call you back," he said to Mark, and hung up. Then he gathered her hands in his and looked at her. "What happened?"

"My mother . . ."

But she didn't want to discuss this with Thomas. There was only one person she wanted to talk to. She snapped her mouth shut and got up, went into the large closet, and put on pajamas. Then she went to the room that was set up for the baby's nursery and texted Adrian.

M: My mother died.

M: I thought you should know.

M: I could really use a friend.

M: . . .

She waited for a response.

MAIKO CALLED CHRISTINE the next day and she came over to the house. Christine curled up with Maiko in a guest bedroom and cried with her.

"I expected more time," Maiko gasped through her tears. "I just . . . I expected—more—time . . ."

"I know, baby, I know." Christine soothed her by wiping the strands of hair that fell in front of Maiko's face out of her eyes. "We all think we have more time."

"It feels just like—" But Maiko couldn't go on. The pain of the baby she and Adrian never had still swept at her every so often, like a tidal wave of grief, pushing and pulsing along the shore.

"I know," Christine said, shushing her. Christine knew all about that baby. How Maiko had wrestled with herself about whether she should keep it.

"When do you want to go to your parents' house?" Christine asked.

"I can't yet. I can't." Because if she did, and her mother was not there, it would be real.

"One day soon you'll have to."

"I know."

Her tears quieted, she lay on the guest bedroom pillows looking at Christine, who was backlit by the window. It must be past noon, she realized. The blinds were still drawn, but the light beyond them was so bright that Christine was more of a silhouette. She wearily wiped her eyes with the back of her hand.

"I could use some good news," Maiko said finally. "Beautiful, happy things. Tell me—how are things with Helen?"

Christine smiled, a far-off look in her eyes. "Good," she said slowly. "We're still taking it slow. We're trying to make sure we don't hate each other by the time we share a bathroom, so we haven't moved in together yet."

"I'm so glad," Maiko said, squeezing Christine's palm.

"She's been very gentle." Christine squeezed Maiko's hand back. "She knows I'm like a scared little rabbit. But Mai? She doesn't make me worry about my soul. So I think it's going well."

Maiko smiled, teary again. "Good."

"Do you want me to stay?" Christine asked.

Maiko nodded.

Christine followed her out to the kitchen as Maiko fixed them some lunch and returned to the guest room to hide from Thomas's gaze. While they ate, Maiko felt Suzume tap-dancing inside her, stomping on her bladder. It grounded her, reminded her that she was still needed here on earth.

35

Jess and Adrian SPLITTING UP
Adrian Dumped Jess!
Watch Footage of the Fight
at Chateau Marmont!

"THIS IS A disaster," Julia, Adrian's publicist, announced. She tapped the tabloids that were sitting on her desk and spread her hands wide, as if to say *What the hell?*

"What were you thinking?" asked Constance, Jess's publicist. The two had teamed up after the Chateau Marmont debacle. The emergency meeting took place at Julia's office near Sunset Boulevard.

"I wasn't," mumbled Adrian. Jess sat next to him silently, sitting on her hands and nodding. They both looked like kids who had been sent to the principal's office.

"Do you want to separate or not?" Constance asked.

The couple looked at each other. Jess imperceptibly shook her head. Adrian sighed.

"Not."

"Then we need to fix this. Jess, do you want to start IVF again?" Julia asked.

"What?" Jess looked stricken.

"Do you still want children with Adrian?"

Jess looked hollowly at the ground. "I don't know—"

That was enough for Adrian to stand up and walk toward the window of Julia's office. They were on the twenty-second floor with a clear view of the Hollywood sign. He leaned on the window, slowing his breaths, slowing his heart.

"It's just," he heard Jess say from her chair, "it's so emotion- ally *taxing*."

"I understand," Julia said. "Would you like to adopt? We can arrange something from a third-world country. Maybe not China. Malawi or something. Get the baby to you fast."

Adrian hated the way Julia was talking. Like a baby was some- thing you just *ordered*. Not something that you carefully and lovingly *grew*. "No," he said, still facing the window. "No babies. Jess, I don't think this relationship is going well." He turned around to look at her. "I'm not bringing a child into this."

Jess slowly nodded. "Okay. It's just," she said for the second time. "It's just . . . I'm running out of time."

"Have you considered breaking up with me completely and getting a new partner who can give you what you want?" he asked. He knew what he was saying would sting, but he had to ask. Her biological clock needed him to.

"I . . ." Jess's eyes darted to the two publicists, who were try- ing not to look like they were absorbed in this private conver- sation. "I remember what you said. About getting those other

girlfriends pregnant. And I think the problem might be me."
She gave a half-shrug with one shoulder. "And if that's the case,
no one I'm with will give me what I want."

"But you could be *happy*. Jess, I know you're not happy."
He had stuffed his hands into his pants pockets and focused his
gaze on the floor in front of him. The square of gray carpet was
threaded through with bits of black.

"But—I write better with you." Her voice was so low, he
had to strain to hear.

"Jess, I want to separate." His voice was firmer.

She stared at a spot on the wall, not looking at him. "Okay."

She didn't put up a fight; she was worn down and tired.
She knew it wasn't working, too. Their relationship had taken
one last breath at a party at Chateau Marmont—where Adrian
joined Jess on the dance floor for one brief moment, before she
laughed at his awkward dancing, and in its last gasps, he'd asked
a nearby blonde to go home with him. Adrian knew what he
was doing would ruin their link, and what's more, he *wanted* it
to. They were both sacrificing their happiness—and for what?

Needless to say, Adrian had come out of the relationship
feeling ragged rather than rejuvenated. He had hired a Teladoc
therapist to help him process his thoughts.

Adrian moved out of the Hills house and into a small town-
home a couple of blocks from his old condo. He wasn't surprised to find that he didn't miss her. She was a lovely person,
but the end of the relationship had curdled their chemistry into
spoiled milk.

————

THE WEDDING OFFICIANT was a movie he'd chosen to do last-minute when Sebastian Stan dropped out, because Adrian had *nothing* to do; he'd been chewing on his cuticles, thinking about how his relationship with Jess was failing. And he wondered, a lot, about Maiko. There were no tabloid shots of her anywhere. Where was she hiding? Was she okay?

His throat hurt sometimes when he thought of the child they could've had—the kid would've been twelve by now. But, of course, he had encouraged Maiko's decision to abort. It's just, in his mid-thirties, Adrian wondered if he was losing his chance to become a father. He didn't want to become a dad at seventy just to pass away ten or twenty years later; he wanted to be young enough to share a lot of firsts with his child—first car, first date, first dances at their wedding. Jerome's absence, even now, well over a year later, stung him in a way he couldn't articulate.

He couldn't just call Jerome and ask him for his opinion on something. When Adrian saw the new 2016 Volvo XC90, for instance, he wanted to ask Jerome what he thought. He could hear Jerome berating it in his mind: "The gas mileage is shit! Why pay for a Volvo when you could get better rates with a Mercedes?" Adrian twisted his mouth into a rueful smile. He missed his dad fiercely. Maybe he'd be a strong proponent of the XC90. Maybe Jerome would've surprised him. Oh well. He couldn't find out now.

"You seem distracted," said the tinny voice on his speakers.

Adrian glanced up at the face illuminated on his computer screen.

"It's nothing," Adrian said.

"Let's continue." The face was solemn and feminine, wearing glasses at the bridge of the nose. Her name was Tahlia and this was their first appointment. Because of his status, Adrian didn't want to go into a counselor's office in person in case he was papped, but he knew he had to talk to someone. She had come recommended by Tim, who was dealing with his addiction issues at last. "You're here because . . . ?"

"I'm here because I'm a mess," Adrian said, with as much self-awareness as he could muster. "I just broke up with a partner of eight years. I'm an addict who hasn't partaken in years but wishes for a good snort every day. Hell, every *hour*. My father died unexpectedly over a year ago and it's still haunting me. I don't know what to do." He rubbed his temple. "I am chaos, personified."

"That's a lot to unpack," Tahlia said in her gentle voice. "Why don't we start at the beginning? How was your relationship with your father?"

"It was fine." Adrian studied his fingers. He had his father's hands. How strange was it, to have the same hands as a dead man? "He was working all the time at his car dealership, so I didn't see him that often. But he still made some time for us. My sister and me," he clarified. "We'd go driving with him. His secretary gave us mints but we couldn't eat them in any of the cars."

As Adrian thought of his father, his throat felt thick. Wiping his face, he continued, "He and my mom had a solid relationship. Each understood what was needed from the other. My dad was the provider; my mother, the nurturer. They were partners. Unlike Jess and me."

"We'll get to you and your ex-partner in a moment. Continue with your parents. How were you raised?"

"My sister and I were both raised to be whoever we wanted to be. I think that's how I got to be who I am today. A successful actor." Adrian sighed. "It was never *'That's not the path for you,'* it was more like, *'How can you achieve your dreams?'* I had really vivid dreams of where I'd be at this point in my life, and it's weird—I *have* achieved them, far more than I ever expected, but I'm still unhappy."

"When was the last time you think you were happy?"

He thought for another long moment. "When Jess and I were first together, I guess."

"When was that?"

"Eight years ago."

"And when was the last time you felt *content?*"

"Probably when I was with Mai." He glanced at his phone.

"Who is Mai?"

"My ex-girlfriend, from when we were up-and-coming. She was wonderful." He was silent for a moment. "I screwed that up too."

"Adrian. Why won't you allow yourself to be happy?"

Adrian didn't know.

And at that moment, his phone lit up. He glanced at the message. He swallowed.

It was from Maiko.

After his session with Tahlia, Adrian sat on the edge of his mattress, staring at his hands. Should he text Mai back? If he didn't, she'd never forgive him. He knew that in his heart. He needed to be there for her.

So he tapped out a response.

A: I'm so sorry. Is there anything I can do?

M: No.

M: Wait, yes.

M: Tell me it gets better. It feels like my stomach is being ripped out of my body and I have to throw up at the same time.

A: It does. Slowly. Although that throw-up feeling never truly goes away.

M: I just keep thinking that I wish I had more time with her. And now that I don't . . .

A: I understand.

M: I know you do. I can't talk about this with Thomas.

A: Shouldn't you be able to, though? That's what couples do.

M: I feel more comfortable talking about this with you.

A: Because?

M: Because it's you.

Adrian paused, wondering what she meant. If he asked—if he pried—he was sure she would shut down and not answer. Another message pinged through.

M: I'm sorry about you and Jess, by the way. I saw the tabloids, even though I try to avoid them.

A: Thanks. It's okay, the relationship had run its course. We're trying to become friends now.

M: I'm glad to hear that.

Adrian blew out a breath. Were he and Maiko *conversing*, like two *grown-ups*?

M: How are you?

He wondered what to say. The cursor in his message box blinked as he considered his words. He was fine, but he wasn't. He was seeing a therapist, and he would suggest she do the same now that Michiyo had passed away. But in the end, he considered her question and realized she was asking a very specific thing.

A: I'm sober. Been on the straight-and-narrow since Romania.

A: I never thanked you enough for that.

M: I'm glad to hear it.

There was a silence after that, and Adrian assumed she'd gone to sleep. He'd taken so many naps after Jerome's death, trying to chase a feeling that was anything but despondent.

He placed the phone on his pillow and waited to hear the telltale vibration of another text coming through.

WITH *THE WEDDING OFFICIANT* wrapping soon, Adrian wanted to have something else lined up to keep him occupied. He found himself picking up a pen and paper during the dragging times on set and starting to scribble away at an idea. The script slowly started to form: a story about two people who are in love but can't seem to get the timing right. And then, when they do, one of them commits infidelity.

He told Tahlia about it during one of their sessions and she asked if it seemed to help his mood at all. Reconfigure his thoughts. He said yes. "Sometimes," Tahlia said, adjusting her glasses low on the bulb of her nose, "writing these extreme scenarios can be cathartic."

Adrian had hopes to film the script when it was done, maybe in the coming year. There was no doubt in his mind that Maiko should play the lead, Sofia. Sometimes, he thought of Mai and wondered how it had gone wrong all those years ago. Pay parity—he didn't have that kind of clout at the time, but maybe he should have pushed for her to get more money anyway. Maybe it had been a mistake to tell her that his money was *their* money, because it made her feel less than, or something.

All she wanted was to feel equal. He realized now that her breakup with him had a lot to do with her insecurity over being a model and not an actress. He should have soothed her; he should have bolstered her confidence.

He hoped that she had forgiven him for not understanding that at the time.

36

Thomas leaned on the doorjamb of the large, en suite bathroom and watched Maiko dab skin cream on her face. "Do you want to talk about it?"

"Talk about what?" Maiko rubbed the moisturizer in.

"Your mom. The funeral is this weekend and you haven't spoken one word to me about it except to tell me when it is."

"I don't *want* to talk about it."

"Maiko, it's not healthy for you to keep things bottled up. I know you've cried, but I haven't *seen* you cry."

Maiko stopped her motions, looking at him in the mirror. "Do you want to watch me cry?" she asked.

"I just mean, I think it's weird that I'm your husband and you won't even discuss this with me. I've been where you are."

Thomas sounded almost kind. She uncapped her eye cream and said, "I know. Thank you, darling." And she smiled at him—the simple, adoring look that she had practiced for years for magazines, a smile that reached her eyes but didn't mean anything in her heart.

THE FUNERAL WAS quiet, understated. Michiyo Nakamoto-Fox had been known throughout many social circles, so it was well attended, but the group of people sat in a hush throughout the entire nondenominational service.

Maiko wondered if Adrian would come. She had texted him about it, but told him not to attend because it would raise more questions than she wanted to answer with Thomas.

Still, she wasn't surprised when, standing at the front of the community center with her father, she saw Adrian materialize out of the group of mourners. He was wearing a dark suit with a dark tie and his hair had been neatly trimmed—nothing like his recent paparazzi photos; his shaggy hair had been for a role, *The Wedding Officiant*, he'd said.

"Mr. Fox," he said to Mark, and outstretched his hand. Mark Fox grasped it. Then he was in front of Maiko, and he held her hand as well. Maiko felt a twinge of comfort from the contact, and his presence. She realized that she did want him to be there—that she wanted his acknowledgment that this horrible thing had happened to her, and that he was attending her grief.

"Maiko," he said softly, and it was like it was just the two of them in that space. She held her breath as he registered her large belly. His eyebrows lifted. He didn't say anything else.

Maiko knew that her being pregnant would stir up feelings for Adrian, considering what had happened between him and Jess. However, she *also* knew that people were allowed to have babies *without* consulting their friends about it first, to make sure that it didn't hurt their feelings. Was the whole world supposed to stop procreating just because Adrian and Jess couldn't reproduce?

Maiko watched out of the corner of her eye as Adrian shook Thomas's hand as well.

As Maiko watched Adrian go, she felt a light touch on the inside of her arm. She glanced down and noticed a dainty hand slithering from where she'd been touched, and Maiko followed it to the body that it belonged to: Elsie Taye, the director for *Surf City*, who was there in an austere black dress and wearing mauve-pink lipstick. "I'm so sorry," Elsie said.

"Did you know my mother?" Maiko asked, confused.

"No, I'm just here as moral support." Elsie's eyes flickered toward Thomas, and Maiko wondered why Thomas would have invited someone they'd worked with five years ago. But soon Elsie was gone, and Maiko held more hands, grasped more shoulders, nodded more times than she could count. Mourning publicly was a rote, methodical thing and she felt numb.

BEFORE LONG, MAIKO had the baby.

Tristan, Thomas's son, came in from out of town to help with Suzume while Thomas figured out a nanny situation. Tristan and Suzume got along immediately; she latched onto him the first time Tristan held her in his arms. "Look," Tristan said softly, "she knows I'm her brother."

Maiko peered at Tristan. He was doing well for himself. He had his own health insurance, he paid his own rent, he had moved up on the career ladder at his publishing house—he was distanced now from the drunk groomsman he'd been at Maiko and Thomas's wedding. But as he toyed with baby Suzume's tiny hand, he whispered to Maiko, "How has he been?"

With that, they were two conspirators on the same side of a coin. Maiko knew exactly what he was alluding to and she wasn't sure what to say. She shrugged, moving her hair out of her face, and let Suzume grasp her index finger.

"I told you he had a temper," Tristan said warily, and Maiko nodded, a lump forming in her throat. But he'd never hit her. He'd never done that. He'd just sometimes be cruel.

Just that very morning, she had been crying because she was so tired and she knew it was just the beginning of her journey into motherhood. There were so many more sleepless days ahead of her, and she wasn't sure if she could do it. But do it she must, and she knew her eyes were puffy, and she held her baby and nursed her at six A.M. anyway. Thomas came out from the bedroom and instead of offering a kind smile or a helpful word, he said, "You look like a mess." Her hopes of having a supportive partner were dashed.

She'd learned not to lash back at Thomas when he was in his moods, because it didn't seem productive. She'd simmer quietly by herself about his verbal jabs and he'd realize his mistake and bring her a peace offering: another piece of jewelry, a new dress. Though the last time he brought her a couture gown, it was in her old size, one that wouldn't possibly fit at the moment.

And in that, the gifts themselves were cruel. She had to pretend to like them, put them in her closet or jewelry box, promise him she'd wear them when she could. But she was just a mother right now, one who had messy hair and wore mesh underwear because she had just given birth and had nursing bras instead of fancy lingerie because that's what her body needed.

Tristan nodded at her, understanding her silence. "He never hit my mom," he continued in a quiet voice, rocking Suzume slowly. "So that's good."

"What happened? With your mom, I mean?" Maiko asked.

He wasn't looking at Maiko anymore, focusing instead on Suzume and her tiny feet, and Maiko was glad. She didn't want to express her relief that physical abuse wasn't on its way.

"She learned that he was toxic. He talks in, like, liberal-arts-college-student-took-psychology terms. Always has. He made his insecurities look like my mom's fault. She finally understood that his nice-guy persona wasn't quite so nice. It's deceptive at first. He can be a real charmer."

Maiko nodded. She'd been charmed, all right. The wining and dining and the hand on the small of her back and the dry kiss at the end of their first date, all hinted at a guy who was shy and vulnerable and sweet. Not this man she now knew.

"Just be . . . *aware* of him," Tristan finished. "He's like a bull in a china shop. He can become destructive."

Maiko's eyes flicked upward as Thomas, now awake, entered the kitchen. "What are you guys talking about?" he asked with a benign smile, one he reserved for strangers.

"Nothing," Maiko said quickly, and Thomas frowned, certain she was lying.

When she'd married a director-producer, she knew that she was going to have to deal with a busy man, that her spouse wasn't always going to be in the honeymoon period with her. Yet she wondered why he was often using her for sex, but without intimacy. No cuddling afterward, no kissing. Maiko's libido had slowed since she'd had Suzume—she felt like she had so many other things to do besides have sex—and his insistence on having a regular schedule felt more controlling than loving. She knew what Adrian meant when he'd said he felt lonely in his relationship. Maiko was being touched *all the time*—not just by her husband, but by her daughter as well—and yet she felt so, so lonely. Thomas, meanwhile, would leave in the middle of the day to "take a long walk" but not invite Maiko or Suzume with him.

One day when Thomas came home from one of his solitary wanderings, Maiko was busy playing with Suzume, and he leaned on the doorjamb of the nursery and watched them. "Have you heard from Adrian lately?" he asked casually.

"From Adrian?" As Maiko sat against the crib, touching Suzume's back, her insides curdled with worry. "No."

"So you won't mind if I check your phone."

"Why do you need to check my phone?" Maiko was even colder now.

"I need you to respect me and my boundaries. My boundaries are that you are not on casual speaking terms with your ex. I need you to recognize that."

"Or what?" she said, sitting up straight, staring at him defiantly.

"Or . . . I might have to reevaluate this relationship," he said. It did not sound friendly.

"There's nothing for you to reevaluate." Too late, she realized her phone was lying on the carpet next to her. Quick as a scorpion, Thomas lunged for it, and Maiko, holding Suzume, couldn't grab it in time. She turned her head, but he grabbed her by the chin and forced her to use the facial recognition to unlock the phone.

"Why are you being so elusive?" he asked. "Do you have something to hide?" His voice was merry, like this was a game. Maiko stood up and backed away from him, moving Suzume out of his way, wondering if she should cut and run. Tristan appeared behind Thomas in the doorway, hovering uncertainly. Maiko realized that he was there to support her, but she wanted to secure her daughter more than anything else.

"Take her," she commanded to Tristan, a plea in her voice. He obeyed, grabbing the baby, and so it was just Maiko and Thomas at an impasse in the playroom.

Thomas was swiping through her texts. "Christine . . . Helen . . . Christine *and* Helen . . . Ah, there it is, Adrian High-tower." He raised a brow. "You haven't talked in months?"

Maiko felt rooted to the spot now. She didn't know what to say or do. She could sense tears threatening to spill over her lashes, but she stopped them, not wanting to let Thomas see that she was upset. "Give that back," she said, holding out her hand, using a firm voice that she didn't know she had.

"He's not sure if he can talk to you now, because you are pregnant? It 'hurts too much'? Wow."

"Seriously, hand it over," she said stiffly, her hand still out-stretched.

But Thomas scrolled further up. "He's writing a script. Ooh. I know. I'll produce it for him." There was a gleam in Thomas's grin, an artificial white-tooth smile that came from years of cosmetic dental work.

"Why would you do that?" Maiko was confused. It didn't sound like a good idea. It felt like a trap.

"Because it's obvious he's telling you so it would be a Madrian film. And I'll be on the set every day, watching you two pine after each other. Because I'm a masochist."

This is why he had gotten so nasty, she realized. He was already a manipulative jerk, with his insecurities coached in therapy terms, but he had increased it tenfold after he'd married her and had Suzume. What was he going to do as Suzume got older? What sort of figure would he be, what type of role model would she look up to?

"Do you regret having her?" she asked suddenly. "Or did you do it just to trap me?"

"I would never do that," he said.

"You probably did the same thing to trap Georgia," Maiko hissed, her rage building. "Well, look at her. She got out."

"Did she, though?" And Thomas smirked. "Not all the way. As long as Tristan is my son, we're connected."

Maiko realized that she had played right into Thomas's hands. "He'll leave," she said. "He's a grown man. He can cut ties with you."

"Not if he wants to keep his inheritance."

And with that, Maiko felt stuck. Because of course Tristan, working in the most expensive city in the country, would want that money.

"I don't want to be with you anymore," she spat.

And then, Thomas laughed. "You don't *know* what you

want. You're addled with hormones. You'll forget we had this conversation by next week. And we both know you won't leave me."

But Maiko did not forget. She held on to the thought like a pugnacious fist.

Part 4

Maiko and Adrian
2019–2020

37

2019

Adrian dated. A few short relationships evolved—these weren't like his one-night stands from before he'd met Jess. He tried to find a connection, but they all paled to the relationship he knew he could never have again.

Adrian was intrigued when Thomas approached him about *Sofia and Max*. "I just wanted you to know that if you want your next project made with Maiko, it'll have to be through me," he said.

What are you, her jailer? Adrian wanted to ask. How would Maiko even agree to be Sofia? Was she on a tight leash with Thomas? Adrian's dislike of Thomas grew—he'd not been a fan of his since the shoot in Romania when he yelled, and swatted, at Maiko. And the thought of Maiko as a docile, whipped housewife angered Adrian further. She should be wild and free. The thought of her smiling at him from over her shoulder after that first date fluttered in his mind, as it often did. *She should always be so happy*, he thought.

Thus, he did want Maiko as Sofia. Maybe, just maybe, she would figure out that she didn't love Thomas and would come back to him.

And so, he agreed.

ADRIAN WALKED INTO the table read with his shirt already sticking to his back with sweat.

It was going to be the first time he saw Maiko in over three years.

On a film that he wrote, that had his characters making up with rough sex after an argument.

In which he would be acting with Maiko.

He swallowed. He found his seat in the mostly empty room and sat down, pulling his baseball cap low across his forehead. He waited.

And then, there she was, striding toward him in long, sure steps, almost like she was on a perpetual catwalk. Her hair was long again, though not as long as it had been when they'd first met. Adrian watched her, spellbound, as she glided to the seat next to him.

"Hi," he said, his voice raspy with dryness.

"Hi," she said, and it was kind. Friendly.

He cleared his throat.

Thomas Whitley walked in as well, and sat across from them in the big rectangle of folding tables and office chairs. He stared at Adrian, who lifted a hand in greeting. A woman stood next to Thomas and spoke into his ear. He nodded and she slinked away to stand in a corner of the room. So, not a costar, then.

When Thomas got the room's attention, he said, "Welcome to the table read for *Sofia and Max*, written by Adrian Hightower." He led the cast and crew in applause. "Let's get started, shall we?"

Setting: a modest house in a suburban area, mid-nineties. An Asian-American woman, Sofia, washes dishes at the sink. Her husband, Max, joins her in the kitchen and leans into her back, holding her stomach. She turns her face to accept a kiss on the cheek. Music wafts in from the living room—there's a record playing on the old turntable, a relic.

Adrian cleared his throat again and said his line: "Hi, beautiful."

Maiko pulled her hair away from her face and spoke. "Hi, yourself."

"Let me take care of those later. Dance with me."

Max shuts off the water and draws his wife in to face him. They clasp hands and sway to the oldie track that's playing. Max buries his face in Sofia's hair.

"You always smell so good. Like . . . lavender," Adrian said. He felt himself start to blush. This was hitting too close to home. Everyone in the room was going to realize that he was still in love with Maiko.

He cursed himself silently. This was a mistake, a giant mistake. Why had he written this script? How had it gone this far? How could Maiko's husband, of all people, have read this and not choked Adrian to death? Instead, he had offered to produce it—why?

Adrian stole a look at Thomas, who had his eyes down at the script, nodding along as Maiko asked, "Where are the kids?"

Adrian found his voice again. "I tucked them in. Alison wanted a bedtime story. Liam wanted a different blanket."

The table read continued, and all the while Adrian was distracted, wondering what he was doing. Was it too late to pull out? Why had he agreed to this? He felt perspiration under his armpits. His upper lip was warm and his cheeks were burning.

Maiko, to her credit, did not waver. She read her lines stoically, as if she were doing Adrian a favor.

When the read was over, Adrian excused himself and walked into the men's room. He splashed water on his face and stared into the mirror. He reminded himself that he was doing this for Maiko.

"Adrian, just the person I was hoping to see," Thomas said, walking crisply toward him after Adrian left the bathroom. Trailing behind him were Maiko and the woman Thomas had chatted with before the table read. "I want you to meet Chelsea Siegfried. She's our intimacy coordinator for this film."

Adrian shook Chelsea's proffered hand. "Nice to meet you,"

he said politely, but he was looking at Thomas, who was still speaking.

"She'll be working with you and Maiko for the kiss and the bedroom scene to make sure there's nothing unprofessional happening."

Maiko nodded, all business. Adrian continued to stare at Thomas. He felt the need to clear his throat, loudly.

There was something funny going on inside Adrian at that moment; besides feeling mildly offended that Thomas thought it necessary to give Adrian a warning, Adrian felt his pulse fluttering wildly. Was it because he was thinking about the kiss? He had written the bedroom scene to be the climax of the movie, where the main characters fought and then made up after angry sex. He was suddenly unsure if he would be able to pull it off.

Thomas gave him a stern nod and walked on. Chelsea followed.

Adrian's hands were clammy and he felt a bit queasy. He swallowed. "Did you want to go over lines together sometime, before we start filming together?" he asked Maiko.

"Okay," she said. Nothing more. Her eyes flicked toward her husband's retreating back. Then she gave Adrian a little nod and walked away.

Her steps were sure and her hair swayed. Adrian felt wistful. So, this was how it was going to be—barely friendly, barely talking, except when the cameras were rolling?

Tim came up to him and clapped a hand on his shoulder. "Hey, man," he said softly.

"What are you doing here?" Adrian asked. It was a small cast and even smaller crew. Tim should be sitting at home, flipping channels on the television, waiting for filming to start the next day, when his skills as a light rigger would be needed—when things would get really crazy.

"Whitley asked me to come in. He wanted to bribe me to watch you. He knows we're friends."

"Say what?"

"I'm telling you this because I didn't take his money. But yeah. He's concerned that you have it for his wife."

"Mai and I are professionals. We can do this film without any weird feelings. We've done it before."

"Yeah, but look at it from his point of view. You're no longer in a relationship with someone else."

"So?"

Tim nodded. "You're right. It didn't matter even when you *were* in another relationship."

Adrian wiped a hand down his face. "It doesn't matter," he muttered.

"Wake up, Adrian. You wrote an entire screenplay about how much you love her. Get it through your thick skull."

Adrian cut a glance at Tim, who gave him a sad nod. "Is it that obvious?" he asked, his stomach plummeting.

"Yup," Tim said, his lips popping with the *p*.

Adrian looked at the doorway where Maiko had disappeared. "I doubt she feels the same way," he said, rubbing the back of his neck.

"I don't know. I think she'll figure out soon enough that her husband is a scumbag who doesn't trust her. And maybe that's when you can swoop in."

Adrian barked a laugh. "Right."

"Anyway, before the schedule gets rough, want to hang out at my place? Catch a game?"

"Nah. I've got a ton of work to prepare. I'll see you."

38

Maiko had driven separately from Thomas because he was going to stay later—production meeting—and she went home to relieve the nanny. When she walked in the door of the house, she stepped right back into the role of Mother Maiko, discovering her daughter crying, with the caregiver unable to placate her. Maiko gathered Suzume in her arms.

Maiko held her hot-blooded child and didn't say anything, just rocked her back and forth. She didn't need to know what had set her daughter off. She just wanted her to feel safe and loved. Maybe this was the wrong way to parent, but Maiko felt an innate sense of comfort in the way she approached Suzume, and hoped that it would make a difference.

Suzume was coming to her senses again: no longer lost in her feelings, she hiccupped and slowed her crying. Suzume was the best parts of Maiko, with her dark eyes and hair, and had Thomas's facial features from the nose down. Maiko peeled herself away from Suzume and rubbed her shoulders. She smiled at her daughter. "Okay?" Maiko said.

The toddler hiccupped. She nodded.

Maiko sat outside on the back patio and gave her daughter some sidewalk chalk to decorate the concrete. She had her sheaf of script pages and double-checked that she'd memorized the next day's lines. They were going to be filming out of order while they had the full cast there with them and eventually, after a few weeks, taper off to film all of Maiko and Adrian's duo scenes, of which there were many. Maiko took a deep breath. She would be able to do this. She was a professional—as much as she could believe it, anyway. She had been on a dozen sets, worked with Adrian a number of times. She'd be fine.

So why did she feel so knotted up and confused?

MAIKO SHOULD NOT have been surprised that Thomas jumped at the chance to get involved with *Sofia and Max* when he heard, through the pipeline, that Adrian was looking for producers. Thomas was anything but impatient. He concocted his plans like a spider spinning a web, waiting to ensnare his target. Maiko was reminded of the way he had wooed *her* into his life, taking her out for a nice meal and saying all the right things, so she would let her guard down on those first few dates.

But she *was* a little shocked when he told her she'd be playing Sofia. "What if I don't want to?" she said, though a part of her wanted very much to see Adrian again, work with him again.

"But I think you do," Thomas said in a soft voice, and she hated how he could read her sometimes. When it came to Adrian, Maiko was apparently an open book.

Ever since she had Suzume, Thomas had been playing her like a fiddle. The nanny, Joann, had been hired, Tristan went home to New York, and then Maiko was left with nothing but time. Thomas had laid low for about a month, but one day while reading the newspaper over his glass of orange juice, he said, "Shouldn't you start prepping for your comeback?"

"My comeback?" Maiko had repeated.

"You know. Get your body back, get back on the screen."

The implication was clear: Thomas did not like her new body.

Maiko had some self-conscious shame over what she looked like now. Distended breasts, cracked nipples, paunchy belly. She had examined herself by shifting her body side to side in the bathroom mirror just that morning: she had stretch marks along her midline and her thighs rubbed together for the first time in her life. She tried not to think about how her actual worth was tied to how she looked and instead gazed at her different tummy, as if to acknowledge the being she had produced from within it. *This is a strong body*, she reminded herself. *This is a mother's body.*

And yet here was Thomas, telling her that she was less than. And she hated it.

So why didn't she leave? It was a tale as old as time, unfortunately: Maiko had wrapped up her money with his. She had had a baby with him. She was reliant on him. She was stuck.

And she was scared.

She and her father had not reconciled the way she and Michiyo had; if she needed help, she wasn't sure if Mark would be there for her. He was too consumed in his own grief to attend to his daughter. Who else did she have? Christine and Helen, who were now living together in Echo Park, and whom she didn't want to disturb. The other Valentina Posh Vixens? No. Just Adrian. And he had stopped talking to her after her mother's funeral. It was an awful feeling.

She'd needed him, and he'd abandoned her.

Maiko stayed where she was, waiting until she had an out.

And maybe *Sofia and Max* could be that for her.

MAIKO AND ADRIAN were two professionals on set for the following three weeks. Thomas Whitley had nothing to worry about—they avoided each other at craft services, didn't visit each other's trailers, and didn't even have any scenes together yet. They were working with their other costars, getting those scenes down before those colleagues took off, but Maiko worried as the days counted down. She wasn't sure she could handle the bedroom scene, which depicted rough but emotional sex.

Maiko was on set while Adrian and his costar Mallory Jenkins were working together. Mallory was playing Max's sister Courtney, discussing his relationship with Sofia.

As the two conversed easily on camera, Maiko couldn't help but admire Adrian's work ethic. He was focused, laserlike in his precision to act; when directed to try something differently in another take, he was a consummate professional, shifting subtly to accommodate the new version of how he was playing Max.

It was this professionalism that had Maiko knocking on his foldout chair as if she were knocking on a door. "Hey," she said, waiting for his response.

Back in the day, on sets, they'd talked. Now, he was on his phone, texting someone, who knows what. When she knocked on his chair arm, he put the phone down and directed his attention toward her.

"I'm concerned," she said.

"About . . . ?"

"About this sex scene."

"Ah." He nodded, though his eyes weren't on hers. He ran a hand through his hair, as if distracted. "Well."

She felt uncomfortable. "Can we run some lines? Just so that we can get to know each other again. As friends and professionals."

Adrian raised an eyebrow, just slightly, and she knew it sounded like a come-on. "I won't touch you," she promised.

"That's not what I'm thinking about. I'm worried about our illustrious producer and director. Your husband."

"Thomas?" She bit her lip, thinking. "Yeah, I'll talk to him about it."

"I don't want to make it seem like you're *his*, but the way he was looking at me when he introduced Chelsea, I want to be sure not to cross him," Adrian said awkwardly.

"All right."

But as Maiko walked away from the conversation, she grew more and more annoyed with what Adrian had said. *His.* Like she was Thomas's property, or something. Like Adrian had to ask Thomas for permission before practicing on his guitar.

So she didn't ask Thomas. She waited a few days, and then, on the day of the shoot, she knocked on Adrian's trailer door. He propped it open with a shy smile, and her heart knocked sideways. He was always so beautiful.

Glancing both ways to make sure no one saw, she climbed the steps and sat down on the little couch that occupied a corner. "Shall we start?" she asked crisply, and Adrian closed the door with a hard snap. He turned to the kitchenette and poured himself a cup of coffee from a carafe.

"Want some?" he asked.

She shook her head, her heart beating heavily in her ears. She was nervous. Why was she *nervous*? It was just Adrian. These were just lines. It would be fine.

He settled on the other end of the couch with his mug and took an experimental sip. Then he turned his attention on her with a gaze so focused, it took her breath away.

"Sofia," he said, already in character, "how could you do this to me? To us?"

Maiko took a deep breath and let it out, remembering that she was supposed to be an enigmatic wife who had cheated on her husband. "I don't know what you're talking about," she said archly, in character as well now.

"With my best friend. You think I wouldn't find out?"

This is where she was supposed to pretend that the bottom had fallen out of her picture-perfect life. "It meant nothing."

"It means *everything*!" he said. Then he looked down at the script on the coffee table. "I'm supposed to yell that part, but I'll save it for the real take. Or do you want me to actually do the whole shebang?"

Maiko nodded.

"It means *everything*!" he bellowed, and Maiko felt his hurt, his anger.

"I'm sorry," she whimpered.

"It's too late."

"It's never too late." She hesitated, then said, "And then I kiss you forcefully."

Adrian had turned toward her once again, and his eyes were so warm, so brown. "Do we need to practice that?" he asked, and it was gentle. "I know you said we wouldn't touch, but if we need to get close to each other again . . ." He let the rest of the sentence trail off.

"Maybe," she said, heart hammering in her rib cage. Would it be cheating if she practiced the kiss now? In private? "I'd have to be Sofia, though. You can't think of me as Maiko."

"Of course."

"Should we get Chelsea?" she asked, the thought suddenly occurring to her. That was the job of the intimacy coordinator: to make sure that everything was on the up-and-up.

"She reports directly to Thomas," he said.

There was a beat of silence.

"Okay, so I didn't tell him I was running lines with you," she admitted.

"I know. Otherwise, Chelsea would be here."

"We can do this ourselves."

"Yes, we can." His voice was low, gravelly. Just the sound of it made her squirm slightly on the couch, and she slid closer to him. He adjusted his arm so that it slung back behind her. Their knees were almost touching. She held her thigh tightly with one hand, wondering if this was a bad idea.

"It's okay," he murmured. "I'm not going to bite."

She remembered how he used to suck and bite her lips, when they were together, and she shivered inside.

"A movie kiss," she cautioned, and he nodded, slipping one hand into her hair, clasping the back of her neck and drawing her face closer.

At first, she was resistant; her mouth was a hard pucker. But soon she melted into his kiss, the softness of his lips, the taste of his tongue, which lightly swiped: a reflexive motion, one borne out of memory.

She remembered the first time they kissed on the couch in her little apartment shared with Helen—how their chemistry was so intense, and how it was the best kiss she'd ever experienced. But this kiss was even better. She moaned slightly into his opened mouth, his other hand now lightly touching the side of her face, moving her hair out of the way so that he could kiss a trail down her cheek to her neck. Maiko felt herself lost in the moment, and as soon as his mouth made contact with her skin, she jolted into awareness.

"Wait," she gasped, and Adrian pulled away just as suddenly, shifting uncomfortably in his seat as he realized what he'd done. She opened her eyes to see him with his bedroom gaze on her, one she'd seen many times before: eyelids hooded, pupils dilated, lips brushed rosy with the friction of their kiss.

"That wasn't even the right kind of kiss," she murmured. "It was supposed to be angry."

"I'm sorry," he said, pulling back even more. "I don't know what came over me. You just . . ." He didn't continue. Maiko knew he had gotten lost in the kiss just as much as she had.

"I've got to go," she said, and stood up abruptly.

"Mai, it's okay, it's acting," he said unhelpfully.

But *was* it acting? The line seemed to blur between what was fake and what was real. At least with *Surf City* she'd known it was just her job. On this day, she was confused, unsettled. She'd felt the tug of *want* so badly. Yanking the door open, she stepped right out.

Into the eyeline of Thomas, who was standing nearby.

Maiko had never seen Thomas so angry. He grabbed her by the elbow and practically shoved her into the makeup trailer. "Out," he bellowed, and the makeup artists and hair stylists evacuated. Maiko watched them go, but she pleaded with them in her head to stay. *He's going to hurt me*, she realized. *It's come to this.*

Thomas was clenching and unclenching his hands, like he was working up to hitting her. "I—" she began to say, but he cut her off by slapping her across the face. She was stunned. He'd never hit her before. She almost didn't believe it had happened. The only thing that made her understand that she'd been slapped was the residual pain on her face, and then the buzzing in her ears. Everything in her brain felt like soft cotton. She couldn't think.

"How dare you disrespect me," he said. It would've been better if he'd shouted. Instead, he'd spoken in a soft tone, one that was laced with anger.

"We were just rehearsing," she said, and she was horrified to hear a tremor in her voice, a soft pleading that came out of her throat.

"Right." His voice was sarcastic.

"I would never—" she began again, but he raised his hand once more and she stopped short.

He hadn't barred the door. She barreled out of it, the world outside blurry and oblong, and she found that she was crying.

"Mai!" Adrian called.

It took everything in Maiko not to scream about her predicament. She had been slapped by her husband. She had a child with that man. She had to *work* with that man.

She had kissed her costar. It had been during rehearsal, but it didn't *feel* like a rehearsal kiss.

What was she supposed to do?

She shut herself in her car and cried. Sobs tore out of her as she remembered Thomas's furious face, his possessive grab of her arm.

Then she called Christine.

"Come over," Christine said, without hesitation.

"I need to get Suzume." She would not leave her baby alone with her husband.

"Get Suzume, and come here. We'll figure everything out after that."

Maiko wiped her eyes and nose and started the car. Before she could pull out of the parking space, however, Adrian appeared in front of her hood. He crossed to the driver's side window. His lips moved, but she couldn't hear him; she shook her head and backed out of the spot.

As she drove away, she could see him looking dejectedly at her taillights. That was another conversation she didn't want to have. What did that kiss mean? Why had it happened the way it had? It was supposed to be Sofia and Max, making up after arguing: an emotional, yet *angry*, interaction. It had, instead, been tender. *Loving.* Maiko swallowed involuntarily.

When she got to the house, she saw Thomas's car in the driveway. Shit. She'd have to confront him after what he did.

She was not leaving without Suzume.

Joann was nowhere to be seen, but Thomas stood in the kitchen, glowering. "We need to talk," he said.

"There's nothing to discuss." Maiko swept past him, looking for her daughter.

"Listen, Mai, I'm sorry about what happened. I'll get you a new car. What do you want? A Jag?"

"You can't buy me off," she said, and he followed her as she walked through the hallways, searching for Suzume, still speaking.

"I don't know what came over me . . ."

"Yes, you do. You were jealous. What Adrian and I were doing was *rehearsing!* You know that I didn't want to do this movie, but I got strong-armed into doing it. And then when I try to do a good job and rehearse with my costar, you go ballistic. I'm not going to stand for it."

Suzume was in her room, playing with Joann.

"You can go, Joann," Thomas said, and the caregiver looked at Maiko for confirmation. Maiko nodded.

"Where do you think you're going?" he said.

"We're leaving."

"This is *my daughter* and I won't have you taking her." He grabbed at Suzume.

"Don't touch her!"

"Let's ask her what she wants. Suzume, sweetie, do you want to stay here with Daddy or leave the house with Mommy?"

"She's not old enough to make a decision like this! You don't know what you're asking of her." Maiko's temper was threatening to blow over.

Thomas held Suzume by the shoulders. "Which is it, honey?" Suzume looked at Maiko with a questioning look in her eyes. Thomas shook her and Suzume whipped her attention back to him. There was fear now, and Maiko couldn't stand it.

"Don't you *dare* shake her!" she hissed, trying hard not to yell. The shake he'd given Suzume was the same shake he'd given to Maiko, way back when, and look at where it had led. Her cheek still felt warm from the slap he'd given her, and she knew—just *knew*—that if they stayed, Thomas would become more of a monster.

"I'm not doing anything," Thomas said defensively, but Maiko wrestled his hands off Suzume and shoved him. He was so surprised that he took a step backward.

Tugging on her confused daughter's hand, Maiko pulled her outside to the car.

"Mama?" Suzume whined.

"We're going to Christine and Helen's. You love them."

"Daddy?"

"We'll see him later," Maiko said distractedly, pulling the car out of the circular driveway and cruising down the street, almost forgetting to stop at the stop sign.

The traffic was stop-and-go, which allowed Maiko to tune

her daughter out and place her mental dominoes in a row. She couldn't believe that she'd been slapped, but when she looked in the rearview mirror, there was still a redness to her left cheek. She chewed the inside of her lip and wondered if she'd deserved it. After all, she *had* been in her ex-boyfriend's trailer, kissing him.

But Thomas made me do this film, she thought to herself, gritting her teeth as fresh tears threatened to flow.

Christine would know what to do, she decided, as the car whispered up to the curb outside her friends' house. Christine was already opening the front door, the outline of her hips blocking the doorway, as Maiko unsnapped Suzume's safety harness. Christine ushered them inside, where Maiko sat down heavily on the couch and tried to bite back her tears.

"Suzume, sweetie," Helen said, "want to watch *Frozen*?" Helen led Suzume off to the living room.

Thus occupied, the two friends turned toward each other and Maiko sagged in her seat.

"Let me make you some tea," Christine offered.

When it was placed in front of her, Maiko cupped her hands around the mug and she dropped the pretense of normality. Tears dissolved in her eyes as she told Christine in a low voice, again, what had happened, including what led up to the confrontation with Thomas.

"You kissed Adrian?" Christine asked. "That's not what I should be asking, but wow."

"It was supposed to be a movie kiss," Maiko said miserably. "Instead, it was . . ."

"It was. . . . ?"

"It was perfect." Maiko sighed. "It felt like old times. But better."

Adrian had grown into his body. No longer just a lean, tall man with a protruding Adam's apple and his dark hair and eyes, he was fuller: broad shoulders, a stomach with a tiny roll of fat that suited him, thick thighs. He kissed like he knew her, and he *did*.

"Shit." Christine frowned.

"What?" Maiko said.

"You still love him."

"I . . . No, I don't."

"Mai, you have that same lovesick look on your face that you had when you first met him. Remember that he used drugs? Didn't support you as an actress?"

"He's been clean since Romania," Maiko said, but tears continued to leak from the edges of her eyes. "And the pay parity thing—he showed me that he got paid the same rate, since *Surf City*."

"And need I remind you that you're a married woman and you have a child."

"A woman married to a guy who hit her," Maiko said fiercely.

"Right. About that. You need to leave him. Divorce Thomas."

"Can I? How do I do that?"

"I don't know for sure, but we need you out of that house."

Maiko's eyes flicked over to Suzume, who was rapt with attention in the next room over, watching ice princesses. She gripped the mug even tighter. "I have to keep him away from her."

"Yes. Yes, you do. Let us help you."

———

Maiko decided that day to never go back to the Malibu house. She left everything behind, including her bedroom of shoes. She bought new clothes, and washed them at Christine and Helen's house. But Maiko didn't have a lot of her own money. She had a bank account with a few thousand dollars in it, which she had before she married Thomas, but it wasn't enough to live off of—she couldn't move into a hotel or a new apartment, for instance. The money was good for paying Joann, who was now commuting to Echo Park to watch Suzume while Maiko was working. Maiko cursed the complacency that she'd been fed—that she would be fine with her finances mingled with her husband's.

Christine and Helen were sweet enough to open their house to Maiko and Suzume, and the two slept on the couple's couch, curled up together. Maiko felt the abject humiliation of the situation: she had no financial leg to stand on.

But she had that bank account. And it was *something*. A seed to start her separation. She could promise the rest to a lawyer after she and Thomas split assets.

And so. She moved forward.

"You filed divorce papers?" Thomas was speaking through her locked trailer door. "Listen, Mai, I'm so sorry about what happened. You have every reason to be upset. I wasn't myself that day . . . and Adrian drives me crazy. But you're filing for *divorce*?"

Maiko ignored him. *Don't suffer fools*, she told herself. If she went back to Thomas, *she'd* be the fool.

Maiko dreaded walking into her trailer and onto the set every day. Thomas was there, lurking. It made for a toxic work environment. Everyone on the close-knit set knew what had happened, it seemed, and Maiko was embarrassed, but tried not to be. After all, it wasn't her fault.

And no one knew what had happened in Adrian's trailer.

It was just a rehearsal, she reminded herself.

She was in her trailer, alone, wondering what was next in her life, when she heard a knock. "It's me," Adrian's voice said. Maiko unlocked the door.

"Hi, Adrian," she said warily.

"Can I come in?"

She didn't offer any refreshments. She resettled in her spot and bundled up on the little couch, one hand resting on her temple. He did not sit.

"I know what happened," he said in a low voice.

She winced. "Do we have to talk about it?"

"Yes, we do. You're not staying with him, right?"

"Of course not." She might have, once. But she knew that if she wasn't worth better, *Suzume*, at least, was worth better.

"Good." He wiped a hand down his face. "I was ready to come in here and tell you exactly what to do, but it looks like you're a step ahead of me."

"Thomas is livid about me filing for divorce. I'm going to ask for sole custody."

"Are you okay on money?" he asked. "I realize how gauche that sounds, but if your finances are tied up . . ."

"I have some money. Christine is helping me with finding a place."

"I can help," he said.

"I can do this without you, Adrian. It doesn't concern you. Is that the only reason you're here?"

"I just wanted to make sure we were okay. You blew out of my trailer that day and then we never talked after that. It's been kind of hard . . ." The insinuation clear: Thomas made it near impossible to get close to Maiko.

"Yeah. I'm sorry about that." She huffed out a breath, a small laugh. "It was weird. We made it weird. Let's not make it weird."

"Mai, it was . . . " He struggled to speak. "It was fine."

"It wasn't in the script."

"No, I mean . . ." His eyes found hers. "It was good."

She smiled lightly. "Yeah, it was good. But it can't happen again. Only on the set."

"Right. So I'll see you on the set, then?" he said.

"Okay." Her voice was very soft.

MAIKO WAS NERVOUS. It was time to shoot the bedroom scene. She knew she could get it right, but it involved being vulnerable in her acting, in a way she was uncomfortable with.

The set was quiet. There was the director of photography, the intimacy coordinator, and Thomas, and that was it.

Maiko was in a button-down blouse and slacks. The script called for Adrian to pull off her top. Toplessness didn't bother Maiko— she had posed without a bra many times as a model—but the intimacy of Adrian's mouth on hers would be hard to ignore.

"All right," Thomas said stiffly. "Let's get this over with."

Rolling!

"It's too late," Adrian-as-Max said.

"It's never too late," Maiko-as-Sofia said meekly.

Adrian rubbed Maiko's cheek with his thumb and breathed her in. His eyes gazed into hers.

Maiko lifted her hand and gently clasped Adrian's wrist. She could feel his pulse racing under her fingertips. She closed her eyes and leaned in.

Their breath mingled before their lips touched.

Her eyelashes fluttered against her cheeks as his lips explored hers. With a sigh, they reluctantly parted.

There was a beat of silence. "Well, that was . . ." Thomas searched for the right word. His face was splotched red and he looked angry behind his glasses. "It's supposed to be full of . . . anger. Passion."

"Right." Adrian scratched his cheek and looked over at Maiko.

"Let's try it again, and this time, try to get it right on the first try. I don't love watching you two."

Adrian nodded imperceptibly. The tension on the set was so thick, Maiko felt like choking on it.

"It's too late."

"It's never too late!"

This time, Maiko had a little more fire in her voice. She grabbed Adrian and kissed him deeply. He fought against her, as if angry with her, but soon he was ripping off her buttoned blouse and shifting the fabric off her shoulders.

He pulled at her hair at the nape of her neck, taking a big fistful as he jerked her head back and began kissing her neck. She gasped in surprise—even though this is what Chelsea had rehearsed with them, it took her breath away—and her hand scrabbled at his collar. Adrian shrugged out of his shirt and went back to kissing Maiko on the mouth, and it was a delicious push-and-pull, as they began migrating to the couch on set. When he was on top of her, he kissed a line from her lips to her belly button. She scratched his shoulders with her fingernails. She was aware of the camera dipping and panning alongside them, and remembered that this was all just for show. But it still felt really, really good.

"And cut," Thomas said, voice shaking. "Print."

Maiko sat up and Adrian adjusted himself away from her. She saw the strong planes of his back, the muss of his hair, and felt tender toward him.

"Could I get a robe, please?" Maiko asked, and Chelsea hurriedly brought her one. Maiko wrapped herself up in it and felt her warm cheeks. It might have been movie magic, but it was a kiss that transcended their roles. There was so much history there. She watched as Adrian stood up, his jeans slung low on his hips, and looked away. She could sense him receding from her, and wondered if she was alone in her feelings.

Thomas approached Maiko as she tied the robe with a cinched knot. "Mai?" he said. "About Suzume . . ."

She shook her head, and Adrian was suddenly there, in between them, playing referee. "I don't think you should bother

her," Adrian said. Chelsea watched with a tense expression, her eyes flicking back and forth like she was observing a tennis match.

"Boss," she said, getting Thomas's attention. "Can I speak to you?"

Thomas followed her off the set and Maiko escaped to her trailer and locked the door.

39

Joann tearily told Maiko the next morning that she could no longer work for her. "He threatened to fire me and leave me with no references. I've been with you guys for several years now and it would look *so* bad if I couldn't list you as a reference . . ."

Maiko understood, but she was without childcare.

"Suzume, do you want to go to work with Mommy?"

Even though going to work meant they'd see Thomas.

She'd have to find someone to watch her daughter while she was on set. Maybe a PA could do it. She felt awful.

Suzume had not grown up on film sets; Maiko tried not to make it a habit to bring her to work. Home life was home life and work life was work life, with a strong delineation between the two. Unless—her heart fluttered—unless she was kissing Adrian Hightower.

So Suzume was holding Maiko's hand as they walked up from the parking lot to the soundstages. As soon as they stepped foot in the shadowy entrance and the air-conditioning kicked in around them, Thomas was there, hovering over Suzume and scooping her up in a big hug. Maiko bit back what she wanted to say, not eager to play tug-of-war with Thomas over their daughter. When Thomas put Suzume down, Maiko possessively took Suzume's hand and held it with a firm grip.

"You can't keep her from me," Thomas said angrily.

"Watch me." She pulled on Suzume's hand and stalked off in the direction of her trailer.

Adrian was waiting there for her, cup of coffee in each hand. "Who's this?" he said, the skin around his eyes crinkling. Maiko took a deep breath to calm down.

"Suzume, this is Mommy's friend Adrian. Adrian, this is Suzume."

Adrian squatted down so he was eye level with Suzume and gave her a sage nod. "Nice to meet you."

Suzume looked up at Maiko, as if to say, *Okay, who is this guy?*

"Here's a latte," he said, straightening up again and handing her one of the cups. Maiko was touched.

"Were you waiting this entire time?"

"Only about five minutes. It's fine."

"Thank you." She sipped. It was hot. Suzume squirmed with her palm in Maiko's hand. "Behave," she said.

"Mai," Adrian said, struggling now. "I'm sorry about how I acted. When you were pregnant. It was wrong of me."

Maiko nodded, eyes averted. "It's fine. I mean, it's *not* fine, but it's what happened, and thank you for the apology."

There was a quiet pause as the two of them stood there, each thinking about their feelings. Suzume tugged on Maiko's hand. "Pudding?" she asked hopefully.

"I've already been in hair and makeup. Want me to watch her while you're in the trailer?"

Maiko raised an eyebrow. "You wouldn't mind?"

"We'll become fast friends."

Maiko normally wouldn't have been comfortable with a man offering to watch her daughter, but this wasn't just any man. It was *Adrian*. She knew him, inside and out. He wouldn't do anything to hurt Suzume.

"Okay." She ducked her head. "Darling, Adrian is going to take you to craft services. You can have a pudding if you're well behaved." She looked at him. "Make sure she eats something healthy like fruit too."

"Got it. Suzume, who is your favorite *Frozen* princess?" He held out a hand, and Suzume reluctantly took it.

"Pudding!" Suzume insisted.

Maiko watched them walk in the direction of the craft services table and then, with a wry smile, made a beeline for the makeup trailer.

FOX AND WHITLEY SEPARATING?

Breaking news: Actress Maiko Fox and director-producer Thomas Whitley are no longer living in the same house, sources report. No one knows why the two are separating, but reportedly Maiko isn't allowing Thomas to see their daughter, Suzume, 3. It's going to be a down-and-dirty custody battle if the two get divorced!

EVEN AFTER MAIKO moved out, taking Suzume with her, Thomas held steadfast against any mention of separation. Maiko wouldn't let Suzume back into Thomas's house after what had happened, and he was understandably angry, but she just couldn't risk leaving her daughter alone with him.

She braced herself for the onslaught of whatever power Thomas had that he would use against her.

But there was still work to do.

Maiko showed up at the studios with Suzume every day, bringing her three-year-old because no one else would dare cross Thomas and babysit for her. Hollywood is an insular town, made up of thousands of hopefuls. They all wanted to make a name for themselves, and they couldn't do that by ingratiating themselves with the actress who was persona non grata to her powerful husband.

Adrian was understanding, and brought Suzume picture books to look at while she sat in a chair in the studio, noise-canceling headphones clamped onto her ears with music piping in so that she couldn't hear the scripted conversations between Adrian and Maiko as they acted their scenes. Production was slow because Maiko kept checking on her daughter after every other take, and all Suzume wanted to do was chat with her mother or anyone who would listen, but Adrian was patient. It was an unprecedented situation, and everybody knew it.

As they finished with the day's work, Maiko heaved Suzume onto her hip, even though she was getting a little too big to be carried, and said, "Thank you for being a good girl, Suzume." Suzume nodded.

"Pudding?" she asked. Maiko sighed, not wanting to reward behavior with sweets, but knew that her daughter deserved a pudding.

Adrian went to grab it for them, and as he peeled the lid off the pudding cup, he said, "You're doing great, Mai."

"I don't know what I'm doing," she confessed.

"It looks like you do."

"I mean—not with her. With my life."

"Mommy!" Suzume was chatty, having been ignored for the past couple of hours. Maiko knew she was stretching the goodwill of the PAs on set with her talkative child, who had to be shushed for every take, and her heart twisted because she knew they weren't being paid nearly enough for their help. "Chocolate pudding?" Evidently, the vanilla cup that Adrian procured was not the right flavor.

Maiko sighed. "Go pick out your own pudding," she said. She released Suzume to go to the crafts services table, and watched as she dashed over, ducking between moving people on the set, nearly tripping a few of them.

"I know it's hard," Adrian said, watching Suzume as well, "but I'm here for you if you need anything."

"Thank you, Adrian," she said, tearing her eyes away from Suzume for a moment to look at him. "If you could think of anyone who would be able to look after her—I know it's not ideal, to have her here."

"Why don't I make some calls?" he suggested, and Maiko gave him a grim smile.

"I've tried everyone I know, and their contacts."

"Ah. But you haven't tried mine."

THE NEXT TIME Maiko saw Adrian, a familiar person was following behind him. Maiko turned a quizzical eye to Adrian, and he smiled. "You know my sister, Leslie. She's offered to look after Suzume for you."

"Don't you live in Florida?" Maiko gasped, and Leslie grinned.

"I rode here in comfort, just to help out."

"I can't accept," Maiko said, her throat dry. "This is too generous."

"You're telling me that my sister flew all the way out here—on a private jet, yes, but she still had to be on a plane for five hours—just for you to shut me down?" Adrian laughed. "I insist."

"I insist too," Leslie said. "I love kids."

"If you feel that strongly about it," Maiko said doubtfully, and her hand, clutching Suzume's, felt sweaty. "Honey," she said, crouching down to be at eye level with Suzume, "this is Leslie. She'll be watching you while Adrian and I work."

Suzume regarded Leslie with a careful eye. Leslie was wearing pink pants and a shirt with Mickey Mouse on it, and apparently that was good enough. She let go of her mother's hand and approached Leslie interestedly. "Read my books?" she asked, and the two walked to the edge of the soundstage.

"I can't thank you enough," Maiko said, and Adrian shrugged.

"It's fine," he said. "Leslie deserved a little vacation from

Tallahassee. And I think it'll be good for her to hang out with a kid. Remind her of her own childhood days, or something."

Maiko stood there smiling at him, and he flashed a smile back. Her insides turned liquid. His kindness knocked her sideways. She could see the red in his hair under the studio lights and she remembered how she'd always been attracted to redheads.

A PA hustled toward them and said breathlessly, "First teams up."

"Let's not keep the director waiting," Adrian said. Maiko stepped forward and, with a quick glance back at him, walked back onto the set.

40

Adrian had his good days and bad days. One never *got over* the death of a loved one. Sometimes, the grief was all-encompassing, pressing on him from all sides. He would find himself with a lump in his throat and a jittery feeling in his hands, like he'd had too much coffee, but it was a tremor from holding back tears.

And other times, it was just *less*. He was aware of his grief, but it was somewhere in the background, always there but not fighting for his attention.

He realized that, though his father was a good man, he had been a flawed man too. Jerome had provided for his family financially, but at the cost of losing time with his son and daughter. When Adrian thought of all the time that Jerome had spent at the dealership, instead of at home, he was somber.

And he knew that Maiko was having the same sort of feelings about losing her mother. All that time wasted when she and Michiyo weren't talking, just because Maiko had had the audacity to follow her dreams and try to become a model instead of a doctor or lawyer.

Adrian tapped out a text:

Grief is not linear.

He hesitated to send it. He didn't know what Maiko's feelings were about unsolicited advice. But then, he hit the little arrow. The response was immediate.

M: How did you know that I needed to hear that right now?

M: I'm just sitting on Christine's couch, head between my hands, thinking about how much I miss her.

M: And this divorce business is not going well. I'm mourning the loss of what I thought my life would be like. But Thomas won't sign. And I'm worried I'll be shackled to him forever.

Adrian chewed his lower lip and contemplated what to answer. He ached to hold Maiko. To let her lean on his shoulder, to stroke her hair, to tell her she wasn't alone.

A: He'll sign eventually. It's all a power play to him.

Adrian wasn't sure about that, but he felt he had Thomas pegged.

M: Can I tell you a secret?

A: Sure

M: I always thought I'd die at 36. No reason why, just that I would cease to exist. Now that I'm 37, it's a mind-fuck. How am I supposed to exist? And why is it in a world without my mother?

A: Thank goodness you're still here. I don't know what I'd do without you.

M: You'd manage.

Adrian shook his head and typed.

A: I don't think that's true. Mai, you're a constant in my life. Sometimes we lose contact, but I never not think of you.

M: That's sweet of you to say, Adrian. Thank you.

Then:

M: You mean a lot to me too.

MAIKO'S DIVORCE STRETCHED out longer and longer, like a piece of taffy being pulled from both ends. Thomas refused to acquiesce, and even contested the paperwork. Maiko continued to go to work on *Sofia and Max*; Thomas continued to be there, directing; and the matter of Suzume seemed to hang in the balance.

The crew whispered among themselves, noting the toxic environment in which they worked. Adrian wondered, again, why he had agreed to Thomas's demands. He should've found another Sofia. He shouldn't even be on this set.

But when he saw Maiko, her miserable mouth in a frown, worry lines creasing her forehead, as she showed up to work every day, he relented. He loved working with her.

He wanted to help her.

He loved her.

Maiko Fox: Cheater!!

We have exclusive photos of Maiko Fox CHEATING on Thomas Whitley, even before she filed for divorce. Now we know why!

Maiko has long been rumored to be in love with her frequent costar Adrian Hightower, and was even engaged to him in 2006. Maiko and Adrian rekindled their romance on the set of *Sofia and Max*, their newest pet project. Scroll down to see all the pics.

41

The film was almost wrapped when Maiko got a flurry of texts from her friends. Christine sent Are you ok??? While Helen sent That bastard. I'll kill him myself.

Her father even called, and Maiko let it go to voicemail. She was on the set and everyone around her seemed to be whispering, which felt pointed toward her.

Adrian walked toward her, his jaw working. "What's wrong?" she asked, and he pulled out his own phone to show her. A gossip site had somehow gotten photos of their choreographed make-out session on set. The photos were grainy and taken from far away, zoomed in, but obviously of Maiko and Adrian.

"But . . . these are from the movie?" she said, her voice rising like a question at the end. "Surely people don't believe that these are real *cheating* photos."

"They do," he said. "It's you, it's me. We're sucking face. It's all they need to make an accusation."

"Can't we release footage from the movie that we filmed, to show that it's just acting?" She felt panic rise in her chest. It would be awful if the impending divorce from Thomas was ruined by her *work*. If her potential custody battle would be affected by these photos, because she was branded a cheater.

"Unfortunately not. The studio won't do it. I've already asked. They think people won't shell out for the movie if we show them what they would have paid to see. It's a Madrian film, after all."

How impossible was it, she thought, *that this is what it all came to?* Years of their shared history, costarring in movies, and *this* is what would sink her life. She was suddenly angry. Angry at Adrian for writing the script that included such a physical scene; angry at whoever took those photos, anonymous as they may be; angry, angry, angry.

"I need some air," she said, and walked past Adrian, out the door of the soundstage, and into the sunlight. But she felt exposed there, too, wondering if there were hidden spies in the crew taking photos of her. She ended up speed-walking to her trailer and pulled the door open, collapsing on the couch.

She wanted to cry. She had known it would be a dirty battle with Thomas, but she hadn't thought that a member of their small, insular crew would betray her like this. They must have a grudge against her.

There was a knock on the door, and without waiting for her answer, Adrian joined her. "Listen," he said. "I know that this sucks. I'm really sorry about all this. My buddy Tim told me that he was offered money by your ex to check up on me. He refused, but somebody else must have been swayed by the money."

Maiko cupped her face in her hands and growled. "I don't

need you to tell me something I already know. This whole movie was a mistake. This was a mistake."

"Please don't say that," Adrian said, placing a hand on the couch near her, but not touching her. Maiko appreciated that. "*Sofia and Max* wouldn't have been the same without you. No matter what, I'm proud of the work we've done here. But I understand if you're mad at me for dragging you into this."

Maiko sighed. She lowered her hands and set them on the couch, too, one hand resting close to his. Their pinkies almost touched, but didn't. She looked at their hands for a moment and then placed hers in her lap. Adrian didn't say anything.

"I *am* mad," she said, sagging a little from the emotional weight of it.

"I don't blame you," he said. She thought he was going to kiss her forehead, but instead, he stood up and made his way across the trailer to exit. "We'll figure something out."

MAIKO WAS, WITH a judge's order, finally able to get her paychecks redirected to her bank account, so she began searching for a new, small place to live with Suzume. Until this point, she had lived on the goodwill of Christine and Helen. She felt like a third wheel in their relationship, with a three-year-old besides. She and Suzume slept on the couple's couch and every morning, she would wake up, shake out the crocheted blanket that she'd slept under, and gather Suzume for Leslie.

She found a little two-bedroom apartment in Laurel Canyon. *Sofia and Max* was wrapping soon, and she was looking forward to the next steps in her life. Would her divorce be finalized sometime soon? (She hoped.) Would Suzume start school soon? (She anticipated.)

And all the while, she and Adrian talked. Not through text, like they had before, but really *talked*. He'd come over to her little place and sit on the new two-seater sofa and just *be there* for her. It was heartwarming, really. Suzume was getting to know Adrian better, and because of Suzume, Maiko kept herself from doing anything rash with her old flame.

Even though she really wanted to.

Adrian Photographed Outside Maiko's Residence

Maiko Fox, who recently served divorce papers to her ex, producer-director Thomas Whitley, had a guest last night! Her longtime collaborator and rumored lover, Adrian Hightower, was photographed outside of her residence, holding takeout containers from a local Vietnamese place. But he didn't stay the night! Adrian was photographed leaving two hours later, looking no worse for wear. Perhaps their tryst was short?! Say it ain't so, Adrian!

42

Adrian toted two containers of pho up Maiko's driveway and wondered what would happen once he was at her door. But when he was there, and she was opening it, all he could say was, "Hey."

"Hey," she said in return, and she stepped back to let him in. There was a flurry of clicking as photographers outside of the gate shot pictures of Adrian walking into the darkened recesses of the apartment before she closed the front door.

"I brought Vietnamese," he said dumbly, even though she had already acknowledged the food by taking the bags from him and setting them on the breakfast table.

"Thanks. Suzume, honey, do you want to eat?"

"No, Mama!" Suzume called from a seat in the living room.

"Come eat, sweetie."

Suzume dragged her feet as she entered the kitchen. Maiko pulled out cans of La Croix from the fridge and set them on the table. They busied themselves with doctoring their soups with sriracha and eating, and after a while, Adrian had the courage to ask, "How'd it go?"

"First day of mediation, done," she said with a tired smile.

Adrian chewed his noodles carefully. "I suppose a few more are to be expected."

"Probably," she said lightly.

"Because—"

"Don't, Adrian." She looked serious, like she might cry. "Don't say anything you can't take back."

"Mai, I want to be with you."

Maiko looked down at her bowl and then fussed with Suzume. "Do you want to watch *Moana*?"

Adrian watched helplessly as Maiko set up the movie in the living room. When she came back to the table, she took a long drink of sparkling water and attacked her noodles again.

"Mai, did you hear me?" he said.

She nodded, not meeting his eyes.

"I think I've always loved you." Adrian felt the words bubbling up out of him. "Even when we were apart. I think that's why I loved working with you, because I could be near you. And when we're apart, I think about you. I know your divorce isn't final—that we can't do anything about this, if you feel the same way, until later—but I needed you to know."

She took a deep breath. "I can't deal with this right now, Adrian. I appreciate you coming by and bringing dinner, but I can't entertain the thought of you in any capacity but my friend at this moment."

If Adrian was less well adjusted, he might have walked out of the house, feeling terrible. But the way she spoke gave him hope. Maybe there was a way for them to be together once all of this was over. She didn't say outright that she didn't feel the same way toward him. And so he smiled.

"That's fine," he said. He began to clean up.

"That's fine?" she repeated, questioningly.

"Yes. You didn't say no. So I'm going to take this as a win."

Maiko stared at him for a second, then burst out laughing. "You bastard."

They grinned at each other and then Maiko said quickly, "I have to get Suzume to bed soon. But if you want—you could watch part of *Moana* with us?"

He settled on the couch with Suzume between him and Maiko, and they watched the movie, and afterward he let himself out while Maiko did bath time and took Suzume to bed. He whistled as he walked himself to his car.

ADRIAN WATCHED FROM afar as Maiko and Thomas's separation grew more and more hostile. He felt helpless, like there was nothing he could do. This was a battle she was going to have to wage herself.

And yet, he couldn't stay away. Despite the tabloids discussing Maiko's supposed infidelity, and with Adrian as a culprit, he found himself bringing takeout over to her Laurel Canyon apartment almost every night and staying for a few hours, spending time with Suzume and with Maiko.

The rags started calling his daily excursions to Maiko's a "pap walk." *Adrian is taking his pap walk to Maiko's again . . .*

After two weeks of this, he had the bright idea to wear the same clothes every time, carrying the same Igloo cooler full of food, so that it looked like the paparazzi were selling photos from the same night over and over again. They started leaving him alone after that, and would go fishing elsewhere for better pics of other celebrities.

Tonight's entertainment was *Coco*. Suzume, four now, loved the dancing skeletons. Maiko and Adrian sat on the small couch, dinner already eaten, as they played a gentle game of footsie.

Maiko wrinkled her nose. "You're going to need to wash that outfit at some point," she teased.

"I do laundry every night!" Adrian said, mock-offended.

"Sure, sure," Maiko said, laughing. She was hugging a throw pillow to her chest, and Adrian remembered that first date, seventeen years ago, when she had done the same thing. He gazed at her, one hand propping his head up, and thought, *You're the same woman I fell for.*

She caught his long glance and said self-consciously, "What?"

"Nothing. Just thinking how much I want to kiss you."

Maiko hugged the throw pillow even closer and gave him a wry smile. "Sorry."

Adrian gave a growl of disappointment. "I'll wait," he said.

"You'll be waiting a long time." She sighed, getting up off the sofa and tossing the pillow to the side. "I'm getting another sparkling water . . . you want any?"

"I'm good." His phone buzzed and he pulled it from his pocket as she walked to the miniature kitchen. What he saw made his heart leap. "Mai."

She sounded unconcerned as she sipped from a can of key lime La Croix. "Hmm?"

"You got to read this tabloid headline."

Maiko took his phone and stared at it.

Thomas Whitley Caught with Pants Off, it said. She read aloud: "'The illustrious director-producer was found getting serviced by an unnamed woman in the backseat of his car.'" She shook her head. "There are *pictures.*" She stared at it some more. "That's Elsie Taye."

"The director from *Surf City*?" Adrian asked, taking the phone back and scrolling down. "Well, whaddya know."

"I wonder if they've been doing this for a while," Maiko said aloud, her thoughts tracing back to the oddly timed showers Thomas took, and the time Elsie attended Michiyo's funeral, despite not having been invited. Had there been other moments as well? Had Maiko missed the signs?

"You know what this means, right?" Adrian said. "His contestation of the divorce is shot." He got to his feet, excited. "You'll be free of him soon."

"The paparazzi, actually doing something *good* for a change," Maiko marveled.

Suzume asked, "Mommy, why are you crying?"

Maiko wiped away an errant tear. "No reason, honey. Mommy is just happy."

43

2020

Maiko Fox Finalizes Divorce from Thomas Whitley

Actress Maiko Fox and director-producer Thomas Whitley have finalized their divorce. According to legal documents, the pair have agreed to share joint legal custody of their 4-year-old child, though Maiko will have primary physical custody.

Last year, Whitley accused his ex-wife of cheating on him with longtime collaborator and fellow actor, Adrian Hightower. However, Maiko was the first to file for divorce, citing that their marriage was "irretrievably broken with no hope for reconciliation."

MAIKO CRIED WHEN Thomas signed the divorce papers. He did it with a flourish, capping his fountain pen like a king, and shoved the papers at her. "I hope you're happy," he said stiffly, and Maiko nodded.

Their lawyers filed out of the mediation room, and Thomas stood up. "I guess we're done here," he said.

"I'll bring Suzume over on Friday," she said somewhat helpfully.

"Right."

And then he was gone, and Maiko was alone in the law office with the chrome table and leather chairs. She pulled out her phone.

M: Guess what?

A: What?

M: . . . I'm free.

A: Celebratory ice cream? My treat?

Maiko laughed out loud. She texted *Will come pick up Suzume* and hustled out of the office.

Suzume was with Leslie, who was with Adrian, so it was easy to see them both. All four of them went out for ice cream, and paparazzi photographed them licking their cones and smiling. Maiko made sure to hold only Suzume's hand and not Adrian's.

But then Leslie peeled off to go back to Adrian's pad, and Maiko and Adrian took Suzume home for supper and bathtime.

Maiko sighed after she put Suzume to sleep. "She should be good until morning," she said to Adrian, rejoining him on the couch.

As they sat on the sofa, him cradling her feet in his hands, Maiko had a déjà vu moment of their first date, when they made out on her tweedy couch eighteen years ago. Should she . . . ? *Could* she be with him now that the ink on the divorce papers was dry—barely?

"Adrian," she said quietly, and he glanced up at her, those dark brown eyes warm with contentment.

"Mai," he said back simply.

"We should have a talk."

"What's there to talk about? I know what you're going to say."

"You know, huh?" she said, feeling a finger of want pulsing inside her chest.

"It's in your eyes, Mai. You love me back."

"You're so arrogant," she said, but he had bridged the space between their faces and kissed her on the temple. He was half-way over her, hands cupping her hips on either side of her body, and she looked up at him for a long moment before she nodded. "I do. I love you back."

He kissed her then, nearly collapsing on top of her.

"Remember the first time we did this?" she murmured, when he moved from her mouth to her neck, giving soft, sucking kisses along her jawline.

"How could I forget?" he whispered, breathing her scent in.

"But Adrian. I'm not that girl anymore," she said, pulling away just slightly. His eyes met hers. "I've had a kid. I'm not some taut twenty-something with no love handles. I'm in my late thirties and I have stretch marks and cellulite and—"

"And nothing. I don't care about all that stuff, Mai. You're the most beautiful person I know, and it has nothing to do with your exterior."

That was the sweetest thing Maiko had ever heard from anyone, and she melted a little.

"Will you hold me?" she asked.

Adrian slipped in between the couch cushions and Maiko's outstretched body, and let her nestle into his chest. They lay there breathing quietly for a while, and Adrian was content just to have her in his arms.

"This can't be some little rebound thing," she said softly.

"You know it's not," he breathed.

"Just making sure," she said, and she kissed his earlobe. He sucked in his breath.

He began peeling off her shirt, kissing her from neck to navel, brushing his fingers so lightly on her belly, tracing the scars there. Maiko was surprised that she wasn't self-conscious about it, not after what he'd said. She could feel his tenderness in his movements, his awe that she had done something so incredible with her body.

"Adrian?"

"Hmm?" He nuzzled the top of her hipbone. She still had the infinity symbol tattoo there, which they'd gotten while on vacation years ago.

"Will you make love to me?"

His face broke out into a smile. "I thought you'd never ask," he murmured. His fingers explored her jeans zipper and pulled it down. Maiko felt the fabric leaving her legs like a snakeskin shedding, and then it was just her, naked, with him, fully clothed, looking at her reverently.

He nudged her thighs open slightly, kissing her hipbones, down into the darkness of where her legs met her body. He began licking her very lightly, his tongue tasting her ever so gently. Maiko felt her legs trembling as she pushed herself closer to his mouth, wanting more pressure, but he drew back, teasing.

"Adrian," she moaned softly, and she curled her fingers in his hair. "Please," she said. "Please."

He slipped off his clothes in quick, fluid motions. She could see his dick in the low-burning lamplight, unchanged in twenty years. It was a familiar sight, one that made her sigh. He dragged it lightly against the side of her thigh so she could feel it coming closer, and he slowly worked it inside her. "*Oh.*" She sighed again, this time contentedly.

It took a few shifts for Adrian to fit all the way comfortably, and Maiko felt herself expanding around him. "Fuck, Mai," he breathed, and his hand lowered down in between them, touching her gently where she wanted to be touched. Her leg twitched in reaction.

"Should I . . . ?" she said, shifting under him, and he shook his head.

"Give me a second." And then he was rubbing her there, where she liked it, and rocking ever so gently between them, moving incrementally, slow, slow, slow. Her breath hitched. She clasped his back with both hands, dragging her fingers down to his hips, which weren't as narrow as they used to be, but that fact didn't bother her at all. They were older; they were wiser; and yet they were rediscovering each other after years apart. Maiko lifted her hips and rocked them down, willing him to go deeper.

"Are you okay?" he asked, and she kissed him deeply in response. He began moving faster, pulling out longer and pushing in faster, so that she was riding his full length. He was still pressing hard against her clit, building pressure inside Maiko, and she longed for release.

"Mai—" he grunted, slowing, but she bucked her hips up against him, wanting to feel him come; he took that as a sign that it was okay to speed up again, to feel her clench against him. She felt the spasm of her orgasm start and she let out a soft moan, which did him in. He gasped deeply, and he laughed out of relief, and soon he was feeling a rhythm and finishing deep inside her.

They lay on the couch, sweaty, hoping that they had been quiet enough not to disturb their sleeping charge upstairs. Maiko stood to clean up, and after she returned to the couch, she snuggled under Adrian's arm and put the flat of her hand on his abdomen. "Thank you," she said.

"Why are you thanking me?" He seemed amused.

"For making me feel beautiful."

Epilogue

Four years later

M aiko rolled over on her beach towel and looked at her companion. Suzume, now eight, grinned back at her. The sound of the surf was soothing, and they were on a lawn close to the public part of the beach so no one was disturbing them. Maiko could hear the shrieks of beachgoers nearby as they played in the water, but she and her daughter were content to stay shaded under a palm tree.

"Lemonade?"

It was Adrian, wearing board shorts and a faded T-shirt, who had come out of the house with two cans of Minute Maid. Maiko shook her head, but Suzume jumped up and took one happily.

"Thanks, Adrian," she said. She still wouldn't call him Dad.

The trio had moved to Maui after they'd left Hollywood, at the insistence of Suzume, who loved *Moana*. The locals didn't bother them when they went grocery shopping, and the tourists didn't know to look for them. They'd lived in relative inconspicuousness for the past four years, living off Madrian residuals and deferring requests for more interviews. Their now-shared publicist knew that they were making the most of their time together and didn't bother them with too much.

Maiko still visited the mainland with Suzume, to make sure she honored her part of the custody agreement, but she flew into Long Beach, where there were fewer paparazzi, and Thomas didn't have much of a target on his back for being photographed anyway. He and Elsie Taye were no longer together, and Maiko didn't think he was seeing anyone. Suzume, at least, didn't know if there was a new woman in his life, which was a relief to Maiko. She didn't like the idea of *anyone* being with a man who would hit his wife.

Maiko and Adrian had done one interview as a couple after they got back together, before they disappeared to the Hawaiian shore. Maiko admitted that she left Thomas because he'd slapped her, and that was enough. Online communities vilified him and called for his cancellation, while Madrian movies were rented, bought, streamed, and rereleased in theaters at the audiences' request. Maiko and Adrian could live off residuals for the rest of their lives and not reenter the world.

Maiko loved living on an island, napping on the lanai, listening to the surf, Adrian by her side. She was happy with her one daughter, not wanting to expand their family any more.

But lately she had been feeling the itch of wanting to do *more* with her life. Not be an actress again, if she could help it; she was too old to model, that she knew; but *something*. "Babe," she said, and Adrian, who was sitting on a chaise longue nearby, said, "Hmm?"

"Why don't we start a foundation?" she suggested. "Sort of like how Jess did." Jess had started an infertility awareness foundation. Its launch coincided with the due date of her first-born, with her new husband—a happy surprise for all.

"What sort of foundation?"

"Like . . . a foundation for young actors. Helping Asian Americans get a leg up in the industry. It was hard for me at first . . . It'd be nice to contribute something back to the world."

"I could get behind that," he said, the skin around his eyes crinkling with his smile. "Although, I do love lounging around doing nothing with you, or surfing."

"We can still do that," she said, feeling her chest puff with happiness. "We could leave the running of the foundation to someone else. We can be as hands-on or as hands-off as you'd like."

"I love being hands-on," he said, sliding off his chaise and joining Maiko on the tiniest slice of beach blanket that was available. Maiko laughed. Suzume rolled her eyes, a teenager in the making.

"Gross," Suzume said, taking her lemonade with her as she left her perch. She stepped through the swinging back door and Adrian put his hand on Maiko's hip.

"Where were we," he said, leaning forward, brushing his nosetip against her hair.

"I dunno," she responded playfully, kissing him on the chin and drawing back to look at him more carefully. "You know," she added, "this aging thing is doing it for me."

"Yeah? You don't mind the gray?" He touched his hair self-consciously, where he had a little bit of salt and pepper going on.

"It makes you look dignified," she said. "Besides, I'm gray-ing too."

"You'll always look twenty-five to me," he said generously.

She kissed him on the mouth and then they grinned at each other.

Acknowledgments

As always, I need to thank my brilliant editor, Asanté Simons. I'm so grateful for her direction and and for her insight into editing this book to be the best it could be. Thank you also to Tessa James for stepping in and riding out the tail end of this book's launch with me.

My agent, Kelly Van Sant at kt literary, has always been a huge supporter for my projects and I can't thank her enough. In fact, the whole team at kt has been amazing.

To my beta readers—Margarita Montimore, Rachael Garza, Kathleen Avera Trail, Lisa Walsh Wittrock, and Lexie Abbott—thank you for your helpful input at various stages of this story.

I asked for help in different social circles and got back so many responses, it's hard to list all who contributed, but I have to acknowledge Sarah Beth, Mari, Jo, Rory, Jacqueline, Helen, Soleil, Christy, and Sarah K. Thanks for answering all of my stupid parenting questions. Massive thank-you to Lindsay Bergman-Debes for her guidance on some sensitive matters. And I can't forget Mike Jordan, for coming up with "Atomic Crusader."

Again, I borrow names from people I know to name random characters, so if that's you, thank you/I'm sorry.

In no particular order, I'd also like to thank . . .

The team at William Morrow, Kelly Cronin, Mary Interdonati, Yeon Kim, Stephanie Vallejo, and Rita Madrigal, who have championed my first two books and this one as well.

Hannah Vaughn at Gersh, my film agent.

Book of the Month for choosing *The Unraveling of Cassidy Holmes* for a pick back in 2020.

The authors who have been so generous with their time and words, to read and blurb my books: Amanda Eyre Ward, Laura Hankin, Ella Berman, Taylor Jenkins Reid, Patti Callahan, Zoe Fishman, Alena Dillon, and Sarah Priscus.

Adrienne Proctor, my *Hit Send* podcast cohost, for working with me every two weeks on that passion project.

My friends, Bao Vo, Matt Mullenweg, Sarah Clarke Menendez, Julie Sugar, Rebecca Lammons, Cathryn Ibarra, Ann Kuo, Rose Kuo, John Tomeček, Caitlin McWeeney, and Beka Vinogradov, for cheering me on.

My family, especially Mom and Dad, for instilling in me a love of reading and nurturing my creative dreams. My sister, who will be my manager one day, if I ever get successful enough. Thank you to my in-laws! Y'all are spectacular.

Walt, my partner in life. Thank you for being the best cat dad to our furry brood.

And you, the reader. Thank you for taking a chance on my books.

READ MORE BY
ELISSA R. SLOAN

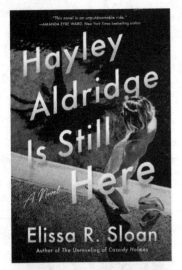

"Elissa R. Sloan has done it again with her whip-smart new novel, *Hayley Aldridge Is Still Here*. Calling all smart readers and gossip lovers alike: this novel is an unputdownable ride, fiction inspired by the narratives of stars like Jennette McCurdy (*I'm Glad My Mom Died*) and Britney Spears. Sloan's examination of money, fame, and control is brilliant, necessary . . . and fun as hell."
—AMANDA EYRE WARD,
New York Times bestselling author

"*The Unraveling of Cassidy Holmes* is a page-turning peek inside the glamour and brutality of life as a pop star. Sloan takes us on a wild ride through the world of music video shoots, expensive hotels, and arena tours—showing us the darkness that threatens just below the surface."
—Taylor Jenkins Reid, *New York Times* bestselling author of *Daisy Jones and The Six*